# THE LATTER HALF OF INGLORIOUS YEARS

Books by Kirk Ward Robinson

## NONFICTION

*Founding Character:*
*Documents that Define the United States of America and its People*

*Founding Courage:*
*Courage and Character in the United States of America*

*Hiking Through History:*
*Hannibal, Highlanders, and Joan of Arc*

*Notes from the Field:*
*A Diary of Journeys Near and Far*

## FICTION

*August Roads*
*Novellas*

*Life in Continuum*
*Stories*

*The Appalachian*
*A Novel*

*The Latter Half of Inglorious Years*
*A Novel*

The Latter Half of Inglorious Years

A Novel

by

~~John Taylor Dean~~

James Trevor Davidson

~~Evan Usher~~

Joplin Dean

**Kirk Ward Robinson**

HIGHLAND
HOME

*Nashville, Tennessee*

*The Latter Half of Inglorious Years*
*A Novel*

A HIGHLAND EDITION

While some of the characters are composites of people the author has encountered, this is a work of fiction drawn from the imagination. Any resemblance to actual people or events is coincidental.

*Nevis Peak*, by Nelson Brooks, is used with permission

Designed by Victoria Valentine/PageAndCoverDesign.com

Printed in the United States of America
HighlandHome Publishing
Nashville, Tennessee
37215

ISBN 10: 0-9996042-3-6
ISBN 13: 978-0-9996042-3-6

Visit www.highlandhome.org

*For Anna, my mother, who has seen as much as Sarah*

# Chapter One

I DON'T HAVE ANY IMPRESSIVE SCARS. That never occurred to me until I got here and saw a shirtless man walking off the dock while hefting a large bluefish by the gills. The man was black with a Spanish cast, drizzling sweat down a back so severely scarred that I would have thought I had been sent back in time to plantation days. He had rope burns across his shoulders, as intricate as a cat's cradle, and a jagged line down the middle of his back where he might have been snagged and dragged by a hook. Other burns were splattered like candle wax, and down near a kidney, an unmistakable stab wound. His scars weren't cruel evidence of an earlier brutal era, but badges he had earned during a life of working hard on the fishing boats and living hard off the docks. He was not a man who had to explain himself. He had done things in his life, the proof was there in his flesh. I envied him.

I'm thirty-seven years old and I haven't done anything. Worse, I've never even tried.

This island is called Nevis, an eyedrop of land in the West Indies. I think there are cruise ships bigger than this place. It's hot and there are mosquitoes, but it's a perfect refuge. Nobody knows anything about anything, and they care even less than that. They don't know me, of me, or why I came. Better yet, my cell phone doesn't work here. I feel completely anonymous. There's safety in anonymity, otherwise you can become famous, or infamous, and either one will ruin you given a chance. I know because I was both, if only for a little while, but long enough to know that I don't ever want to be either again.

Morgane sent me down here to escape the social media frenzy back home. I thought she would send me to Martinique where she's from, but she said I wouldn't like it there, that they only speak French on Martinique and this would make me crazy. Left unsaid in her lyrical accent and aloof demeanor was that on Martinique I would probably stumble across her family sooner or later, an encounter I'm pretty sure she'd rather avoid. So she picked Nevis instead, where she is unknown and where the people speak English—mostly.

I don't know what I have with Morgane. I made the mistake of telling her once that I loved her. She laughed, her eyes glittering with mirth as I stumbled through a quick retraction, trying to turn it into a joke. When I couldn't perform later that night she just shrugged. "Okay Joplin," she said, neither discomfited nor disappointed. "No problems." Then she rolled over and went to sleep, leaving me alone to puzzle it out for myself. Sometimes, when she's not enticing me with her savvy Gallic body, I'll think that I don't have anything with Morgane at all; and I'll wonder why we're together, if that's what it is.

The people here are congenial enough, if a bit blunt. "Why you be on Nevis?" a black woman tending bar at the Double Deuce asked me. She was gracefully proportioned, tall, with a high forehead, wise espresso eyes that had probably seen more than I would ever know, and a reserved smile that was whiter than my pale, home-office complexion. It was late afternoon so there were only a few people at the bar. She usually gave her name as Shelly, although her real name was Shelisa. She was my age if that, poised, with an authentic air that said, *Don't you dare lie to me*.

Then why did I lie? Because suddenly at that moment I felt that I needed her approval more than anything else I could lay a finger on in my life. She saw right through me anyway. I came up with something unimaginative, like I'd won a free trip so here I was. She paused at that, her eyes unmoving, not even a twitch to her lips, and yet I could sense disappointment crossing her face like a riptide. Something utterly intangible in her expression offered me a last chance, and when I didn't take it she just pushed back from the bar, said, "Then have you a nice stay," and moved on.

I sat there, more alone now but with enough rum in my glass to keep me occupied for a while. An older man with a clean face and a nautical bearing came in and sat at the other end of the bar. He sounded British, maybe Australian. Shelisa poured for him, and in return he said something that made her chuckle. She leaned on her elbows, laughing gaily as he told a boisterous story. His gestures were wide and wild, his cheeks ebullient, his eyes bright with enthusiasm. Others gravitated toward him, sweaty beer bottles laying cold wet trails his way. I envied him.

My rum went down, so did the sun, and a mosquito bit me on the ear. When my mind was sufficiently numb I called a taxi to take me back.

I awoke the next morning as the sun broke above Antigua. The wind was raucous and damp and had kept me up most of the night, but at least it was cool and held the mosquitoes at bay. My ear itched.

Settling into a lounge chair on the veranda, I scratched my ear, sipped coffee, and tried to fathom how people could laze around like this, doing nothing for hours at a time. Mom would love the place. She would organize her days around highballs, sea views and local gossip, and be perfectly content. Without cell service, though, my sister Kessie would be miserable. I was somewhere in between.

I hauled myself up, walked from one end of that long veranda to the other, looked down into the jungle below and startled a monkey, which loped into the bush for cover. The wind picked up and the fan palms strummed music on themselves, castanet clicks and low bow notes. I returned to my chair. The view out to sea hadn't changed in those minutes, still watercolor layers rising from slate waves through purplish haze to orange-limned clouds. The far-off silhouettes of Redonda and Montserrat looked like the backs of whales breaching the surface. It was all very pretty, but I had seen as much in pictures.

I went inside for a refill and then plodded over to my laptop. At least there was internet on Nevis, otherwise I think my notoriety would have been compounded by insanity. I gazed at the keyboard and felt the tug. Just one click and it would all come in like a flood, those who supported me, those who didn't, those who had nothing better to do with their time, and the inevitable thousand questions why. Just graze a key, I thought guiltily, and my blog would come up. My readers might still want to know what was going on, but one update would alert them and everybody else, and then the frenzy would start up again, growing crazier until it found a way to reach across the sea and find me.

And I wasn't ready for that yet. Still, how long could this go on?

I sipped my coffee. The view beyond the veranda had changed, still in watercolor hues but the sun was higher now, beginning to drip gold from a train of vestal clouds. The day would be clear, the sea would be blue, and the beers at the Double Deuce would be cold. I knew what I had to do, and somehow I thought she would listen to me, so I showered and I dressed and I called a taxi; and I took myself on down to the Double Deuce to tell Shelisa about *The Latter Half of Inglorious Years*.

## Chapter Two

WHEN I ORDERED A BEER, Shelisa looked at me with such dubious incredulity that I winced.

"It be only nine o'clock, mon," she scolded me, hands on hips and hovering there like a schoolteacher. "Why you be drinkin' so early?"

"I, uh—"

"Coffee does be better for now," she added with finality.

The place didn't actually open for business until eleven or so, I had just caught Shelisa in early getting everything set up for the day. She hadn't seemed put out when I showed up, she'd even gestured me to a stool at the bar. We were alone, the kitchen staff wouldn't show up for about another half hour.

"Coffee's okay," I said meekly, feeling self-conscious for imposing myself on her.

Shelisa spun through the door into the kitchen, where I heard the clatter of dishes. Her speech was really not that heavily inflected, no more than any stray accent back home, but I got the sense that, away from tourists and expats, she could adopt a local patois that would be unintelligible to outsiders.

She returned a minute or so later with my coffee, effortlessly balancing the whole set-up: cream, sugar, spoons, cup, saucer and napkin, along with a placemat rolled under her arm. She arranged all of this as if it were regular hours and I hadn't interrupted her work.

"You don't need to go to any trouble," I offered, embarrassed.

"What trouble that be?" she asked as she adjusted the cream and sugar spoons just so. When she was satisfied how everything looked, she spun off again to continue her work.

The Double Deuce was open to the air, a corrugated tin roof over a bare wood plank floor, wooden tables and chairs, and a long bar in the back. Nets and buoys hung as decor, along with national flags from all over and an impressive collection of American license plates. A sticky sea wind rustled the flags. Although it was shaping up to be a gorgeous morning, the beach was still quiet.

A motorcycle growled up out front and a young black guy with dreads came in. He nodded at me like I was a regular and then made for the kitchen. They chattered at one another back there, words coming so fast and strange that they must have been in that local patois. When I came here I thought the residents would probably sound like the Jamaicans I'd seen on TV, but they don't, it's as different as Massachusetts and Mississippi.

Shelisa returned from the kitchen after a bit, grinning back at her co-worker and carrying her own cup of coffee. She set it to the side, then propped herself on the bar across from me.

"Okay, mon," she said, her eyes reading me like white paint on a clear glass pane. "So what is it you want to talk about?"

"Huh?" I said, startled enough to rattle my cup.

"Why else you come here so early and order beer?" she grinned. "Go ahead, tell me your tale."

It's what I had come for, but her frankness unnerved me. I stammered a few thoughts, mumbled a few more, averting my eyes, although her penetrating expression made that hard to do.

"We gawn be open soon, mon," she said not impatiently, "so you best get on with it."

Her smile was a salve, her honesty reassuring. I began to speak, and then faster. Things came out that I hadn't meant to say, but it didn't seem out of line to say them. I had found it in my father's desk, I told her, the complete manuscript. It was a good two inches thick, typewritten on crisp white paper without any hand-written notations or even dog-eared corners, and all held together with a big black binder clip. I described the title page to her—

*The Latter Half of Inglorious Years*
*A Novel*
*by*
*John Taylor Dean*

—to which she exclaimed:

"The mon who save the little girl...he be your *father*?"

There was the approval I yearned for, as evident in her expression as her amazement. Even if it was for my father and not me, at least I could bask in a tangential ray of it. More than that, I suddenly noticed that I could breathe, effortless breaths, as if a weight had been lifted, although my father would have found a better metaphor than that. No matter, it was liberating. Shelisa was the first person to ever come at me with anything other than, "The guy who died in the video...he was your *father*?"

///// 

A DOZEN PHONES CAUGHT MOST OF IT. Their videos crowded the internet for a day or two, but only one of them was serendipitously pointed in the right direction before the screaming started. This was in Houston, a little over a year ago. It was a Saturday in November, one of those rare, crisp fall days when northerly winds clean the air and turn the sky a miraculous shade of blue. The woman who shot that video has somehow managed to keep her name out of it. She had been out jogging along Buffalo Bayou with her baby in a stroller, and had stopped at that spot to take a video of the butterfly that had landed on her kid's nose. The woman babbled baby talk at her kid, whose eyes were hilariously crossed trying to focus on the butterfly. If it hadn't been for what happened next, her cutesy baby video itself probably would have trended for a while.

It all happens fast, seconds, less than seconds. At the top of the screen, above the edge of the stroller and off in the distance, you can clearly see a little girl dressed in white. She's three years old at best, alone beside the jogging path, and then out of nowhere she toddles clumsily into busy Allen Parkway. The woman with the butterfly baby hasn't seen this yet, she's focused on her kid, but then there's a shriek, the woman looks up, her phone following her eyes. The little girl is now in the middle of the street. A woman off to the right is screaming and racing toward the child, but it's too far and too late. A gray SUV is shooting around a corner to beat the oncoming traffic—and you feel a sickening lurch because you know that the little girl in white is going to be hit, first by the SUV and then by a succession of oncoming cars, that it's going to be ugly, that it's going to be horrible, and that you ought to look away but you can't; for some reason you just can't.

The woman with the phone cries out, *"Oh my God! Oh my God! Oh my God!"* Butterfly baby is bawling now, but below and out of view. Beneath that you can hear the collective anguish of the onlookers, susurrating gasps of helpless horror.

A jogger races into the frame, a tall man, fit, but too far away to be able to make out his features. In one instant he is not there, and then he is, sprinting full-out into the street, his arms pumping and then reaching, diving, fingers outstretched like fragile branches, which seem to barely touch the little girl and yet she is shoved off her feet and into the median, just a white blur now, like a plastic grocery bag blown out of a pick-up's bed; and the man is hit by the SUV, tossed up into the air like a knot of laundry, coming down near the little girl, half in the median, half in the street, with cars careening around his legs, which lie at odd angles on the pavement; and the little girl gets unsteadily to her feet, crying and confused, her mother shrieking from the other side; then the little girl, with her arms opened pitiably toward her mother's cries, begins to go back into the street, into screeching traffic that hasn't yet figured out what's going on; and the man, with a wrenching cry of pain that is clearly audible, rolls his broken body, takes the little girl by the leg and holds her there in the safety of the median while the little girl jerks to get away...

...and he is still holding her there when he dies, his white hand in sharp juxtaposition against the little girl's black skin.

*/////*

I THINK BUTTERFLY BABY'S MOTHER must have posted the video even before my father's heart stopped beating, because the video got to me through social media long before Kessie called.

I was at my apartment in Nashville, staring blankly at my laptop screen while trying to come up with the first word of the first sentence of a new blog post. My mind was as blank as my gaze, and my coffee had gone cold. I was vaguely thinking that I should probably get up and get another one when an email came in. I didn't recognize the sender, one of my readers, probably.

*"Holy crap! Check out this video."*

I got that kind of thing all the time, so I ignored it and went back to contemplating getting up for coffee.

Our morning in Nashville was similar to the one going on in Houston, clear, cool, and with a brisk north wind that swirled the autumn leaves into circular deposits in the parking lot beyond my window. Morgane had left the apartment before I woke up, off to Vanderbilt to audit a class on comparative politics, part of her *plan*, as she pronounced it with her French accent, a plan of which she had shared few details. I had the television on in the background. A red *Breaking News* banner popped up and caught my eye.

The volume was down so I couldn't hear, but they were playing a video, poor quality, of a guy running into a street. He shoves a kid and then a big SUV is right there. The video was frozen at that moment but I could tell what would happen next. And then I thought about that email, and I wondered, so I brought it up and I clicked it, and yes, that's what it was.

"Holy crap," I whispered to my screen.

It was as I said—I couldn't look away. That video made me realize that action scenes in movies really are bogus, that flying bodies in the real world break and don't get up again. I didn't recognize the jogger as my father, the video was shot from too far away for that, but I could tell that the guy had probably been killed, and I wanted to know who he was.

I brought up a news channel in a window. At the bottom of the screen it said: *Jogger Killed Saving Child, Houston, Texas*. Houston? Hmm...I wondered if Kessie was watching this. A reporter had corralled a black woman and was interviewing her. Police were stringing crime scene tape behind them. There were more flashing patrol lights than seemed warranted for what had happened, but no ambulances, so I guessed enough time had gone by to move the body. The black woman must have been the little girl's mother. I had seen her in the video, and was able to recognize her now because of the bulbous purple rastacap she had on. She spoke calmly to the reporter, although her eyes were wet and her lips trembled from time to time. She was a handsome woman, but looked a little old to be the mother of such a young child, mid-50s, maybe.

The little girl's name was Persimmon Banks, the second youngest of four kids, and the woman she was with was not her mother, but her *great-grandmother*, Eugenia Washington. The jogger—who had died at the scene—hadn't been identified yet.

The video was going viral while reporters were still canvassing the area. A GoFundMe account had already been set up for Persimmon, and someone at the University of Houston had made a Facebook post promising her a scholarship. Little Persimmon was only alive because a guy who hadn't even been identified yet lost his life while saving her, and now she would be showered in the largesse of social media—and perhaps get a free ride through college—for doing nothing more than being in the wrong place at the right time; and if the day did come that she could cash in that scholarship, it would have to be like some nebulous prophecy to her because she probably wouldn't remember any of this.

I had my blog post. It came to me in a fit of pique, not that I begrudged Persimmon or her family anything, but that this is what social media does, throwing money and attention at random events, like a lottery for the misfortunate. I typed it up right then, while the news crews were still circulating through the onlookers, making the thing go on as long as possible and still seem urgent. I clicked keys in a fury, read it over quickly and thought it was brilliant, posted it on the spot, and then my phone rang. It was Kessie.

"Hey, Kessie. Have you seen this *video*?"

"*Oh, Joplin—*"

Her voice was so drawn with anguish that it pulled me up short. I straightened myself and held the phone closer to my ear.

"Kessie, what's wrong?"

She started crying, crying hard, and must have lowered her phone because now her sobs were muffled.

"Kessie?"

Kessie and I didn't talk often. We weren't close. She was nine years younger than I was, born the same year that Mom and Dad divorced, so her childhood had been caught up in that turmoil; and then when I was eighteen, and she a fragile nine, I had fled to college. We only had those few years when she was little, going back and forth between Mom and Dad's houses. All I knew of her life since then was in bits of information I picked up in passing, sometimes a year or more between, and then time leapt and now she was twenty-seven. When had I seen her last? That occurred to me as she sniffed wetly and her sobs drifted off. Did she have a boyfriend? I wondered. Is that what it was about? Why on earth would she call *me*, then?

"It's Dad, Jop," she exhaled in a tremulous breath.

"Huh?" but then she started crying again, and I tried to picture her there, and I realized I couldn't recall her face, how she looked now. Something caught in my throat, squeezed at my temples. "Andy?" I said. That had been my pet name for her when she was little. Kessie Ann Dean, *Ann—D*. She had liked that name. Sometimes I had called her *Andean*. She hadn't liked that one as much, but then Dad had taken it one step further and had come up with his own pet name for her, *Inca*, which she did like, but only from him.

She sniffed again, and I imagined that she had put on a pained smile, although I couldn't quite picture how it would have looked.

"The video," she managed in stutters, "you saw it?"

"The one from this morning? Yeah."

"Oh, Jop," and she started up again, an aching cry that reached inside me and squeezed hard. "Jop, that was *Dad*."

///// 

WHERE'S THE GUIDEBOOK that tells you how you're supposed to act when someone close to you dies; that tells you how you're supposed to feel, what you're supposed to do? Dad and I weren't friends, we weren't even friend*ly*, and yet I felt a cold stone in my chest just the same. But I didn't cry, not even close, and this had me worrying that my dispassion would give me away, that people would call me out for my heartlessness. I studied myself in a mirror, made my lips tremble, tried to draw tears the way an actor would but I couldn't. Trembling lips would have to be enough.

I used Morgane's account to buy tickets to Houston. I hoped she wouldn't be too mad, but I didn't have the money so what else could I do? I also had to use her account to rent a car. Kessie didn't have a car, and as I thought about it glumly, in that huge city we didn't have anyone else.

Morgane was uncharacteristically sanguine that I had used her account. I promised to pay her back as soon as I could, but she waved that off. "He was your father," she said pragmatically, "so you must go."

She drove me to the airport a couple of hours later, and when she dropped me off I looked into her eyes for some recognition, some acknowledgement of some emotional connection between us, but all that looked back at me were her usual enigmatic eyes, the stormy green of a tornado sky. Her lips were slightly parted, showing the crooked front tooth that made her smile so exotically alluring. She kept her dark brown hair feathered lightly above her ears, and she never wore makeup, only some freckles high on her cheeks, yet she could, when she wanted, look as feminine as a runway model. Her chin was softly pointed, enough to make you want to hold it in your fingers, although she would jerk away whenever I tried. She had never met anyone in my family. I could have introduced her to Mom the previous summer, but something had come up for Morgane at the last minute, and afterward it all seemed to have worked out for the best.

She stubbed out her cigarette and blew the puff out the window.

"Call me and tell me what you are doing," she said flatly, and then with a thought added, "I am sorry about your father."

I brushed the hair above her ear with my fingers and she let me, even leaning into my hand a bit, and that was enough to make my heart stutter and make my lips tremble for real.

"It'll be all right," I said. "I'll call you."

"Okay," she said, and with that I got out, pulled my suitcase from behind the seat, turned my back and walked into the airport.

# Chapter Three

MY PHONE PINGED A FEW TIMES as I went through security. A TSA agent threw me a dirty look, so I grudgingly shut my phone off and put it in the tub with my laptop. On the other side I got back into my shoes, gathered everything in a rush and took off for my gate. I didn't get a look at my phone again until I was in my seat, an aisle seat with a hefty guy in the middle whose girth forced me to lean away and get bumped by everyone heading to the rows behind us.

Comments were coming in about my blog post, which I had titled *The Social Media State*. Some of the comments were the usual unimaginative one-liners—*good post; liked the post; interesting*—but then I scrolled down to one from someone called *5pointsprogress* that was a full paragraph in length and mostly all caps: *WHAT A RACIST RIGHTWING PIECE OF TRASH...*

"What?" I hollered indignantly. The big guy in the middle gave me a malevolent look, and then I got banged in the head by a flight attendant who was closing the overhead bins. She leaned down and, with a soft voice backed by impatience, asked me to turn off my phone for take-off. "Sure," I fumbled. "No problem. Sorry." And when she had moved on I went back to my phone but the big guy was having none of it.

"She said turn it off, man," he said smugly, as if he alone had been elevated to enforce such things.

I grumbled under my breath, but turned the phone off, then ground my teeth for two hours until we landed in Houston—and during that time a storm had brewed up and was now blowing with righteous fury. I stumbled into it going down the jetway, when I scrolled back to the comment from *5pointsprogress* and saw that it had turned into a scathing thread: *@5pointsprogress, JoplinD is just another hater who can't take it that we reelected Obama, #joplindracist; @5pointsprogress, Cons always blame the victim. Why do people read this trash, #joplindracist, #dontreadjoplind...*

I felt a fuzzy tremor and a little sick to my stomach. My *People & Places Nashville* blog was, while I wanted to think of it as serious writing, ultimately light fare that drew just enough ad clicks to get me by. Dad had called it a hobby masquerading as snobby journalism. That had been when he was feeling charitable. Later he called it something much worse, and while that had just about been the final straw between us, inside I knew he was right, then and now. My blog simply never got this kind of attention. Sometimes people disagreed with my restaurant or movie reviews, but their comments had always been more humorous than hateful. I couldn't understand what was going on. Why were they calling me a racist? That's not what *The Social Media State* was about.

And then it went from bad enough to worse than that, this from *mywhiteamerica: JoplinD tells it like it is. The libs hate that, #whitenation; @mywhiteamerica, The hell with political correctness, #joplindean said it right. We have to put and end to the socialist welfare state and bring back our conservative american values...*

Sprinkled throughout was language that made me cringe. I made the mistake of opening my Twitter feed. It was a chaos of hatred and profanity and dripping scorn being thrown both ways, and those defending me were people who made my skin crawl. My stomach roiled. I sidestepped into a restroom and bent over a toilet but nothing came up, so I sat in the odiferous quiet of the stall while people shuffled in and out beyond the steel door.

I didn't know what to do; I didn't know what this meant. I called Kessie but only got her voicemail. She lived with a gaggle of roommates somewhere in the Heights, or maybe it was lower Washington Avenue, or maybe she had even moved again, I wasn't sure. I couldn't think of anywhere else to go but Dad's place. I knew where he hid the key, and under the circumstances I didn't think he would mind if I went in. And then I thought about that, grunted at the irony, and went out to get my rental.

Dad lived alone in a condo off Briar Forest Drive. I hadn't been there since...well, I wasn't sure, but I think it was when Kessie graduated, four years, maybe. I could take Beltway 8 around, though. I remembered the way.

It was well after dark. The air was still crisp and clean, the sky a rosy hue from the towering vapor lights along the Beltway. Traffic hurtled past me, big SUVs with ultra bright LEDs seizing lanes with an air of entitlement. I found Dad's street and slowed. It was dark under the canopies of oaks, but there was a bubble of searing light ahead. I could see people milling around. The street was jammed with parked cars, so I took the first open spot I found, about a block short of Dad's place. Coming up the sidewalk, I soon discovered that all the activity was in front of Dad's condo. News vans had pulled up onto the sidewalks to make room in the narrow street, forcing me up into the grass.

"*Is that the son?*"

"*It* is *him. It's Joplin Dean.*"

All those milling people gathered into a front that swarmed around me in moments. Microphones were thrust into my face.

"*Joplin?*"

"*Joplin?*"

"*Joplin, look over here.*"

"*Joplin, tell us how you feel.*"

"*Where were you when you heard about it?*"

"*Have you talked to Kessie, Joplin?*"

"*Are you proud of your father?*"

We see this kind of thing on TV all the time, but I had never experienced it; I had never even been near it, except one night down on Broadway when Miranda Lambert had come out of a bar on the arm of a guy who wasn't Blake, but I had been too far back to really get a sense of...*this*. The lights make you feel naked, and the cacophonous questions grub at you like filthy fingers. At first you attempt to answer them, as if you had a duty to do so, but before you can speak one word a dozen more questions are hurled at you. They feel like painful thumps on your eardrums, and then you're overwhelmed and all you want to do is run, to get away somehow, but you're tangled in it, like a web.

My head felt gauzy and distant. I raised a hand against the deafening glare, clenched my teeth and pushed blindly through the throng. By the time I reached Dad's front step I felt bruised and dirty. Reporters were tripping over themselves trying to squeeze into the alcove with me, hemming me in so tightly that I couldn't reach down into the flowerpot for the key. My shadow quavered around me. It was so close in the alcove that I could feel the sickly warmth of aftershave and armpits and cigarette breath. I gasped for air, squared my shoulders and turned back to the glare, raising both hands to shield my eyes. I wanted to scream at them, and I think I was about to when a surreal hush scythed across the crowd. A reporter stepped forward, a sober looking woman in her early thirties. In the glare of the lights I couldn't make out much more than that, but she exuded a quiet authority that seemed to cow the others. I would learn later that her name was Doreen Ybarra.

"Mr. Dean," she said forthrightly, "your *Social Media State* blog post is being called a racist screed, while your father died saving an African-American child. Would you care to comment?"

"*What?*"

I sputtered this incoherently, and then the door opened behind me and I fell backward.

# Chapter Four

I CAME DOWN ON MY ELBOWS, heard the door slam and then suddenly it was dark. I lay there in a daze, sucking cleansing breaths while my eyes adjusted.

"Oh my God, Joplin! Are you okay?"

I looked up in the dim light of a single table lamp and saw that it was Kessie. I recognized her right away, even though I wasn't certain up until then that I would. Her nose was deep red, her eyes round and wet. She was wearing jeans and a maroon T-shirt, and had her hair done in rows. In the subdued light, I couldn't tell what color her hair was now.

I grunted as I got to my feet, swaying for a moment until I found my footing. It was tomb-like in the condo, with the blinds closed and the curtains pulled. Only a little of the glare outside leaked around the edges, like the first glow of morning. I couldn't hear anything from out there. I was about to speak when Kessie wrapped me in a shuddering hug. It was startling, as if some stranger off the street had come up and embraced me. I held my arms out in indecision, but then folded them lightly around her shoulders. I'm not sure I had ever hugged Kessie, maybe when she was a girl. I felt a solid figure beneath my arms, not muscular but taut. She sobbed into my shoulder, and after what seemed like a reasonable amount of time, I pushed back gently and looked into her red-rimmed eyes, trying to make out their color in the low light because I really didn't remember.

"How long have you been here?" I asked in lieu of a host of other questions that I couldn't bring to mind.

Kessie sniffed and ran the back of her hand across her nose.

"Since this morning," she said, dropping her eyes to her hands. "They called me. I didn't know what else to do."

"How long have they been out there?"

"All day. They won't go away. I had to unplug Dad's phone, it wouldn't stop ringing, and then they blew up my phone so I turned it off. It's been horrible. They even knock on the windows, so I've been staying in my old room upstairs."

I went wearily to the kitchen, found a bottle of wine, poured a healthy measure then flopped on the couch. Everything looked the same as last time, whenever that had been, clean, ordered, masculine browns. Kessie was still standing, following my every move like she was waiting for something. I could see now that her hair was a sandy color, darkening toward natural. The cornrows made her look like a beach girl. She had a nice tan. I sipped the wine, red and bitter. Dad would have thought it was great. I sipped more until I finally felt loose enough to go on.

"So," I asked, "what do we do now?"

Her brow wrinkled.

"I thought *you* would know."

"*Me?*"

"Well...you're older."

"Have you called Mom?"

She bristled. "Why would I call her? She's got nothing to do with this."

"C'mon, Kessie. Mom might know what we should do."

Her cheeks reddened to match her nose. "If it's something she thinks we should do, then I'll do something else."

"What is it with you two?" I asked, beginning to bristle myself.

"What do you care?"

"Ugh," I groaned. I needed more wine if we were going to get into this. I cast another look around, noticed some familiar furniture, some things on the walls that had once hung on other walls. I had never lived here. Kessie had, but I was long gone by then. The wine helped stir the ashes.

"Dad was never there for me," I mumbled bitterly.

Kessie propped her hands on her hips and came back with venom. "Mom was never there for *me*."

"She was there when you were born."

"So was Dad."

"No he wasn't. I know because *I* was there."

Kessie was puffing indignantly through her nose, so angry now that if it weren't for the crazed crowd outside I would have fled to a hotel. We stayed that way for a while, the simmering tension thick enough to cut and freeze and save for later. As my head began to swim, our spat seemed less important. What could Mom do anyway? She lived in Florida and probably hadn't seen Dad since Kessie was in high school. I didn't care about any of that. I wanted my phone. I wanted my laptop. I wanted to get online and find out what was happening, try to figure out what had gone wrong, but all my stuff was in the car.

"My suitcase and everything is in the car," I muttered at last.

She dropped her arms then. The heat drained from her face.

"You can sneak out the back," she offered; then, said plaintively enough that maybe she was afraid I might not stay, "I'll help you."

"I'm scared to go out there," I admitted.

"Me, too."

"Look, I'm wiped out and I smell like ass. I need a shower and some sleep. Maybe they'll be gone in the morning."

"Okay. You could wear some of Dad's clothes."

The thought made my stomach heave, not because Dad and I hadn't been close, but because, well... Kessie had perked up, though, and I saw no reason to pull her back down.

"Sure," I said. "Good idea. I'll sleep on the couch."

"Okay," she said again, this time with a tenuous smile, and in that I could sense how alone she was, that she didn't have anyone else but me, and it wasn't fair.

/////

IT WAS THE QUIET OF NIGHT. Kessie was asleep in her room upstairs while I was wrapped in a sheet on the couch and trying to parse the dark. I had dozed for no more than a few hours, and now my mind was too busy for sleep. I needed my laptop. I needed my phone. I needed to know what to do about my blog. I had no idea what to do about Dad.

I got up, clutched the sheet around my shoulders and tiptoed across the living room, careful not to bump into anything, not for fear of waking Kessie but for fear a reporter might be lurking just outside the window, attuned toward even the faintest hint of activity in the condo. I stood beside a window, slipped a thumb and finger behind the curtain then gently parted the blinds. I could see nothing outside in the still of a streetlight, just a halo of haze and a fluttering moth. I could hear crickets chirping, and surely that was a sign that the reporters had given up the siege. But there was a van down the way, almost completely melded into the dark of the trees. It could belong to a news crew or a soccer mom, there was no way to tell.

I sighed and stepped away, and then it occurred to me that Dad would have a computer in his office. Why hadn't I thought of that earlier? His office was in what would have been the master bedroom. I entered stealthily, unable to shake the feeling that I was sneaking around his house and might get caught. That sounds as silly as it felt, but Dad had always guarded his privacy. He wouldn't like me going in his office. I had to remind myself that he wasn't here, that he wasn't going to be here, and that I didn't have to be thinking these thoughts, I could just go in.

The door creaked as I opened it, loud enough, it seemed, to alert any loitering reporters if not also wake up Kessie, who might chastise me in Dad's absence, I didn't know her well enough to know. I held there, scanning the quiet, which remained quiet so I exhaled and eased the door closed. Kessie must have been in here earlier because these blinds and curtains had also been drawn. I was able to see well enough in the telltale lights of his electronics to cross to Dad's desk, and I could also see that it was the same desk he'd always had, a broad block of dark oak that must have weighed a ton. I fingered the polished wood and was conflicted in my thoughts. Guiltily, I wondered if Kessie would let me have this desk. She seemed to have priority, having lived here, but maybe the priority should be mine. After all, I had watched Dad working at this desk long before she was born.

We lived in Bellaire then, in a comfortable house with a nice yard and a pecan tree out front that attracted the neighbors once a year. Kessie lived there for barely months, and only as a baby, so that house would mean nothing to her. Even if she drove by it now it would mean nothing. But to me it was everything, the foundation of my life, and when that foundation broke everything else seemed to break as well.

Then, too, Dad had an office, a back bedroom at the end of an avocado-colored hall. Sometimes he left the door cracked and I would peer around the corner as he worked, sitting at this desk and clicking away at his type-writer, rubbing his forehead, pausing in thought, then clicking some more. I had wanted nothing more than to click that typewriter myself. I snuck in once and tried it. Sitting in his chair, my head came just high enough to see the keys, and when I plunged them with my fingers the keys stuck and I panicked and I ran out of there. Dad never said anything about it, but one day sat me in his lap, took my index fingers in his hands, and showed me how to do it. From that day on I wanted to be a writer like him.

Dad wasn't a real writer, although I now know of course that he really was. Dad sold refrigerators and stoves and washing machines at a store on Bellaire Boulevard. He was good at that job. He might have been good at writing, too, but he was better at selling stoves. That store went out of business some time before Kessie was born. Dad stayed home and worked at his typewriter for a long time after that, raising stacks of paper on the side-board and making regular trips to the post office until Mom told him to find another job, and then he sold memory-foam beds, and he was pretty good at that, too. They started arguing around then. Dad began to spend less time behind his typewriter and more time at work. Mom went off to real estate school, I went off to fourth grade, and then Kessie came.

I lowered myself into Dad's high-backed leather chair and rested my arms on the desktop, and the first thought that came to me was that I could look down at his keyboard now, not up at it. It was such a part of him that I was sure Dad's old typewriter was still around somewhere, maybe in a closet. I wouldn't have minded having it for a conversation piece, but the idea of actually using it felt as archaic as clipping a Walkman to my belt. Dad was still using a desktop machine with a wired keyboard and mouse, which was almost as bad. I shook my head, reached down to the box on the floor and pushed the power button. It took a long time for the machine to boot up. When it finally did, it was password protected. I tried my name and Kessie's name, caps and lower case. None of that worked, and I couldn't think of anything else.

I sat back in frustration and sighed. The monitor cast a ghostly light, enough to see by but not enough, I hoped, to signal a reporter who might be encamped beyond the window. The desk was cluttered with cables and a printer, a green-shaded banker's lamp, some reference books, and some paperback copies of his novels. Whatever he had been pecking away at when I was a child, the only things he had ever published were four detective novels that he had written in the 90s and penned under the name J.T. Dean. I had never read any of them up until then. They had been published by a vanity press, so not many others had read them either. They all got a few good reviews online, just never went anywhere. He had been selling cars by then, and was much better at that than getting his name in print.

I rummaged through his desk drawers, looking for nothing in particular except maybe a clue to his password. The top drawers were cluttered with supplies, paper clips, rubber bands, a mess. A lower left drawer had dividers, and between those were short manuscripts, some so old that the paper was yellowing. I pulled one of the older ones out and looked it over, wondering if he had written it while I spied on him all those years ago. It was a short story titled *Onward Until,* and the opening line went: *Cities mean to crush those who have no fear.* A pretty good line, I thought, if not a little over the top. The manuscript wasn't dated, so could have been written anytime up to and after Mom left him, since it was typed. Dad didn't start using a computer until the early 90s.

Then I noticed the rejection letters paper-clipped to the back of the manuscript, quite a few of them, mostly from magazines that I didn't think were around anymore, maybe online if that. The letters were all pretty standard—*does not meet our needs at this time*—and all dated in the early 80s. So I might have watched him write this one after all. That thought gave me a pleasant surge of nostalgia that then collided with the obvious evidence of his failure to get the story published. Suddenly those stacks of paper on the sideboard and those trips to the post office took on new meaning, forcing me to ponder something that I would rather have kept down where it was harder to notice. Failure is a lonely profession.

I shook off those thoughts, slipped *Onward Until* back into its place, then moved to the right side of the desk. That's where I found it, in a middle drawer all by itself, as if it occupied a reverent place, deserved special notice—as if it should have been wrapped in velvet and kept with the fine silverware. I have already described it, a hefty stack of clean white paper. It wasn't dated either, but the ink smelled fresh and the paper was so clean that Dad could have typed it out yesterday. I flipped to the last page, being careful, without thinking about it, not to crease the pristine pages, and there it said *The End*. So whatever it was, he'd finished it, and he'd signed it with his full name, not the *J.T. Dean* of his detective novels.

*The Latter Half of Inglorious Years* was something different, something special to him. I thumbed back to the first page and read the opening paragraph, a paragraph that I couldn't have come up with if I'd had my whole life to ponder it:

James Trevor Davidson came to life at 8:48 one morning as the sky raged. He breathed as windswept rain lashed my window, as lightning scorched the clouds, his chest heaving off the page until he could stand fully formed, a human of invention but true in every way. After all the work, finally, I knew him, and I loved him. He was the character I had always envisioned him to be.

I sat back and whistled. Really. This was heavy prose for Dad, written in the first person, but then the voice changed in the next paragraph, that is if I could follow what I was reading:

*The author reviewed his handiwork and he smiled. Lacing his fingers behind his head, he leaned back and looked into a future that would read like a novel yet feel like the life it told, of an author haunted by the pum-*

*meling inanity that permeated every cleft and crevice of his existence. And he had found the voice to tell it—he had found the voice of James Trevor Davidson. It seemed simple now, after the frustrations, the rewrites, the days that had passed one to the next without the pages to show for them. It was all in the name. His character hadn't lived because the original name he had conjured for him wouldn't fire, so at 8:48 on a stormy morning, in a moment of desperate inspiration, he had changed that name to James Trevor Davidson, and James had taken a first breath, and then a second, and now his story could go on.*

It goes without saying that I had to change his name, too. *James Trevor Davidson* was just too close to *John Taylor Dean*, so I renamed him *Evan Usher*. The story still worked fine. It won awards, after all.

/////

"WAIT A MINUTE, MON," Shelisa interrupted, her brow furrowed in puzzlement. "You are everywhere with this. What tale you be tellin'?"

"I'm telling you the story of my father's book."

"Sure mon, but who be tellin' that story?"

"A third person. He's not a named character."

"Then who be this Evan Usher?"

"That's just the name I gave James Trevor Davidson."

"But you say he already had his name change before?"

"Yeah. The author thought he had given his character a weak name, so he changed it."

"So this author be your father?"

"No...yes...well maybe—but in the story he's the first-person narrator that the third-person narrator is telling about."

"The *what?*"

I could feel a headache screwing into my right temple. What I wanted to do was skip the afternoon beers and go straight from coffee to good island rum, but it was still morning. I exhaled and tried to assemble it all in my mind.

"My father wrote a book about an author who is telling the story of another author who is also telling a story. What I'm telling you is my story about my father's story."

Her eyes went as round and white as demitasse saucers.

"Mon, that sound crazy."

"Yeah…" That's the only response I could come up with.

"So what happen nex in this crazy story?"

# Chapter Five

I WAS STILL SITTING AT DAD'S DESK, puzzling over the very thing that would puzzle Shelisa, when the door creaked and Kessie stuck her head in. I dropped the manuscript and jerked back as if I had been caught looking at porn.

"Sorry if I scared you," Kessie said gently, her face pallid in the silver glow of the monitor. "I thought you might be in here."

"No, uh, you didn't...well, yeah," I stuttered. The manuscript had landed precariously on my knees. I squirmed until it scooted securely into my lap, praying all along that I wasn't being too obvious about it.

Kessie didn't notice. She padded over and lowered herself into a chair adjacent to the desk, hooked a smooth leg over the arm, folded her other leg on the seat then leaned back on her shoulder. She had her sleeping clothes on, baggy white boxer shorts and a white T-shirt. I found myself inadvertently looking where I shouldn't have been. Fortunately it was too dark to see anything that would have then carved itself guiltily into my mind forever. To my eternal relief, Kessie didn't seem to notice, either my discomfort or my stray gaze.

I raised my eyes to meet hers, opalescent in that light, like a night owl's eyes. I nudged the drawer closed with my knee without giving anything away, and shifted my hips so that the manuscript slipped between my legs onto the chair and I could almost sit on it.

"I was trying to be quiet. Did I wake you up?" I deflected while this was going on.

"No," she shook her head. "I can't sleep. I came downstairs to see if there was anything to eat. I saw you were up and figured you had to be in here."

"I haven't been in here long."

"Have you found anything?"

I casually adjusted the sheet around my shoulders so that it fell across my lap.

"I mean," she went on, "I looked earlier, you know, for something—I don't know what."

"And?"

"Nothing. I didn't look hard. It didn't feel right, like I was going through his personal stuff. It made me cry more, so I left."

"We're going to have to deal with it sooner or later."

"I know," she said, dabbing at her eyes, "but not now. Okay?"

"Okay."

Kessie bit her lip and looked away. We sat quietly, the silence enveloping, just a static hum from the monitor. I fought not to drum my fingers on the desk.

"I keep thinking he's here," she said at last, looking off to a darkened wall as if it held his shadowed image, "like this can't be real." Her voice broke and she seemed to focus more intently on the wall. "I know it happens," she said after a pause, "I just never thought about it."

"Well, you were closer to him than I was," I said, and then winced at the heartless way that sounded.

She turned to me slowly, her expression seemingly caught up in some inner debate. After an unfocused moment she asked, "How come you and Dad didn't get along?"

Her voice was contemplative, not a hint of rebuke in it. I squirmed in my seat again, but this time it had nothing to do with the manuscript.

"I guess I could ask you the same thing about Mom," I replied, working to keep my own voice level.

"It's all right, I'll tell you. It's no secret anyway."

"Okay."

"I wanted to live with Dad. That's it. But you know how Mom is."

"Uh, huh." Mom had never talked to me about this, but I could picture the scene. She would have thrown a fit.

"It was like I betrayed her, like because I wanted to stay with Dad for a while I didn't love her or something. So Mom told me I should go if that's what I wanted. She never called or anything, and she wouldn't help when I needed her, so Dad had to deal with all that stuff by himself. It wasn't fair."

"Stuff? What stuff?"

"Girl stuff."

"*Oh*," I mouthed. Kessie had been twelve or thirteen when this went down. Where was I at that time? About to drop out of college, I think.

"I never knew about any of that," I said after an awkward moment. "Mom never said anything. Or Dad," I added.

"Seems stupid, huh?"

"Yeah, I guess," I said with a dulled edge. What stung was that I had wanted to live with Dad once, too, and he'd said no.

"So what about you?" Kessie asked, turning a frown into a mischievous smile that seemed out of place, considering what we'd just been discussing.

"What about me?"

"You and this Morgane. Is she really French?"

"Ah…" I laughed nervously and wished I'd had something to keep my hand busy, like a glass of wine or something. Kessie had gone from morose to merry in a moment, and now she was grinning and tapping a tooth in anticipation of something juicy. "Yes, she's really French," I answered with a sigh.

"And?" She pulled her knees up and hugged them, waiting expectantly.

"And what?"

"Oh, c'mon, Jop. Tell me."

She looked like she would have thrown a pillow if one had been at hand. That made me chuckle, and I looked at my sister in a new way. Kessie was girlish yet self-composed at the same time. She had Dad's worrying brow and his sage, dark eyes, but the rest of her looks came from Mom, her tapering face and delicate lips. She was so eager, so instantly buoyant, and though we barely knew one another, I felt at ease with her all of a sudden, like we'd been sharing confidences all our lives. I liked the way that felt. I think I craved it.

"Okay, okay," I waved in surrender. "What do you want to know?"

"Do you talk to her in French?" she asked playfully.

"No, I don't speak French, but I can understand some of it now, especially when she's mad."

Kessie snickered at that, then asked, "How did you meet?"

"It wasn't something I was expecting," I recalled fondly. "She's a travel agent. I wanted to take a trip, you know, Cancun or something, so I called this agency in Belle Meade and got Morgane. She talked me out of going to Cancun and turned me on to a cruise instead. She had some kind of sponsorship thing with the cruise line, and wound up on the same ship. So we met face to face and hit it off."

"Wow, serendipity." She squeezed her legs and rocked with glee, like a teenager in a love story. "How long ago?"

"A year...no, a year and a couple of months."

"So, are you two gonna..." she trailed off with a coy grin.

"No, it's not like that," I answered weakly.

She was leaning on her knees now, her face cupped in her hands and intent on my every word. Her brow knitted in a cute way as she pondered that.

"You mean you aren't together?" she asked in a disappointed voice.

"Well, kind of. It's—"

"OMG!" she exclaimed, shooting me her coy grin once more. "You mean she's your FWB?"

"*FWB?*" I shot back testily.

"Your friend with benefits."

"My *what?*"

I almost leaped up in umbrage, but caught myself in time to keep the manuscript from fanning onto the floor. Why was I bothered? Because after a year of trying to figure out what Morgane and I had together, Kessie had come up with it in a second, and in textese of all things. I didn't know what was worse, realizing that Morgane and I weren't going anywhere and probably never would, or being able to succinctly spell out what we did have together in three letters. It made it seem so trivial.

Kessie wasn't put off by my tone. "Hey, it's no big deal," she said with a casual shrug. "Everybody does it." She was still grinning, in a knowing way that would have made me blush if I hadn't been looking for more with Morgane than just the benefits. Kessie didn't know that, though. She wasn't being critical, just curious, so I eased up on the umbrage and diverted her with my own question.

"So what about you, then? Got a boyfriend?" I tried to match her grin but couldn't muster that much enthusiasm. Still I smiled, maybe in a brotherly way.

"I've got friends," she said, completely unabashed. "Sometimes we hook up. It's no big deal."

"Really?" Now my brows knitted. "So no regular boyfriend?"

"Why? That would ruin everything." She said this as if it should have been obvious, that I should have been able to see it for myself. Times change, I guess, but then that thought sobered me because it meant that I had aged out of whatever group Kessie belonged to, and that was startling because I didn't feel old enough to have aged out of anything, and *that* meant it was time to change the subject.

"You had a coffee bar, didn't you?" I asked.

"Yeah," she sighed, "me and some friends. It didn't work out."

"What happened? Did you all start arguing? They say it's hard to be in business with friends."

"No," she seemed taken aback, "of course not. That would never happen. We just ran out of money, that's all. We're going to try again, this time with a food truck so we don't have to pay so much rent. My friend Jason is writing an app. We're going to do bicycle deliveries downtown, coffee and maybe sandwiches and stuff. We just have to save some money first, and my college loans...man." She slapped her forehead for emphasis. "But there's five of us," she went on, "so it won't take too long."

My jaw dropped in amazement. Kessie and her friends threw ideas into a pot and stirred until something gelled, and if things didn't work out they just shook it off and tried again. Something like that would never have occurred to me and my friends. We'd meet over beers or wine, talk big, get wound up, and still be having the same grandiose conversations a year later. It wasn't like that with Kessie and her friends. I felt vaguely jealous.

"So are you working now?" I asked.

"Yeah," she said, "at Starbucks on Voss."

"Oh," I said, not knowing if Starbucks was a step up or a step down for her. Considering the upbeat way she was talking, I don't think she even looked at it that way.

"I've read your blog before," she said then. "I thought it was pretty good."

"Really?" I perked up. "Did you ever post any comments?"

"No, I didn't think about it. And I've never been to Nashville, so I wouldn't know what to say anyway."

"Well, yeah...I can understand that."

And that brought it back, what was going on with my last post, what Dad had said about my writing, all of it. The smile slipped off my face then. My mood darkened. Kessie must have thought she had said something wrong, because she went on quickly like she was apologizing.

"Hey, I didn't mean anything. I liked your blog."

She wore a worried look now, her lips parted expectantly, like she'd be ready to turn her smile back on if she could undo whatever it was and get us back to where we were. But it wasn't Kessie, it was me. I rubbed my hands as I debated whether to go on. She'd given me her story about Mom, then she'd shrugged it off with a sweet smile like it wasn't worth dwelling on. Why couldn't I be that way?

"Okay," I mumbled after a moment, still rubbing my hands. "Here it is—Dad didn't respect what I do." I looked at her harshly. "So, there."

"You mean your blog?" She put her feet on the floor and leaned forward.

"Yeah. He said it was just a hobby. He said worse than that. He told me once that it was amateur, that it was—get this—that it was amateur masturbation. He couldn't believe I got money from it."

"Daddy *said* that to you?" She looked hurt, like her hero had just lost a leg and was tottering on his pedestal.

"Uh, huh."

"Oh Joplin, I'm so sorry." She hopped up and put her arms around me, rested her head against mine and I could smell the freshness of her skin. "Dad was old-fashioned," she said close to my ear. "You know that. And he wasn't happy. His writing...you know?"

The manuscript was secure beneath my thigh, so I wasn't giving any thought to it just then, only Kessie, and a well of hurt that was deeper than I had thought.

"So you're making excuses for him?" I asked, pushing her back so that I could see her face.

"No." She pulled back farther, studying me closely before she lowered herself back into her chair. "No, I'm not. He wasn't perfect, I know that, but he was always sweet to me. It's hard to understand."

"So he never said anything to you about it?"

"No." She shook her head sadly. "Sometimes people would ask him about you. I know I did a lot back then. He said you were a successful writer in Nashville. He said he wished he had as many readers as you did."

"He didn't say that," I came back heatedly.

"Yes he did. All the time."

That wasn't going to be enough salve for this wound, but it did force me to reappraise my father, especially since it came with Kessie's earnest expression.

"I wish he would've told me that," I said petulantly.

"I don't know, Jop. Maybe he meant to, maybe he would have, I don't know. Sometimes I think...I don't know—maybe because you're so much older. You knew Dad when he was younger than me. I didn't know him until he was your age."

"So what?"

"So people change, Jop, like they make a mistake and they don't know how to fix it."

"I don't think that's what Dad thought."

"I don't think the Dad I knew and the Dad you knew were the same person."

"That just sounds wrong, Kessie."

"No, I don't think so." And now she had sharpened her voice to match mine. "I think it sounds just right."

I groaned and sat back, and so did she, and what glowered between us seemed to put an end to the little bit of sincerity we'd found between us. The manuscript was beginning to press uncomfortably into my thigh. I shifted a bit to ease the pressure, and that gave me a thought.

"Was Dad working on anything?" I asked as if to fill the silence.

"Writing, you mean?"

"Yeah."

"I don't think so. He said he was tired of it."

"Really? He was always writing something. I used to watch him on his typewriter when I was little."

"Me too," she said, and that caught me because I guess I thought of those memories as mine alone. "But I think he quit. He told me everything was so cheap now, with the internet and e-books. He said he didn't want to be a part of that."

That sounded like Dad, all right. It was why nobody bought his books. I barely had time to mull that before Kessie leaned forward again.

"Listen, Jop," she said contritely. She looked wounded, and that made me want to protect her, and then I felt guilty.

"Yeah?"

"I wish we wouldn't argue. I didn't mean for that to happen."

I couldn't think of anything except to take the blame myself, to act the big brother that I'd never been.

"No, Kessie. I'm sorry. It was me, not you."

"No. It was both of us together. Okay?"

I had no defense against such candor, no choice but to agree.

"Okay, Kessie. It was both of us...together."

And with that her smile was back, a little embattled but it was there, and just as I discovered that I was glad to see it, it went reflexive, became a tight line of thought.

"When you saw me tonight," she said, not looking at me but at the wall again, at solid shadows that appeared only to her, "you said Dad wasn't there when I was born. Did you mean that?"

I could destroy him with a word, I knew it, but that power left me cold because it wasn't just him, it was Kessie too, and I couldn't do it to her. I couldn't.

"I was just mad," I said with a fake smile. "Of course Dad was there. Where else would he have been?"

She didn't ask, which thankfully relieved me of the burden. Kessie's hero was intact, her smile proved it, and so was her naive optimism. It was an elixir, her smile, a medicine I hadn't known I needed.

Gray oozed around the curtains, a new day, but there was still business from yesterday.

"Do you have any idea what the password is for this computer?" I asked her.

She gave me a beatific look and chirped, "Of course. Couldn't you guess? It's *Inca*."

## Chapter Six

THEY FOUND MY FACEBOOK PAGE. I was amazed at how crafty they were, how ingeniously they skirted the profanity filters. I made a try at deleting and blocking the worst posts, but that was futile. There were too many, and they kept coming. Finally, in exasperation, I just unpublished the page. I did the same with Twitter, which left only the comments on my blog. They were less about me now, instead my blog had become a platform for people to argue with one another, or rather, to hate one another. It was depressing that so many people had enough spare time in their lives to waste on this. Maybe it was a better way for them to vent their anger, though, better than in person, in the kind of road-rage confrontations that got people hurt. I just wished their anger didn't involve me.

Some of the more recent comments had started a new, unsettling thread that seemed to have come out of nowhere. The language might have been cleaner, but the result was just as mean. *exlibris41* wrote: *Can't believe this is the son of J.T. Dean. Shows you can't inherit talent; @exlibris41, I love J.T. Dean, can't believe he's gone, #ripjtdean; @exlibris41, I read all his books. Loved them, especially the first one, Houston Storm. Loved his characters. I don't know why he wasn't more popular The father was great, but the son not so much. Sad, #ripjtdean, #houstonstorm, #houstonlights, #houstonstreet, #houstonrising.*

I pushed back from Dad's computer, gaping at what was on the screen. That fuzzy tremor came back. My stomach felt sour. I brought up my blog and re-read it, searching for clues to this fiasco. All I had done was criticize the syrupy excesses of social media, the philandering and self-gratification. People didn't get involved in causes, didn't see them through, instead they tapped keys at a distance and congratulated themselves for their generosity.

That's what social media had done for Persimmon Banks, one of four siblings without a father, a mother in jail, a grandmother in rehab, for God's sake leaving a *great-grandmother* to look after them all, and with some cousins in the mix as well? It would be hard enough for *two* parents to ride herd on so many kids, but because of this family's circumstances one little child had gotten loose, Persimmon, and now she would be awash in excess, none of which would solve her family's problems, and none of which would prevent her or her siblings from turning their great-grandmother into a great-great-grandmother within the next ten years, and the woman was still plenty young enough for that to happen.

There it was. That's what had done it. I groaned and squeezed my temples between my palms. Everything I wrote about Persimmon's family had come from news reports except for that last speculative sentence, which while plausible, perhaps even probable, had nevertheless segued my argument into the rage of racial politics. I could fix it easily enough. I could go in, edit the blog, delete that sentence, but something told me that would make it worse, that if I thought it was bad now, imagine *that* storm. I visualized what the responses might be, like headlines in a newspaper: *Blogger Tries to Cover His Tracks; Blogger Bows to Pressure.* No, it would burn itself out faster, I thought, if I left it alone.

Kessie was upstairs in the shower, and the manuscript was double-wrapped in plastic grocery bags on the couch. It was fully light outside now, another crisp and clear morning. I chanced a look through the blinds, saw no one. The van from last night was gone, whatever it had been. A woman crossed the street to her car, juggling coffee, keys, and purse. Her door slammed and the engine started. Leaves skittered along the sidewalk, and acorns made cracking sounds as they fell. That was it. All clear.

This looked like my best chance, so I took it. Easing out the back door with the manuscript under my arm, I made my way through the condo complex to the next street over, and then the long circle back around to my rental.

After paranoid glances up and down the street, like I was a spy being tailed, I quickly unlocked the door and dove in. With peculiar relief, I shoved the manuscript under the passenger seat, then allowed a moment to ask myself why I was being so secretive about it. I didn't dwell on it too long, though, because my phone started vibrating. That stimulus took precedence over everything.

It was Mom. I didn't want to talk to her just then because of an irrational fear that a reporter's microphone might be close, so I sent her a text telling her what had happened, then I sent Morgane a text, saying about the same thing. Mom texted back right away. *Find his will*, she wrote. *Get in touch with his lawyer.* If it had been anyone but Mom I would have questioned the coldness of that advice, but from her it just seemed like normal pragmatism. Another text from Mom came in like an afterthought: *I'm sorry. How's your sister?*

I had to smile at that. Any concern from Mom was a watershed. Kessie wouldn't believe it. We texted back and forth for a few more minutes, enough for Mom to instruct me on about everything Kessie and I would have to do, from identifying Dad's body to contacting a funeral home. It was complicated. It wasn't going to be easy, especially having to identify Dad. I didn't want to do it. I didn't think Kessie could, or even if I should let her. Mom asked if I wanted her to come do it. I wrote that I would let her know.

That ended my conversation with Mom, and then Morgane texted me: *The people are very mad with your blog.*

///// 

KESSIE WAS AT DAD'S COMPUTER when I got back to the condo. I was short of breath after hauling my suitcase and all my stuff the long way back around. I leaned against the office door, panting, and she looked up at me with her brows dipped in concern, but not for my health.

"I just read your blog," she said. "Do you know what people are saying?"

"Yeah," I mumbled wearily.

"Why would you write something like that?"

"It's not what I meant," I found myself pleading. "I was only trying to—"

"It's okay, Jop. I understand."

"You do?"

"I think so. I'm not sure I agree with you, but I still think these trolls are awful."

"Well thanks...I guess."

She mulled that for a moment, then noticed my suitcase through the doorway.

"You went to your car?"

"Yeah."

"Any people?"

"I didn't see any."

"Good," she spat, and with such force that if any reporters had strayed past the window right then I think Kessie would have jumped through after them. And she looked the part, rugged in camo cargo pants and a brown pullover sweater.

"Listen," I said hesitantly. I went to the chair Kessie had sat in last night, lowering myself into it before going on. "I talked to Mom."

Kessie stiffened.

"What did she have to say?"

"She asked how you were."

"I doubt that."

"No, it's true. She did. But she also told me the stuff we have to do."

"Like?" she asked skeptically.

"Like we're going to have to go down and see Dad."

She sniffed and looked away, and I chided myself for being so blunt.

"Look," I said soothingly. "You don't have to. I can do it."

"No," she snapped, and when she turned back to me her eyes were red. "Us together. Okay?"

"Are you sure?"

She covered her face then. A little cry squeaked out.

"Uh, huh," she said wetly, nodding with her face in her hands. "They told me yesterday. We have to."

It took a little while for this to pass. I stared at the carpet, chewed my lip and waited, pretended not to be looking when she wiped her eyes and nose. After a few sniffs she asked, "What else did Mom say?"

"Are you sure you want to talk about it now?"

"We have to, Jop. It's okay."

"Okay." I went on carefully. "We need to look for his will, and see if he had a lawyer...and some other things."

She was nodding as I said this, then pointed to a closet.

"He has a lock box in there. Everything's in it."

"Okay."

"But before we do that, I want to go where it happened. Take me, will you?"

"Oh, Kessie." My chest hurt at the thought. "Why do you want to do that?"

"I need to see it, Jop. I have to see it."

I groaned but said okay, and after a breakfast of nothing but coffee and toast, we went.

///// 

DAD HADN'T BEEN A JOGGER when I knew him. I asked Kessie why he took it up, but she wasn't sure.

"I think maybe he was just getting older, you know? Like he was worried about his health."

"You mean like a heart attack or something?"

We were on I-10, about to take the Yale Street exit. The traffic was abominable and fast, and I had both hands on the wheel. Kessie was navigating because I didn't remember anything on this side of town.

"Don't say it like that, Jop. It sounds mean." She had her sunglasses on against the glare of white concrete. They made her face look wider and she older, old enough to scold me the way Mom would. "Exit here, go all the way across, then turn right."

She steered us across Memorial Drive, through some tangled cloverleafs and then into a pullout off Allen Parkway, where we got out and left the car. The jogging path was clean and white, hemmed in by Buffalo Bayou on our left, speeding traffic and then office buildings on our right.

"It's that way," she said, pointing.

Cool as it was, I was beginning to sweat in the sun. Kessie pulled off her sweater and tied it around her waist. She wore a white T-shirt underneath, which formed to her tightly, making her look like an urban tough girl.

We didn't have to walk far before we could see a spray of color ahead. People had been leaving flowers, so many that they resembled a manicured garden alongside the path. A few scraps of color clung to the median, lifted and blown like litter as cars rushed past.

To our left was a broad grassy area, bordered in the back by some nice shade trees. It had been a good place for Eugenia Washington to bring the kids to play, plenty of room away from the street, easy to keep an eye on them all, except she hadn't. Somehow, Persimmon had wandered off unnoticed. Eugenia would have come running across the grass right there. The woman who shot the video with butterfly baby would have stopped up ahead by that streetlight, and Persimmon would have toddled into the street just...there. And then Dad, jogging in this direction, pure coincidence. He didn't have that far to run, not as far as it looked in the video, but if he had been a half a step slower he wouldn't have made it. And that's what made him a true hero, they said, because if he hadn't made it he would have been hit anyway.

There were people ahead, the usual joggers, who glanced curiously at the flowers as they went by, but other people as well. I stopped and stiffened at the sight of a reporter and cameraman. They were moving through the people, catching interviews where they could. A group of kids followed ahead of them, showing off for the camera. Kessie stopped with me, took my hand and squeezed hard.

"You want to keep going?" I asked her.

"They won't know it's us."

"You sure?"

She didn't answer, just shook her head and pulled me along.

There were candles with blackened wicks among the flowers. Sympathy balloons bobbed in the breeze. People had left crosses, which caught me as ironic because Dad wasn't the least bit religious. None of us were. I wondered what would happen to all these flowers. Would someone come and gather them up, or would they be left here until they wilted and blew into the bayou? And what about the other offerings? Would they just become trash? Should Kessie and I take some of them? I didn't want to, but maybe Kessie would.

We stopped directly across from where it happened. Kessie leaned into me and covered her face. I felt wooden, no tears, but thankful that there wasn't a smear of blood or anything else on the pavement. That would have been hard to bear, yet at the same time it felt wrong that there was no mark, no stain, nothing physical left at the scene to bear witness. If it weren't for all of this, we could have walked past and never known.

*Cities mean to crush those who have no fear.*

"Mr. Dean," someone said behind me. I spun around and saw that it was the reporter from last night.

"Oh, hell," I said.

Kessie tensed like she was ready to pounce. The look on her face should have driven this woman back a few steps, but the woman stood her ground, resolute and unintimidated. Her cameraman edged around to her right to get all of us in the frame. We didn't attract any other attention. These interviews had probably been going on since sunrise, so were taken for granted now.

"Ms. Dean," the woman added with a nod. "I'm Doreen Ybarra from Channel 2. I'd like to talk to you."

"No way," I growled. I took Kessie's hand and started to shoulder past Doreen. Kessie felt unbendable. She kept her eyes locked on Doreen as we went by.

"Mr. Dean, please," Doreen said after us, keeping her voice low. "I'm sorry for your loss, but what I want to talk about is your blog."

That pulled me up short. I turned back to her, causing Kessie to step on my foot and bounce off my hip.

"What do you mean?" I asked suspiciously.

I thought I saw Doreen smirk, but that wasn't it, just the muscles in her face relaxing a little.

"Why don't we go over there?" she said, pointing to the grassy area where Persimmon's family had been.

"Okay."

"*Jop*," Kessie mouthed with her teeth clenched.

"I think it's okay, Kessie. Please?"

She grumbled but stayed with me as we casually wandered away from the crowd. The cameraman carried his camera in front of him, I guess to hide it from those behind us, and Doreen clasped her hands behind her back as if she were just out for a stroll. I stopped in the shade of an oak tree, far enough away, I thought, not to attract attention.

"How's this?" I asked Doreen.

"Looks fine," she said.

The cameraman began to raise his camera but Doreen waved him down. "Let's just talk for a minute," she said to me. "Okay?"

"Fine."

"Then let me start again by saying how sorry I am for your loss. Your father was a brave man."

"Thanks."

"I guess you know that racial tensions are high all over the country." That was a statement, not a question. I nodded for her to go on. "So something like this goes a long way. Which is why I was surprised when I read your blog."

"It's not what I meant," I said defensively.

"Then tell me what you did mean."

"Only that people knee-jerk to everything that happens, then social media turns it into a big deal."

Doreen's brows went up.

"That's a pretty big deal," she said, gesturing toward the growing memorial like it was self-evident.

"That's not what I meant either," I grumbled.

"I believe you," she said, "but words can come loaded with all kinds of meanings. As a professional you must know that."

I flinched a little at that, enough that Doreen noticed. Her face betrayed nothing, but I got the sense that she had pretty much sized me up, could intuit that I had never really thought of myself as a professional. The truth is that I always felt like I was pretending, that sooner or later someone would catch me, and maybe they had. Maybe that person was Doreen.

"Anyway," she continued, "please take my card." She held one out and I took it, gave it a glance, saw *Pulitzer Prize* and some other journalism awards. No wonder the others had quieted down for her at the condo last night. "If you ever feel that you need to talk, please give me a call." She nodded at her cameraman, who sighed. *No story here after all*, his expression seemed to say. They started to head off.

"That's *it*?" Kessie asked after them, her hands on her hips. Doreen looked over her shoulder.

"That's it," she said, and then she paused. "One other thing, though. Those books your father wrote? I'd find a literary agent if I were you. You're going to need one."

# Chapter Seven

DAD DIDN'T HAVE A LAWYER, so Mom called one for us, someone she knew from the old days. His name was Leonard, and for the longest time I thought that was his first name. Leonard was supposedly no older than Mom, but he looked like he'd been around about twenty years longer. He even smelled like age, that kind of musty drawing room smell I remembered as a child from our visits with Mom's mother, the only grandparent I ever met. Dad's parents had died long before any of us were around, and Mom's father had died when I was still too little to remember him. Kessie had never known a grandparent at all, a concept that must have been as far beyond her as an ancestor in the Civil War.

Leonard was attentive though, and spoke with us like an old family friend, which I guess he was in a way. He had known Mom when she was young, and had met Dad before Mom and Dad got married. He said he had seen me once as a baby. He went on about that for a while, spreading his knotty hands to show how small I had been. My cheeks warmed at this talk, although I kept a loose smile on so I wouldn't seem rude. Kessie leaned in, girlishly rapt, egging him on, which made it hard to change the subject.

Dad's will was simple, Leonard explained, something Dad had downloaded over the internet. Dad didn't have a lot, but he did well enough. We would have to sell the condo to pay off the mortgage, his car and other things. There would be a little left after debts and expenses, and Kessie and I were to divide that equally.

Kessie seemed pensive as we drove back to the condo from Leonard's office.

"Are you okay?" I asked, thinking she might still be upset from our visit to the morgue that morning.

"I'm fine," she answered quietly.

It turned out that we could have been spared the morgue after all. They had identified Dad by other means, but there had been some kind of miscommunication, probably because of the media frenzy, so when we showed up it was a surprise to everybody. For me it was a reprieve, like I'd been rescued at the last minute, but Kessie was adamant. She wanted to see him, there was nothing I or anyone in the coroner's office could say that would change her mind.

I went gray at the thought of going in there. Kessie clung to me tightly, burrowing so deeply into my chest that we must have resembled a couple of terrified characters in a horror movie. The place was unnaturally cool, with a stinging smell of disinfectant that barely masked another, more sickening odor. We squeaked ahead with halting steps, pausing well away from the steel gurney like we might catch something. The sheet was pulled back and I saw Dad's mannequin face, him but not him. I swallowed hard and fought for an untainted breath. Kessie turned one hesitant eye that way, and then with a shivering squeal pressed her face even harder against my chest.

Dad had written something in one of his detective novels. At the time, I couldn't figure out where or when he had experienced such a thing that he could write about it so vividly. It went:

*When you get death on you it sticks, a ptomaine stench that clings to your skin, and no matter how much you bathe you can't get it off.*

We rushed back to the condo after we left the morgue. I showered, changed clothes, and as we met with Leonard I could still smell it. I couldn't get clean, and wondered if I ever would.

*/////*

WE CONTINUED ON BY ROTE toward the condo, stop and go in the traffic, with Kessie gazing trancelike out her window.

"We need to plan the funeral," I said as gently as I could.

"I know," she whispered.

"He didn't say anything in his will. Do you know what he would have wanted?"

"No, he never talked about it." She still had her face to the window. I could make out her reflection dancing on the glass. Her eyes were dry, her mind elsewhere.

"Kessie, what is it?"

She turned to me at that, her face a mask.

"It's not fair, that's all."

"What do you mean?"

"You heard what Leonard said about Dad's books."

Oh, that. It seemed like from one day to the next all four of Dad's books had become bestsellers on Amazon. There were going to be some big royalty checks coming in. Those would go to Kessie and me, too, but if this went on it would get too big for us to handle. We needed an agent. Doreen Ybarra had said that yesterday, and now I understood. Leonard knew someone who would be in touch.

"Yeah, I heard what he said. Why isn't it fair?"

"Because it's all Dad really ever wanted," she said. "To be an author, for people to read what he wrote. You know that. You saw all those stories in his desk, didn't you?"

I tensed at that. How far had she explored Dad's desk?

"Yeah...I saw them."

"Did you *read* any of them?"

"Only a little," I said, and now I looked away, pretending to be keeping my eyes on traffic.

"Well they're good, Jop. They're really good. But nobody would ever publish him. He had to publish his detective books on his own, and now look. Suddenly he's famous and people think his books are great. It's not fair."

She crossed her arms in a huff and turned back to the window, while I swallowed a guilty lump in my throat. I had to ask, just to be sure:

"Did he write any other books, I mean besides the *Houston* books?"

"No, just those stories in his desk. But there's enough of them for at least two books, maybe three."

I exhaled inwardly. "So we can get them published, then. He would have liked that."

Now she turned to me, wound up tight and as red-faced as an argument about Mom.

"That's not the point. He didn't get to *know*. Don't you understand?"

I pulled back a little. She was serious about this. I would recall this conversation later on, something that Dad had written:

*To know that no one will ever read your words is death. To know that characters brought lovingly to life will never be met is to murder them at birth. To know that others might someday reinvent them and call them their own is purgatory.*

"Damn. I'm sorry, Kessie. I didn't mean anything."

She halted in mid-breath, and then her shoulders slumped and she seemed to deflate into her seat.

"No, I'm sorry, Jop. I thought maybe...well, because you write, maybe you would understand. But what you do isn't the same, I know, so *I'm* sorry. Let's not talk about this anymore."

And then I had to puzzle out what she meant by that. Did she mean that what I did didn't measure up to what Dad did? It was the same old criticism, but from her this time, the hobby, not worthy of one of Dad's opening lines.

I ground my teeth but didn't say anything. It was easier to just brush it off. When we got back to the condo, though, I retreated to the office and slammed the door, rerunning it all through my mind. What I could do was go through that damn drawer and shred every story I found, and I was mad enough to do it, but then as if by a saving grace Kessie knocked lightly on the door and came in.

I took Dad's chair, *she* could sit in the other one. I fumed while she settled herself.

"Jop, I'm sorry," she said.

"Sorry about what?" I snapped back.

"I didn't realize...I compared you to Dad, didn't I? I didn't mean to do that."

"But it's what you sounded like you meant," I said, completely oblivious of the irony.

"I know," she said sadly.

I could tell that she was sincerely miserable, and while I knew that I should calm down, I just couldn't make myself do it. The strain was eating at me now, all of this, but also the comments on my blog, which hadn't let up, no, but had actually gotten worse: *Does anybody actually read this guy's blog? It's amateur stuff. Could he really have come from J.T. Dean? That apple fell pretty far.*

The video was still circulating, like a fire that kept leaping to another tree, and now his books had become instant bestsellers. The *Houston Chronicle* was going to run a feature in next Sunday's *Arts & Entertainment* section. Their people had managed to get through to Kessie. They did a short phone interview with her, but hadn't asked to talk to me at all, like they'd read my blog and decided they didn't want any of that sullying their story.

"C'mon, Jop. I'm *sorry*," Kessie offered again, this time leaning forward and reaching for my hand. I pulled back, berating myself even as I did it. Kessie pulled back too, and now her face was hardening.

"You know something?" I said after I exhaled a hot breath. I thought I was keeping my voice low and reasonable. The way Kessie reddened and crossed her arms said otherwise, but I pressed on anyway. "I've been doing my blog for a long time. I make *money* from it, not a lot, but enough. You know what's really ironic? I've had so many visits since I put up that damn post that now I'm going to have some real money coming in. Even the people who hate it are making me money. Right? So Dad never made any money from his books, not enough to do anything. He sold cars, Kessie. So which one of us had a hobby?"

She gaped at me, not trembling but close to it.

"I can't believe you would talk about him like that," she hissed through her teeth.

"It's what he said to *me*," I shot back, hard enough to make her jump, which pierced me with shame but I just couldn't let it go. "Look," I went on imperiously, "I want Dad's desk."

"No."

That was it. She didn't hesitate, she didn't raise her voice, just that one steel word. I looked her over. Her demeanor was immovable, her gaze narrow. My self-righteous resolve began to wilt right then.

"Why not?" I asked, flustered.

"Because of the way you said it."

"Huh?"

"If you want Dad's desk then take it, but don't ever to talk to me like that again."

That was Mom's voice, Mom's demeanor. I knew them well. Taken together, they declared a line that would not be crossed. I could have said as much to Kessie but she would never have accepted that her implacable strength didn't come from Dad.

"Okay," I said wearily, hoping that would bring an end to this.

"And..."

I groaned. No, that wasn't the end of it.

"And?"

"I want Dad's stories."

"What? *Why*?"

"Look—you want his desk, I want his stories. It's a trade. So...?"

That set everything roiling again. I could feel the heat rising back into my cheeks, but I could tell from Kessie's granite expression that it would do no good to argue.

"Take 'em, then," I conceded in disgust. "Why should I care?"

And to my surprise she got up and came right over, bending across me to open the drawer as if daring me to get in her way. She took the stories out an armload at a time, filling a file box she found in the closet. When she was done she hefted the box with a grunt and carried it off, leaving me there to ponder what had just happened.

/////

THE NEXT COUPLE OF DAYS ran together as we made arrangements, took care of the things that had to be done, and dodged media requests. Reporters or other media people would still come to the door a few times a day, but there had never been another crowd of them like that first day. We would answer the door, politely decline, and after that they were good enough to go away. Neither one of us wanted to sit for interviews, even if some of the networks obliquely offered to make it worth our while. It seemed that every time there was a tragedy or event, it had become routine for people to parade themselves from camera to camera, from morning show to morning show, turning themselves into temporary celebrities, entertainment for others. Not us.

The temperature between Kessie and me cooled to the point that we were getting along pretty well again, but there was still something between us, a vague tension that wouldn't ease. Trust is fragile, it chips easily. You might be able to glue the broken parts back on, but you would still be able to see the cracks.

I was given a chance to mend those cracks when Mom showed up unannounced at the door, but as I should have known, there was no way I would ever be able to gather the broken pieces between her and Kessie.

I stepped back from the door in shock and surprise.

"Mom?"

"Joplin!"

She opened her arms in her exaggerated, motherly way, and I stepped into them numbly so that she could hug and squeeze and fawn over me, and then Kessie came up behind us.

"Oh, Inca baby," Mom gushed, brushing past me with arms wide.

"I've asked you not to call me that," Kessie said in a firm, controlled voice. She had her arms at her sides, not crossed. She didn't look angry, just unyielding.

Mom dropped her arms, and I could sense the exaggerated smile sliding off her face.

"All right then, Kessie," Mom said tightly. "How have you been holding up?"

"We're doing fine," I said, closing the door and stepping between them. "You didn't say you were coming."

"Do I need an invitation?" Mom asked, keeping her eyes on Kessie. "You're my children. You need my help."

Kessie was about to sputter something when I interjected again:

"And we appreciate it, Mom. We took your advice. Leonard has been great. Kessie's already made most of the arrangements, though, so there's not really anything left to do."

"Hmm," Mom said. She flicked an appraising glance at Kessie and then took off on a self-guided tour of the condo. Kessie leapt after her, and I leapt after Kessie, feeling completely impotent to do anything to avert what I was afraid was coming.

But for their hair and clothes they could have been the same woman. Mom was in a powder-blue pants suit with a white sweater, her hair a little brassy now but still in her signature shoulder flip. Kessie was in jeans as usual, and a T-shirt, which just happened to be a similar shade of blue. Mom's hands were on her hips, Kessie's were on hers. Mom bulled ahead, pausing to examine Dad's bric-a-brac, some photos, a painting of a city street in the rain, everything smeared gray except a woman in a yellow raincoat hailing a black cab. Kessie stayed right with her, poised like she was getting ready for a showdown.

Mom seemed to sense this. She glanced over at me with that wry smile of hers, then turned back to the painting.

"That's me, you know," she said, jarring me out of whatever strange state I had been in.

"Really?" I said as Kessie simultaneously mouthed *bullsh*—

"Yep," Mom went on. "We had a friend—you can ask Leonard." She turned to me, ignoring Kessie. "In case you can't tell, this is London." She turned to Kessie. "Did your father ever tell you about this painting?"

Kessie seemed confused at the change of tack. So was I.

"He never told *me*," I said, probably more dumbfounded than Kessie because this painting had hung on a wall in the house in Bellaire. It was a part of my childhood memories, but no one had ever said that there was anything special about it.

"That's where we met, you know," Mom said.

No, I didn't know. And from the look on Kessie's face, neither had she.

"Uh, huh." Mom seemed to be relishing this. "Summer of Love—ever heard of *that*, kiddos? Except we went to London, but it was pretty much the same. I had a friend, Marc." She gave me a wink that made me cringe. "He painted this. He called it *The Woman in Yellow*. There was a place in Camden Town we hung out at, a little cellar called Jo—uh, hmm." Something caught in her throat. She coughed lightly before going on. "Well, it was a dark little place down some narrow stairs. Have you heard the song by Petulia Clark, *I Know a Place*?"

Kessie and I looked at each other then, both mouthing, *What?* Mom continued as if whatever the hell she was talking about made complete sense to us.

"So one night your father showed up down there. It was dark—only gaslight, you know—and at first I thought he was George. I loved George back then."

"*George?*" Kessie and I asked at the same time, both of us flailing against abject confusion.

"Oh, yes, George." Mom hugged herself in fond memory, then she looked at us, annoyed like we were idiots. "George Harrison? *Beatles?* You've heard of them, right?" She didn't wait for an answer. "Most of the girls loved Paul or Ringo, but I loved George, and that's who your father reminded me of when he came down that night. Marc was brokenhearted, of course. He gave this to your father when we left London, like a trophy for the victor." She tapped the frame with a fingernail and then added reflectively, "I'm surprised John kept it."

This was more information about my parents than I was sure I wanted to know. Still, I had a dozen questions to ask at once, but Kessie put the kibosh on that like your girlfriend dumping a cold coke in your lap at the movie theater.

"What do you want, Mom?" she asked abruptly.

I flinched at Kessie's tone, but Mom didn't shift a muscle. She was still gazing at the painting when she sighed and said to herself, "You never stop thinking of them as children. Hmpf." And then she turned to Kessie. "I came to pay my respects at the funeral tomorrow, honey."

And with that Kessie was dismissed. Mom walked past her, took my hand and said as pleasantly as if Kessie hadn't spoken a word, "Walk me to my car, would you?"

Mom had parked on the street. We went outside and down the sidewalk toward her car, with Mom holding my hand just tight enough that I knew from experience she was furious. I took one look back at Kessie. She was standing in the doorway with her arms tightly crossed.

When I thought we were out of earshot I asked, "Mom, why do you treat Kessie like that?"

"You don't have children, Joplin," she sighed. "Sometimes I wonder if you ever will." She looked at me with a haunting glimmer of Kessie's earnestness. "You and the French girl? That would be fine with me if I could get a grandchild out of it."

"*Mom!*"

"No, really. I'm sure she's a nice girl, but something tells me you all aren't going down that road. Am I right?" I looked away guiltily. Mom seemed to deflate. "I thought so," she said with another sigh, "and Kessie will probably never— Well anyway, what were we saying?"

"I asked you why you treat Kessie like that."

"Like what? You mean like a petulant child?"

"Mom, she's not a child."

"Are you sure?"

"She's no more a child than I am."

"Hmm. Interesting comparison."

"Huh?"

"Oh, it's nothing, Joplin," she said as we approached her car. "Let's talk about this some other time, okay? I need to get going. Ted came with me and we have some old friends to see." Ted Percy was Mom's husband number three.

"How is Ted?"

"He's fine. You'll see him tomorrow." She opened her door and slid in. "Oh," she added, about to pull the door. "I have a friend who'll be calling you. She's a realtor here and can help you with John's condo...that is, if you want."

"Sure, Mom. Thanks."

"And one more thing."

"What's that?"

"Hang onto the painting, would you? If not, I'd like to have it."

"Okay, uh, yeah, we'll do that."

She nodded, satisfied, then pulled the door closed and drove away.

## Chapter Eight

KESSIE MADE ALL THE FUNERAL ARRANGEMENTS by herself, her eyes fixed on her phone, her thumbs in a constant choreographed dance. Up the stairs, down the stairs, sitting for a bowl of cereal, curled in her comfy chair, tattered jeans, bare feet and clasping her toes, it was like a mission for her, absorbing all her attention. It wasn't so much that she excluded me, but that she seemed to need the distraction. It gave her something to do, something to keep her mind busy. If it made her feel better I was happy to stay out of the way, maybe even relieved.

After our experience at the morgue, Kessie didn't want an open casket. I was okay with that. I didn't know if I would ever be able to get past my issues with Dad, but I did know that I didn't want my last picture of him to be the waxen one beneath the lid of his casket. I was having a hard enough time trying to forget what I'd seen at the morgue. And since it would only be Kessie and me, Mom and Ted, some friends of Dad's from work, and maybe Leonard attending, we were only going to do a short graveside service. There would be no wake or visitation, and no other formal service. I thought Kessie made a good decision there, too.

The service was scheduled for noon, and even with traffic we would probably be home by 1:30 p.m. or so, which brings up the part of Kessie's planning that had me shaking my head. For such a brief service, I thought she went overboard on what the funeral home called *amenities*. One of their limos would take us there and back, and Kessie had rented a black suit from them for me, along with all the bling and extras. It seemed excessive, but I kept that to myself. This had become her day, like a bride planning her wedding. She knew what she wanted, and money was suddenly not a problem, so why not?

I was peering through the blinds when I heard Kessie come down the stairs. "The limo isn't here yet," I informed her as I looked up and down the street. "I think they're late."

"You look nice," she said.

I turned at the unexpected compliment, and what I saw defied anything I could ever have imagined. Kessie was in a black dress, which hugged every curve of her, from her shoulders to her calves. The neckline was low but not indiscreet. Her shoes were black pumps with enough heel to give her an extra inch in height along with a startling profile. But most of all it was her hair. She had teased out her cornrows somehow, forming them into a soft bob that delicately framed her face. I was speechless.

"Well?" she asked. She didn't reveal a hint of awkwardness, like she dressed this way all the time.

"Kessie, I...you're..."

"Well thank you, Joplin," she said with a trace of amusement.

"I mean...you look..."

"You didn't know I could dress up, did you? Dad did, though. That's why I wanted to do this. For him."

I had to remind myself that we were going to a funeral. A *funeral*. The only concession to that was the sheer black veil that came down only as far as her brows, otherwise, especially with a limo on the way, we could have been heading out to the Schermerhorn Symphony in Nashville. It wasn't lost on me in my amazement that Kessie was beautiful, and in her I had to picture Mom in those London days, even if she would have been almost a decade younger than Kessie at the time, eighteen years old, in fact.

And then it occurred to me that when Mom looked the way Kessie did now, she and Dad had already traveled the world, independent and intrepid, exploring and experiencing things that I couldn't conceive of. I doubted

that Kessie could either, or any of our friends. The rules had shifted somewhere along the way. We had all been sheltered, planned, even if sometimes
those plans hadn't worked out. Suddenly I felt that I had been cheated out
of something fundamental, something I couldn't put words to.

I shook that off.

"You look great," I beamed. "Dad would be proud."

"Thank you," she said, her voice breaking ever so slightly.

There was a double-honk from outside. I looked through the blinds to
see a shiny black limo at the curb.

"It's here," I announced.

"Okay," Kessie said expectantly. She blew a couple of breaths then
looped a glossy black purse over her shoulder. "Let's go."

The limo driver seemed indifferent until Kessie stepped outside. The
moment he caught sight of her he was out and scrambling around to hold
her door, which was comical because he was a pretty heavy guy. Kessie and I
slid in, sitting across from one another in that cavernous space. It felt odd,
just the two of us in there, like we were going to a prom. I hadn't actually
gone to a prom when I was in school, but I had friends who had, and this
is how they described it. I didn't know if Kessie had ever gone to one, but
the prom crowd didn't seem like it would have been her crowd.

The outside glided past tinted windows like a separate world. The
weather was still clear and sunny, like it had been all week, but that clean
northerly breeze had shifted around to the southeast. It had become almost uncomfortably warm, and now the air carried a haze from the re-
fineries along the ship channel. We were on Westheimer Road. The lunch
traffic was stacking up at the red lights, but we seemed to waft through
this like a boat on a calm sea.

Kessie gazed out the window absently, looking regal sitting in that
wide leather seat. She wore some thin bracelets: a gold chain with small
charms, a braided string, and a plain silver bangle.

"I never saw those before," I said, nodding at her wrist. She fiddled
with them and smiled.

"Dad gave me this one on my sixteenth birthday," she said, fingering
the gold charms and seeming to lose herself for a moment. "This braided

one...I made matching ones for Dad and me. I couldn't find his, though. It was a long time ago. I don't know what happened to it."

"And the silver one?"

She chuckled. "That one's from my boyfriend in the twelfth grade."

"You had a *boyfriend*?" I laughed. "I thought you didn't do that."

"Hey, I was just a kid." She acted offended but it was obvious from the mirth in her eyes that she thought this was funny. "We didn't go together long. He was all hands. His name was Ben...Bennie," she laughed. "I don't know where he went after we graduated."

"But you kept the bracelet?"

"Sure, why not? It's pretty."

There was no obvious follow-up to that, so our conversation drifted off, and then I thought of something, something that hadn't come up but in retrospect probably should have already.

"Kessie?" I asked hesitantly. "Didn't Dad have a girl—uh, a woman friend or something?"

"No." She shook her head and seemed sad. "Not for a long time."

"Why not?"

"You'd have to ask him," she replied testily.

"Hey!" I snapped without thinking. She exhaled and looked away.

"I don't know, Jop. He said he liked being alone, that it was easier that way."

"Easier than what?"

"I don't know."

I sat back and mulled that. Dad had never remarried, not like Mom. Now I wanted to ask Mom about all of this, even though I couldn't explain to myself why it mattered.

We continued on through traffic, getting close to the cemetery. The traffic was getting worse. Our driver's name was Carver. I could see him cursing under his breath as he tried to weave that long limo through the congestion. I checked my watch. It looked like we were going to be a little late. We inched forward a bit at a time. People were honking and cursing and throwing up their hands. The air looked hoary and foul from all the exhaust. Ripples of heat wavered above baking hoods.

In his frustration, Carver nosed the limo onto the curb and sidewalk, and then made progress in lurches between the gas pedal and the brake. Kessie and I were jolted this way and that, balancing on our seats with flattened hands and sharing the same apprehensive look.

"What's going on?" Kessie asked with a note of concern.

"I don't know."

And then I did know, because I could see it ahead.

"What the hell?" I muttered under my breath.

Kessie twisted around to see what was going on, and then immediately jerked back in alarm. The sidewalk ahead was mobbed with people, some of them spilling into the street, many of them carrying signs and placards spouting horrible, sanctimonious words and slogans. Then I understood what was going on, I just couldn't believe it. I'd heard about these people, a crazy church from the Midwest somewhere. They showed up at the funerals of soldiers, preaching hell and damnation and worse. They were trash, worse than that, but what were they doing here?

"Jop?" Kessie said tremulously. "Who are they? What do they want?"

The mob spotted us before I could answer. They began to swarm toward the limo, shouting curses, shaking their fists. Kessie jumped across to my side and fell in next to me, pressing herself against the far door as if those people would be in among us at any moment.

Carver growled something. He was big and black and I could see his simmering eyes in the rearview mirror. He looked like he was about to get out and wade into those people, like a bouncer at a busy bar. He lowered the partition and hollered back at us:

"I know who your daddy was, and man, this ain't right."

A group of elderly black people formed a line between us and the crazy church people. Quickly, as if they had practiced this, those elderly people unrolled a large banner, large enough to mostly block the filthy signs behind them. The banner held a bible verse, John 15:13—*Greater love hath no man than this, that a man lay down his life for his friends.*

A police officer on a motorcycle came up beside us and motioned us forward, while another officer directed traffic out of our way. Once we made the turn into the cemetery, all of the craziness seemed to evaporate behind us. Still, we were both shaken.

"Y'all okay back there?" Carver asked. His gaze in the rearview mirror was uncomfortably penetrating yet concerned. Kessie nodded.

"Yeah, we're okay," I said.

"Them crazy people," he muttered to himself, shaking his head as we drove on. "*Crazy* people."

We eased around a circular drive, finally coming to a stop at a shaded arbor set with white folding chairs. Dad's casket was there, resting on a platform that was draped with green outdoor carpet. People were standing off to the side. I spotted Mom and Ted. I didn't see Leonard. There were only a few other people, maybe Dad's friends from work, but beyond them was a large crowd, a sprinkling of white faces, but mostly black folks dressed in what looked like their Sunday clothes. They kept a discreet distance, like they were waiting for permission to approach and not sure they would get it.

Carver rocked the limo as he got out. He straightened his tie, buttoned his coat, then opened the door for Kessie. He helped her out and then I followed, still unnerved from what had gone on out on the street.

"Miss Kessie?" Carver said, towering over Kessie but looking oddly gentle at the same time. "I'm s'posed to take the car away before the service, but I wanna stay and pay my respects if that's okay wit you."

"Sure it is," Kessie said. "You don't mind, do you Jop?"

"Uh, uh," I said with a shake.

I walked with Kessie toward the arbor. Mom's eyes went round when she saw Kessie. I thought she was about to smile, or even grin, but if that had entered her mind she swallowed it quickly.

"Joplin, Kessie, you look…" She seemed to have run out of words. "It's terrible out there. Did you have any trouble?"

"No, not really," Kessie answered flatly.

"Kessie," Mom said then, "this is Ted."

Ted stepped forward uncomfortably, his hands trying to decide what they should do. Kessie hadn't met Ted. I was afraid she would say something rude, but she held out her hand and smiled sincerely. Ted seemed relieved. They shook hands and chatted for a moment, just pleasantries.

Ted was a nice guy, good looking if not in Dad's rakish way. With Ted it was more that he was comfortably weathered, with a golf-course tan and white hair that managed not to make him look ancient. I liked him well enough. He put up with Mom, after all, and had always seemed to know what subjects to leave alone.

After Kessie introduced me to some of Dad's friends from work, I began to migrate toward the arbor, thinking that might draw people along, but when I looked back I saw that Kessie was now speaking with some of the black people who had been standing back from us.

No one at all had followed me, and now I felt foolish. I made my way back casually, like I had just been checking on the arrangements, and as I drew closer I saw that it was Eugenia Washington talking to Kessie, with little Persimmon standing at her great-grandmother's knee. I was about to back away when Kessie noticed me.

"Here he is now, Mrs. Washington," Kessie announced. She motioned me over, so now I was involved in it, whatever it was.

I sidled in uncomfortably while Eugenia looked me over with weary eyes that were full of memories and emotions that I couldn't possibly comprehend.

"Jop, this is Eugenia Washington," Kessie said.

"Yeah, I recognized you," I said nervously, and because that sounded stupid I added, "uh, from the news."

"It's good to meet you, Mister Joplin," Eugenia said evenly. She didn't offer her hand, which was holding onto Persimmon, and I didn't offer mine because that would have felt weird.

I looked down at Persimmon. She was in a little black dress with a frilly collar, and little shiny black shoes with white socks. She had black beads woven into her hair. Eugenia's black dress would have been fashionable in the 1950s, like it had been stored in a wardrobe trunk all this time. It was satiny, with buttons at the neck and delicate lace at the sleeves.

It was quiet all of a sudden, just the breathing of all those people. I looked from them to Kessie, saw Mom, who had a perplexed look, then back to Eugenia, who seemed to be waiting for something. Sweat popped out on my forehead.

"Uh, I didn't mean what I wrote," I blurted. Eugenia smiled, but sadly.

"You wrote some bad things about my family," Eugenia said in a voice so calm that I felt even guiltier.

"It's not what I meant," I said, feeling weak in the knees.

"I believe you, Mister Joplin," Eugenia said in that same calm voice. "But it *is* what you wrote in your story."

"I know." I lowered my eyes. Persimmon's were right there, meeting mine curiously. She had a soggy finger in her mouth. "It all came out wrong," I said to Persimmon, and then to Eugenia, "I'm sorry."

"Don't worry about it, Mr. Joplin." And now she offered me a reassuring smile. "People are saying bad things about you too. I know they must be wrong. Put it out of your mind. We came to thank your daddy for this little girl's life—"

"*Amen,*" someone said.

"—and to thank you and Miss Kessie for letting us be here. This little girl is gonna be a good one. And she will always know who your daddy was, I promise you. So don't feel bad, Mr. Joplin. Don't feel bad."

My mouth opened without producing any words. I *did* feel bad, I *was* sorry, and the things people were saying about me *were* true. I couldn't hide it here, not under the scrutiny of so many forgiving eyes. I looked around for some place to go but I was surrounded. Even more people were coming in now, those elderly folks out on the sidewalk. They were carrying their banner and singing a hymn, sweet voices in perfect harmony. My God, but there was nowhere to go.

"Okay, Jop, it's time," Kessie said, taking my elbow and steering me toward the arbor. It was a relief just to have my back to those people. I took deep breaths.

The arbor was only large enough for twelve chairs arranged in three rows of four. Kessie put me into the far right chair in the front row, sat down beside me, then motioned Eugenia and Persimmon into the remaining two chairs to the left. I kept my eyes fixed forward on Dad's casket, picking out patterns in the swirling grain of the polished wood, a cat, a Munch-like face, an ocean wave. Mom, Ted, and the others shuffled into the rows behind us. The rest gathered behind us, forced to stand in the sun, except for those elderly folks from the sidewalk, who formed an arc on the other side of Dad's casket. They had rolled up their banner and had left it lying on the lawn.

"What's going on?" I whispered to Kessie.

She leaned over and whispered into my ear, "They're from Eugenia's church. The reverend wants to say a prayer."

"But I thought—"

"It's okay, Jop." She patted my hand the way Mom would. "They wanted to do this. Dad wouldn't have minded."

It's not that I really minded either. Funerals seemed to need some kind of religious service to give them weight, it's just that this meant the service was going to go on longer than I thought, and I felt a hundred eyes boring into my back.

The church people sang some hymns, which I have to admit were very soothing. I was able to almost lose myself for a little while, then the reverend said some words about love and brotherhood, not in booming revival tones, but in a gentle, paternal voice punctuated by warm exhalations of *Amen* from the people gathered behind us. I was getting antsy, and was about to shift position when I heard a final, *Amen*, and Kessie stood.

I exhaled a long breath, shifted in my chair and used that motion to glance at my watch. We were running way late. Kessie leaned down to me and whispered:

"Do you want to say anything, Jop?"

I replied with a short shake of my head, then found that Munsch-like face in the wood again.

"It's okay," she said. "Don't worry about it."

I looked up as she walked to the head of Dad's casket, some folded papers in her hands, her purse resting in the chair beside me. She positioned herself where everyone could see her, licked her lips, and shakily unfolded her papers. She scanned the papers, and when her eyes came back up they were wet.

"Daddy," she started out, her voice cracking and probably too low for the people in the back to hear. She took a breath, smiled nervously, and tried again. "My father," she said, firmer now. She took another breath and ran the back of her hand quickly across her eyes. "My father was a writer.

He loved words. He also sold...*Lexuses*?" That made her laugh. "*Lexi*?" She laughed again.

"It's *Lexuses*," one of Dad's friends chimed in with a humorous assist. Kessie smiled at him like an angel.

"And that's the exact kind of thing that would have made Dad...would have made my father crazy." She ran her eyes across everyone, squared her shoulders and continued. "He used to tell me that words were too important to get wrong. A word like Lexuses," she paused to chuckle, "would have bothered him because it sounds weird."

"It does," the same voice from behind me agreed with a laugh. Kessie rewarded him with another smile before she went on.

"He would have tried to find a better way to write it," she said, "or else he would have gone through all of his word books to make sure he was at least spelling it right.

"When I was in high school he made me sit down and listen while he went through the newspaper, showing me all the words they were using that he didn't like, like, well, *like*." She smiled prettily. "I know, I do it too, but my father would have said that I spoke *as if* I had never gone to school, not *like* I hadn't; and I went to four schools, not four *different* schools, that's obvious."

She paused there and I looked around, thinking that people would be rolling their eyes, but they weren't. Some of Dad's friends were even smiling and nodding, and I caught a glimpse of Mom. She seemed rapt by what Kessie was saying.

"Sometimes I watched the news on TV with him. I didn't learn so much about what was going on in the world as I did about words. He despised the word *horrific*. He said it was pretentious and overused. He thought that was lazy, even *horrible*, sometimes *horrendous*, and if they said it too many times he thought it was *terrible*.

"He told me that there were no *civilians* in warfare, only *combatants* and *noncombatants*, and people who fly on planes are *passengers*, not *customers*.

"I could go on and on, but I won't." She smiled brightly and batted her eyes. A few people laughed. "But there's one more overused word that he really disliked, *hero*, because he thought no one ought to be called that for doing what *anyone* would do. He said overusing words made them cheap, and there are some words that should never happen to."

"Amen," someone said.

Kessie took a moment to swallow while that sank in, and then she added, "So while my father is *my* hero, he wouldn't want other people saying that about him. He just did what anyone else would have done if they had been there instead of him."

An *Amen* sounded from behind, but in a collection of voices this time. Eugenia was wiping at her eyes and nodding, and I was thinking that Dad had never said anything like this to me. Ever. I hunched down, and suddenly I didn't care what people thought about me. Someone patted me on the shoulder. I looked back sharply. It was Mom, and the look on her face said she knew what I was feeling. I smiled insincerely, then turned back to Kessie, who was just starting to speak again.

"So to finish up," she said, "I'd like to read something my father wrote in one of his stories." She puffed her cheeks before continuing, exhaled a hesitant breath. "The story is called *Comes Now, Achilles*, and it goes like this:

> *And if the mountains fell they might read my words and wonder what they had buried. Your immortality is in the things that only you can know, so you must write them down, and write them well enough to endure. You must choose your words with skill because you are writing not just for your own age, but for ages yet to come. So find me in these words beneath the mountains, and I will tell you tales you cannot imagine.*

Kessie's face screwed up then. She lowered her head like—excuse me, *as if*—she were praying. Her shoulders shook. Murmurs of approval rose into the stagnant air. They all heard something sermon-like in those words, but what I heard was a bunch of self-indulgent crap. Dad always did have a hyperbolic streak, a flourishing imaginary life shot full of destiny and delusion. That's why he created James Trevor Davidson, I bet, and gave him three degrees of separation, so he wouldn't lose himself in his own fantasy.

I had my arms crossed now, and my eyes were surely red. Someone was pushing lightly on my shoulder. I turned and it was Mom, gesturing toward Kessie and then urgingly back to me. The glower that answered this made her sigh. She stood then, straightened her dress and shuffled through the aisle and around to Kessie, who stepped into Mom's comforting arms as if she and Mom had always been close. And then Eugenia went up, leaving Persimmon sitting there and me wondering if the little girl would get away again. They all hugged and cried—well, Mom wasn't crying but the others were. And then everyone was up, blocking my view. The church people started up with their hymns again.

And I sat there.

## Chapter Nine

*Why do we idealize the things we long for? Why do we delude ourselves? It's as if we aren't endowed with enough will to face all of our eventualities, so we have to weave fantasies to preserve our sanity.*

I WAS IDLY THUMBING through the manuscript when that passage caught my eye. It sounded as if James was having a Hamlet moment, or else Dad was, and if so then exactly what was it he was longing for? I was about to scan the rest of the page for an answer when Morgane's voice brought me back to the present.

"What is that you are reading?" she asked. Her eyes were fixed on the road ahead, her fingers keeping their usual frenetic touch on the steering wheel, as if she were reading Braille. I let the pages fall, then slipped the manuscript back into my bag.

"It's nothing," I said. "Just some papers."

"I saw the video of your sister," Morgane said. "It was very beautiful."

Yeah. The reporters weren't allowed close enough to record anything, but that didn't stop someone from catching it on their smart phone. Now Kessie's speech at Dad's funeral was going viral, and that passage from *Comes Now, Achilles* had become a damn meme. People were wallowing in Dad's pompous prose, teasing meaning from words that I bet he hadn't ginned up until after a few too many glasses of wine.

"Yeah, Kessie gave a nice speech," I said sourly. Morgane chanced a glance my way, her brows dipped.

"Are you sure you are feeling okay, Joplin?"

"I'm just tired," I said. That seemed to satisfy Morgane for the moment. She was a woman of few words anyway.

We turned a corner and the mid-morning sun blazed through the windshield. I sat back and rubbed my eyes. I had caught the first flight out. It was still early but it felt late, and that left a long day ahead to get through, so it goes without saying that the movers were at the apartment with Dad's desk when we arrived.

"Oh, God," I groaned.

"What is this happening?" Morgane asked in confusion.

"It's my dad's desk," I answered wearily. "They weren't supposed to bring it until later."

"Desk?"

Morgane threw the car into park then turned to me with the look that said I was about to hear a lot of French.

"It belonged to my dad," I told her. I didn't like the pleading tone in my voice.

"But where will it go?"

"I don't know, the living room, maybe."

"But Joplin, there is no space for this." And then, because she was going to have to get it in there sooner or later, she added, "You did not tell me what you were doing."

"I'm sorry, Morgane. Everything was so crazy. I told you how bad it was. I just forgot, that's all."

The movers were annoyed that no one had been home. They already had Dad's desk strapped to a pair of large dollies. The ramp was down and they were ready to go. Morgane took one look at the size of the desk, then turned in a huff and stalked inside, muttering *incroyable, incroyable,* as she went.

Morgane went into the bedroom and closed the door. I barely had the energy to stay on my feet, but had no choice but to tug the couch out of the way by myself while the movers stood and watched. After that I told them to just get the desk in and leave it. I wanted them gone, the door closed, the lights off, and some time to readjust my headache.

Minutes later I had all of that. I fell back on my dislocated couch, rubbed my temples, and when I felt strong enough to open my eyes, I did. Dad's desk—I was a long way from being able to think of it as mine—overwhelmed my living room. I scanned the room from wall to wall, feeling overwhelmed myself, so I left it there and went to take a hot, much needed shower.

When I came back out, feeling marginally better, Morgane was grunting and pulling furniture and hissing *merde*, but she had cleared a space under a window, and while the front of that magnificent desk would be hidden by the wall, at least I would be able to look outside while I worked.

"You didn't have to do that by yourself," I said sheepishly.

"And what were you going to do? *Prendre une douche et te coucher?*"

I got the gist of it. That was something about showering and sleeping.

"No, Morgane, I wasn't going to bed." I said this apologetically. It was best to grovel when Morgane got this way.

Together we were able to slide the desk across the carpet and put it in place, and with that there was peace. Morgane left to go back to work at the travel agency, and between Kessie's and Dad's videos taking up everybody's bandwidth, no one had any time left to bother with me.

I set my laptop up on Dad's desk and set myself to write a blog post, but nothing came to mind. I made coffee and it went cold. I debated whether or not to get up and make more.

And then Dad was there, hovering in my memory, sitting at this desk and regarding me as if he had more important things to do. How old had I been? Kessie's age, I think. I don't know what it was that brought that particular episode to mind. I was able to avoid that mannequin image of him at the morgue by superimposing the scrutinous look he put on whenever he was about to trot out the paternal wisdom.

"A *writer*? *You*? Joplin, where would you get an idea like that?"

With even older memories at this very desk, I have always wondered if he knew how shattering it had been for him to say that to me.

"It's what I want to do," I came back testily, so sure I was on firm ground that I didn't remember how unsure I had been an hour earlier.

"Maybe if you'd stayed in college...I don't know. But I do know you can't make a living at it."

"I think I could if you helped me." I knew that sounded weak even before I said it, and before Dad dismissed me out of hand.

"Help you? How? To be a writer you've got to have stories."

He brought that knife down with such disregard that my eyes welled.

"But..." My lips trembled. "I have stories...I have stories."

"Tell me one."

"I...I can't. Not just like that."

He studied me for a moment, nonplussed, then turned his attention to something else.

"Go back to college," he said as an aside. "Or find something to do that you would be good at."

/////

A WHITE MAN CAME IN and pulled up a stool next to me, halting me in mid-breath. Shelisa grinned as wide and white as a beacon at night.

"Barber," she enthused. "Good mornin' good mornin'."

"Mornin', Shelly. Get us a Carib, would ya?"

"Yeh, mon."

Shelisa bent down to the cooler while I felt suddenly outcast. The man—Barber—hadn't given me a glance. Shelisa slid him a frosted bottle of Carib, which he picked up but then held an inch from his lips as if he had forgotten where he was.

"What you doin' today, Barber?" Shelisa asked him.

"Oh, yeh." He found himself and took a pull on his beer. "Be limin', darlin'."

What did he say?

"Y'ain hear," she came back, her grin still blazing, but then she caught a look at me and seemed to remember that I had just been spilling confidences. "Sorry, Joplin. That be our local talk. Barber, this mon is Joplin."

Barber turned to me and began to raise his hand, but then something ticked behind his eyes and he went vacant; just for a second, though, and then he gave me a yellowing smile and shook my hand.

"Nice to meet you, Joplin."

"You, too," I said without conviction. His hand was cold from his beer bottle, and he had an odd accent.

"I used to know a place in London called Joplin's. You ever been there?"

"No," I answered curtly.

"And there's Janis Joplin," he carried right on. "You ever know her?"

"No," I answered again, this time in exasperation.

Barber seemed disheartened. He looked me up and down as if to be sure, then mumbled, "Well, yeh, you look a little young for those days." His eyes had been on a downward pass when they went vacant again. He recovered quickly, then bluntly asked, "So why are you on Nevis?"

I wasn't about to start from scratch, and definitely not with this guy. Wearing khaki from his roasted throat to his roughened knees, he looked like an absentminded archeologist. He had a patchy gray beard, a deeply tanned and lined face, fading blue eyes beneath unkempt hair, and an annoying tendency to lose his train of thought. Shelisa noticed my mood darkening even if Barber was tactlessly oblivious. She stepped back in quickly.

"Joplin win himself a contest," she explained with a wink, "so he gets to miss the cold north for our nice island breeze."

"That so?" Barber said. "Well, you're a lucky man, Joplin."

"We open now, Joplin," Shelisa informed me before I could say anything else. "I gawn do some work, but gawn to come back. Okay? Talk to Barber a little while. He got chat."

And with that, I was stranded with Barber. I learned very quickly that he was a South African, had expated himself to England in the 70s and then here in the 80s. And he really was an archeologist. For years he dug for artifacts in the ruins of seventeenth-century sugar plantations until the government cut his funding a while back. He spent his time doing odd jobs now, mostly manual labor.

By the time he got all of that out, my coffee was cold and his Carib was warm. I was debating whether to signal Shelisa for a refill when Barber said:

"So tell me a story then, Joplin."

He wasn't being flip, or as he might say, *cheeky*. I got the sense that this was how he passed most of his time, especially considering the skill with which he could nurse a beer.

"I don't have any stories," I admitted glumly.

"Nonsense," he harrumphed. "Everybody's got stories."

I gave him a wretched look that had him averting his eyes uncomfortably.

"Everybody except me," I said.

/////

IT WASN'T TRUE that I didn't have any stories, it's just that they all mostly involved some form of alcohol and had become more puerile than priceless before I had even turned thirty. No matter. It was the ability to organize them into a coherent string of words that eluded me. I sat at Dad's desk and I expected it to give me something, some inspiration, some insight, some fonder memory, *something*, but I got nothing from it. I felt nwo imaginative spark. None of Dad's clever wordplay leached through the varnish. It was just a desk.

I pushed back from it in frustration. There was no blog post in me either, nothing that I cared enough about to expend the energy. And then why should I? Money was no longer a problem, and the way the *Houston* books were selling, it wasn't going to be—ever. Kessie and I had hired the agent Leonard recommended. Her name was Marcia Garretty, a savvy operator about Mom's age who concealed more than she revealed, and seemed to have all the dots mentally connected within minutes of meeting us. She presented us with a contract from Knopf by the close of business on the Tuesday following Dad's funeral, while Leonard was in the process of setting up a company to manage it all. The only thing I had to do was accept the checks when they came.

I rose to my feet and had a look around. I didn't have to argue with Morgane about anything, I could get a bigger apartment and I could get it now. Hell, Marcia was already talking about film rights. I could probably get one of those new McMansions in Green Hills if I wanted.

If I wanted...

I flopped back down at the desk, parked my elbows and rubbed my temples. What would Dad have written about this if he'd wanted to make it a story? How would it have ended? I couldn't see as far as the coffee maker in the kitchen, let alone visualize a story arc in any of this. Trying to think up things to write makes you tired, it really does.

The manuscript was still in my bag. I drug it out and returned it to its place in the middle right drawer, as if it should be kept hidden away like the One Ring, which was not an unreasonable simile when I thought about it; and just like those characters, I was drawn to it, and so I brought it out instead, arranged it neatly on the desktop, and finally, without the distractions of Kessie or Morgane, I read it; and I read a long time, and I admit that what I read reignited the childhood reverence I'd had for Dad, but what it also did was raise questions, especially when I got to this passage:

*The Woman in Yellow crossed the street beyond his window twice a day. He called her The Woman in Yellow because that was her best color. Yellow roused her complexion; yellow set her hair aglow like a new sun. In yellow her face was radiant. It was a pretty face, often harried, too often worried, but always pretty.*

*Every day he watched her; under an umbrella on rainy days, in heavy coats on winter days, and in the flimsy chiffon of summer; yellow in the heat, blue in the rain, gray in the cold. She crossed the street alone, never otherwise, and from that he inferred a certain reserve, an unalloyed essence. His words flowed in the mornings, returning in the evenings like a tide. He loved her. One morning he stood up from hollow words and gazed long through his window. He cast a last glance at empty pages, then he sent James out to her.*

*Her name would be Clarissa.*

/////

I HAD TO TAKE ALL OF THAT OUT. It was a shame to sacrifice Dad's evocative prose, but the other *The Woman in Yellow* now hung somewhere in Mom's house in Florida. I renamed Clarissa as Hannah, and set Evan Usher after her so that they could complete their story more or less as Dad wrote it. Still, there was something perplexing about that passage. It wasn't just the startling change of voice.

Exactly who was Clarissa?

# Chapter Ten

Clarissa worked in a downtown office on a street that still had a trolley ring past every half hour or so. She usually took lunch at a corner cafe on the ground floor of her building, so that's where James went to watch her. He understood how this could be perceived, but his intentions weren't nefarious by any distortion of the imagination. He simply found her intriguing. Perhaps, if he was careful in his attentions, he could eventually introduce himself, even befriend her.

That would take time and familiarity, though. For now he was content just to be able to see more of her, to learn about her. He observed that she liked sandwiches with the crusts trimmed, and she always left the chips on her plate. Sometimes she would only have a salad and a cup of tea, which she seemed to prefer over coffee. There were times when she was ebullient, gracing the cafe with her infectious smile. He witnessed the effect, not only feeling buoyed himself but also noticing how moods lightened from table to table, ranging out from wherever she was sitting, like a pearl into a pool.

There were other times, though, when the stress of her day was apparent in a darker shade beneath her eyes. On these days she would sometimes surreptitiously slip out of a shoe, reach down and massage a foot. Even this he found endearing, so much so that after she returned to her work, and he to his, the words would flow across his pages like a pure, unbound spring.

He began to question certain things. Her solitary nature, the quality that had first attracted his attention, seemed wrong now. He never saw her in the company of others, never observed the camaraderie of coworkers or a peck on the cheek from a boyfriend. She remained as alone at her table as she did crossing the street. He interpreted this as a guarded protectiveness shielding an inner wound, a state in such conflict with her obvious nature that it made no sense, and yet the evidence sat right there across the way, sipping tea and nibbling thoughtfully on a trim sandwich. It was abstruse to the point of absurdity. He couldn't reconcile it, so he returned to his work, crafting stories one after another in search of an explanation.

She became, in his pages, a woman of mystery. She was at once a seductress, an ingénue, an orphan, an amnesiac. His stories expanded until they could have filled a volume of their own. He wrote her as a foreign agent, a forsaken lover, a fortuitous heroine. She had lost a husband, a brother, a parent...a child. Her stories were poignant, adventurous, thrilling, and sometimes crushing. They were multifaceted, complex and real, and yet none of them, not one, could capture the paradox of a beautiful woman who was always alone.

When the day at last arrived, it was so perfect that he would never have written it that way for fear of pandering to the pedestrian. It was a joyous day of its own, the scent of flowers on a soft breeze, the sky alight with the varied hues of life, of abundant sapphire and islands of pure white. Remarkably, she wore yellow that day, entering the cafe with a poise and beauty that drew eyes, raised smiles, and interrupted conversations along the way. If she was aware of this she did not show it, and never had. Her expression was neither dovish nor disingenuous, her stride neither beguiling nor benign.

The cafe had a stone tile floor with an uneven finish, and in retrospect it seemed odd that something like this didn't occur more often. It so happened that his table was next to hers on that day, another of the unlikely coincidences that he would never have written but was nevertheless the case. She weaved between tables toward him with her lunch tray, soup as a not too uncommon change, and of course a cup of tea. Her eyes grazed his in no particular recognition, but he felt the charge of contact just the same. He wasn't concerned about the proximity, having spent enough lunches in the cafe by then to have become a part of familiar surroundings.

He watched her only peripherally as she approached. Anything more might reveal his interest, and that was something he wouldn't risk. He did acknowledge his good fortune, though. In the crowded cafe, she would be close enough that he might be able to catch her scent, perhaps even feel her warmth. His heart sped up, pounding such that it would surely give him away. He swallowed hard to ease his breathing, wiped a sweaty palm on his pants, and at that moment her heel caught on the uneven tile, and with a gasp and an expression of horror, she pitched forward.

He was up in an instant, even as her tray flew past him; and without thinking, without knowing—as if he were writing the scene—he positioned his arms perfectly and caught her before she fell.

The tray crashed, the soup splattered, and the teacup skittered and spun between the legs of startled diners like a golf ball through a gaggle of geese. He was immediately immersed in the moment, a kind of stop-motion trance in which every sense was heightened to be almost unbearable. He had her under her arms, their chests pressed together, hearts thumping as if answering one another, her breath tickling his lips. He dared not raise his eyes to meet hers for fear of what he might reveal, and yet as still as the moment was he could feel her eyes on him, flashing from chagrin to gratitude in a blink, and also the envious eyes of others, who could only have fantasized about being in his place, and wondering why, if it was destined to happen, the man at the opportune moment had to be so much older than she.

And then he blinked, the hollow sounds of voices intruded, and his senses resumed their usual state.

"Are you all right?" he asked with a practiced smile, standing her upright and pushing back to a decorous distance.

"Oh my God," she exhaled, her cheeks reddening. "I'm so sorry."

"No reason to be sorry," James said in a soothing voice. "It was an accident. No one's hurt," he looked around to be sure, "but I'm afraid some tea spilled on your dress, Clarissa."

He knew he had made a mistake even before her name had fully passed his lips. He expected her to stiffen, cast him a narrow look, but her brows dipped only just slightly instead.

"How do you know my name?" she asked without accusation.

"Oh...well, I, uh...I've seen you here before. I must have overheard it."

That explanation couldn't possibly work, but it was the only one he could think of in that disconcerting moment. He had never overheard her speaking with anyone. As a matter of fact, he had never heard her voice this close, only from across the bustle in the ordering line, and now he loved her voice as much as the rest of her. It had a peculiar quality, a gentle huskiness, but no accent that he could detect—

The author shook his head at what he had written, sat back in disgust and rubbed his eyes.

"No," he mumbled to himself. "No. This is not the way it would happen. James doesn't know her name. How would he know her name? And Clarissa would be...flustered and yet composed. She is not a fragile flower, do not write her that way. James wouldn't write her that way, and he would never fumble over his emotions like a boy. There would be none of that kind of tension, he's old enough to be her father for God's sake! He would...he would...he would be much the same, only more secure with himself, entranced to be sure, but he would keep it in perspective."

The author searched through his window for The Woman in Yellow, but she was off to wherever she went each morning and returned from each afternoon. She had been in blue that morning, the color of his mood. It had been a gray morning, damp, no rain, but the streets had been slick, were still slick as noon approached, her lunchtime wherever that might be.

He stood and paced, his hands clasped behind his back. He ran the scene through his mind, iteration after iteration until he had it firmly fixed, and then he returned to his work.

—He watched her only peripherally as she approached. Anything more might reveal his interest, and that could ruin everything. He did acknowledge his good fortune, though. With their tables so close, he might be able to catch her scent, perhaps even feel her warmth, two more pleasant additions to his store of knowledge.

Her faint shadow slipped across his table, her purse rattled onto a chair. He chanced a more direct view, and at that moment her heel caught on the uneven tile. With a gasp and an expression of horror, she pitched forward.

He was up in an instant, even as her tray flew past him; and without thinking, without knowing—as if he were writing the scene—he positioned his arms perfectly and caught her before she fell.

The tray crashed, the soup splattered, and the teacup skittered and spun between the legs of startled diners like a golf ball through a gaggle of geese. He had her under her arms, their chests pressed together so closely that he could feel the actual beat of her heart, could feel her warm breath on his lips. He looked into her sea-green eyes, saw them flash from chagrin to gratitude in a blink. Around him he could sense the incredulous expressions of others, who could only have fantasized about being in his place, and wondering why, if it was destined to happen, that the man at the opportune moment had to be so much older than she.

"Are you all right?" he asked evenly, taking her by the shoulders and guiding her to her feet.

"Oh my God," she exhaled, her cheeks reddening. "I'm so sorry."

"No reason to be sorry, it was just an—"

"Oh, look what I've done!"

She wrenched out of his hands and bent past him toward the mess she'd made. In the next moment she was down on a knee, fussing with the mess, trying to corral it with a sodden napkin into a more manageable mess. The cafe employees were among them at once, mouthing apologies as they pulled tables and chairs aside to wipe them down. Order was restored even before Clarissa could be coaxed back to her feet. Her table was cleaned and moved back into place, and with embarrassed pleas she was invited to sit, assured that a duplicate order would be brought to her shortly.

James was still standing as the other customers resumed their tables and conversations. An exasperated employee rolled a mop and bucket past him, dealing efficiently with what remained.

His table had come through unscathed, his coffee resting there still, steaming. This was the moment, perfectly written. There would be no better opportunity. He took his cup and saucer, then turned to her.

"May I join you?" he asked.

A brief frown crossed her lips, but then she restored it to a thankful smile and gestured him forward.

"Of course you can." She pointed to a chair. "Please."

He had never heard her voice this close, only from across the bustle in the ordering line. Her voice had a peculiar quality, a soft huskiness, foreign somehow but with no accent that he could detect. He found that he loved her voice as much as the rest of her.

He took the offered seat and positioned his coffee. "Well, that was more excitement than I'm accustomed to here," he commented with reassuring good humor.

"I'm so embarrassed," she said, glancing around as she said it. No one was watching them now. A strand of golden hair had come loose, which gave her a harried look. He brought it to her attention with a slight nod and a lift of his brows. "Oh," she mouthed in surprise. She worried the strand back into place and then fixed him with a pretty smile. "Thank you," she said. "And for catching me, too. That would have been...well, that would have been embarrassing."

"You're welcome. I'm afraid we can't save your dress, though."

"What?"

She chinned down for a better look.

"It was the tea, I think," he said.

"Oh, no." She examined the stains as best she could, then rested her hands on the table and sighed. "Well," she said in resignation. "That won't come out."

"I'm sorry," he said. "It's a pretty dress."

"My favorite, too. Oh, well..." she trailed off.

"I'm James, by the way." He offered his hand along with an inviting smile. "James Trevor Davidson."

Her brows arched for a moment, but then she took his hand. Her grip was strong, defying her graceful fingers. He wouldn't have guessed that.

"It's nice to meet you, James Trevor Davidson. I'm Clarissa."

"Clarissa," James mused. A pretty name, and not prone for shortening. For her age he would have guessed Jennifer, perhaps Alexis. Jenny or Alex...no, Clarissa was perfect.

Clarissa's lunch was brought out then, another bowl of soup, another cup of tea. It was tomato soup, with a sprinkling of cheese and a sprig of basil.

"It's a good thing that didn't get on your dress," James commented, gesturing at her soup.

"I wish it had," she sighed. "That I could have gotten out."

"But you would have looked as if you'd been injured in a traffic accident."

"Well...yeah. That would have been worse."

"And you would have smelled like basil."

"But I love the smell of basil."

"Okay," he smiled, lifting his cup to his lips. "Just the traffic accident then."

She smiled in return, then took up her spoon and dipped it into her bowl. He didn't want to stare at her while she ate, not so obviously, so he used his coffee to distract his eyes. She ate quickly, probably because she was now running late. The stains on her dress had mostly dried to a darker hue. She put down her spoon and brushed at the stains.

"I can't go back to work looking like this," she said more to herself than to him. She reached into her purse and brought out her phone. "Excuse me a moment, okay?" James nodded and pretended to be interested in some art on a near wall. Clarissa called her work, explained what had happened, and after a long silence in which she nodded periodically, she thanked whomever she had been speaking with and hung up.

"Well, I've got the rest of the day off," she exhaled in relief.

James felt a moment of expectant elation. Here was an opportunity, perhaps, to join her for a walk, another addition to the string of happy coincidences that morning, but when she abruptly pushed her bowl aside and stood, he sensed that his unlikely good fortune had come to an end.

"It was nice to meet you, James," she said pleasantly, although she didn't offer her hand. "Thank you so much for everything."

"What? You're leaving?" His tone seemed to catch her off guard. She eyed him curiously.

"Yesss," she said, drawing it out with a questioning expression.

James realized his error immediately. He stood and corrected it with an innocent smile.

"It was nice to meet you too, Clarissa," he said, carefully masking his disappointment. "I hope you can get those stains out."

He resumed his seat and lifted his cup, and this erased whatever suspicions Clarissa might have held. She gave him a quick parting smile, and with that she left.

James settled in at his desk that night with a feeling of profound contentment. He inventoried what he had learned, then set those words to paper. He wrote and he wrote, and he reveled at the life in it. Even after her lights went out across the way, still he wrote, imagining her dreams.

/////

YOU HAVE TO READ *The Latter Half of Inglorious Years* with patience and attention. It doesn't have to be exhausting, not if you learn the characters and the voices, not if you flow with them from scene to scene. But then I really don't have to explain it, do I. Enough readers figured it out on their own to make the book a bestseller—twice.

For me though, on that first reading, I was faced with a staggering admission. I could fantasize all I wanted. I could make excuses. I could scratch at my blog, maybe even conjure a story worth telling, but no matter what I did, no matter how hard I might try, I was not this good and never would be.

# Chapter Eleven

MOVING INTO A NEW HOUSE would take energy, while buying a new car would only take an afternoon. It was a revelation to discover how easy the process was when you didn't have to worry about financing or payments. I had an embarrassing moment when it came time to pay and I had no idea how to do it. My salesman sighed inwardly and gave me an abiding look that spoke legion, but it only took a call to Leonard to straighten it all out, and then my salesman brightened, brought me a cup of artisan coffee, and suddenly we were best friends.

I admit I felt a twinge of guilt in all of this, but that didn't last long. When Morgane got home from work I was able to show off my brand new BMW 328i, with the bright red paint and the throaty roar. I should have known better than to think she would be impressed. "But I liked your Honda very much," she said disconsolately, nevertheless I could tell that she was enjoying herself as we spun onto West End Avenue and played zigzag in traffic. Her smile might have been subdued, but it was still a smile.

And now I went out most nights, often with Morgane. She had never been taken with country music, Nashville's signature theme as it were, but there was still the odd dance club in the Gulch or the East Side that sometimes played her kind of syntho music. This hadn't been our scene previously, I had never been any good at dancing, but the sight of her in tapering black jeans and a glittering sheer top, with her arms over her head and bouncing with the beat, compensated for a lot. Whiskey helped, too. I eventually graduated to the high-end stuff, Makers and such, and that helped even more.

I bought a Rolex.

Morgane went off to Martinique to be with her family over Christmas and New Year's, which left me alone. Mom and Ted were on a cruise, and Kessie was...well, I hadn't heard from her. She was probably doing Christmas with friends. There was no need for me to interrupt that, and besides, I was used to being on my own during the holidays. No big deal.

The New Year's Eve *Bash on Broadway* was the biggest ever, so crowded that I couldn't get within a mile of it. All of my friends were in there somewhere, texting me every couple of minutes—*where r u; cmon jop; hurry, ur missing it; this is the bomb*—and then abruptly going silent as the countdown neared. I finally gave it up and drove home, heard the popping of fireworks behind me.

It was quiet in the apartment, late but I couldn't sleep. An idea for a blog post was dipping in and out of my head, catching here or there on words and phrases that seemed uncommonly insightful. I raced to write them down, splashed some whiskey into a glass and tried to focus. Is this the way it had been for Dad, stray thoughts that congealed into a story in fits and starts? Thoughts that could vanish just as quickly if you couldn't get them down fast enough?

There were post-its all over the desk now. Another whiskey helped me organize them, and another after that brought it all together. The post was *Nashville and the Costs of Fame*, my first post since *The Social Media State*. I felt reasonably confident with what I had written, but a prickle of fear had me reading it over and over until I had practically memorized it, just to make sure I hadn't set any traps for myself like last time. The sun was coming up. My stomach felt as sickly sour as a Sunday morning back in college. I tapped the key and exhaled, then stumbled to bed, where Morgane's lingering scent tugged at me, lilac and musk with an acrid trace of cigarettes. When she got home, she would be furious that I hadn't washed the sheets. I laughed as I fell onto the bed, and that was that.

/////

THOSE FIRST DAYS OF JANUARY were cold and quiet, and for a time I could feel that things were normal again. I hadn't been out late since New Year's Eve, Morgane would be back soon, and my new blog post was getting good comments.

It was almost as if *The Social Media State* had never happened. I appreciated the blasé comments now—*good post; interesting; I agree 110%.* Dad would have torn into the *110%* commenter for poor comprehension of the whole, but I could have hugged him or her, probably a him considering the post-game show nature of his excess. Regardless, 10% more than *completely* was fine with me.

But there were also longer comments that sent my chest swelling. I read them again and again, as if I had missed something the first few times: *A very perceptive analysis of our present conundrum; Joplin Dean really knows Nashville; JD is right, Nashville is getting too big too fast; Can't even go to the clubs on Broadway anymore because they're all full of drunk tourists.* But above all there was one comment that filled me with pride, and maybe love, too: *Very well written, Jop. I feel as if I know Nashville, and I've never even been there...Andy.*

Sweet Kessie. All of this gave me enough confidence to turn my Facebook and Twitter accounts back on. I felt elated, and then I slept, and the next morning I sat at Dad's desk, gazed through the window at naked trees and austere gray, and found no words to write. None.

But it was winter, after all. I kept that in mind as my coffee went cold. A hot cup of coffee would get me going, I thought, or maybe I should give hot chocolate a try. I pondered that. A redbird flapped at the window, bumping angrily at its reflection. It didn't know any better, and then it tired and gave up.

///// 

WATCHING TV CAN BE PAINFUL. You would think they would know what they were doing, but everything about TV seems designed to drive viewers away, the incessant drug commercials with their hokey brand names and grating dialogue, the asinine reality shows, the news that you already know, and the vacuous talk shows. But streaming content on the computer takes energy, so sometimes it's easier to just lie on the couch and let the TV run in the background, which is how I saw Kessie on a morning show.

I didn't know what channel the TV was on, but the host of the show was the bald guy with the smirk and the bottled tan. I wasn't really watching, the TV was just a blur beyond my coffee cup, the audio nothing more than shower noise. I was thinking that a trip might help me, and wondering why I hadn't put my foot down with Morgane and demanded that she take me with her to Martinique. She would be home tonight, bright as a Caribbean beach and as dark as a coconut shell, and people would ooh and ahh and be envious. I was envious. It was cold outside, man, and I couldn't string three words into a sentence worth writing.

The comments had tapered off. They always did when they were good comments. It was the bad comments that stuck around.

I puffed my pillow, reached for my coffee, took a sip and grimaced because it was cold.

The TV was all *blah, blah, blah*, figures shaking hands and then sitting on too-tall chairs. I thought that Nashville had some nice parks, Centennial, Shelby Bottoms, Percy and Edwin Warner, and I wondered what they were like in the winter. Maybe there was a blog post in that, but damn, it was cold outside. The figures on TV were jibing back and forth, saying nothing that registered on my brain until I heard *John Taylor Dean*.

"Huh?"

I rolled off the couch and took a stance in front of the TV like a football lineman at scrimmage, the only way I could get up close to the screen now that the desk took up so much of the living room.

It was Kessie. I had to rub my eyes to be sure I was seeing right, but it was definitely her. She could have walked in the front door and I might not have recognized her, and this time not because I hadn't seen her in a while, but because she was dressed as I doubt she had ever dressed before in her life. She was wearing a pleated white skirt with black hose and a black turtleneck sweater, her hair held back from her ears with white barrettes. Her cheeks were pink and powdered, and her lips were ruby red. She had the fresh look of a New England college student on her first tour of campus, when things still looked exciting and innocent.

The show was being broadcast live from New York City. So Kessie was in *New York City*? What was she doing *there*?

"...I haven't read the whole book yet," the host was saying, "but I came across this line and would like your thoughts: *Cities mean to crush those who have no fear.* That's a potent statement, don't you think?"

"It is," Kessie smiled. She betrayed no nervousness at all, but didn't elaborate, which left the host hanging and then grasping for words.

"But...okay, what do you think it means? Is it saying that we're afraid all the time?"

Kessie shook her head thoughtfully.

"I don't think so. That's from the story *Onward Until*. There's another passage in that story that I think kind of explains what it all means. It goes, *You come under attack whenever you think up something someone else should have thought up but didn't.*"

"Oh—kay." The host puffed his cheeks, and I'm pretty sure he rolled his eyes. What a smug bastard. "So walk me through it then," he led on. "What do you think your father was trying to say in this story?"

I realized just then that my mouth was hanging open.

"What I think Dad was trying to say is that everybody wants to be safe all the time, but they don't want to be responsible for it, so we have 911 and EMTs and Homeland Security, all of that. So if you get in trouble or hurt yourself or something, you make it somebody else's problem to deal with. Okay, fine, but if you try to stand up for yourself, people come after you. They want everything to stay the same, where it's safe."

"Uh...huh."

The host pretended to ponder that deeply, even stroking his lip with a finger; then abruptly, as if he had been on a timer, he held up a book, faced the camera and announced:

"The book is *Comes Now, Achilles and Other Stories* by John Taylor Dean, the Houston author who bravely gave his life to save that little girl; and edited by his daughter, Kessie Ann Dean. Kessie will be signing copies at Barnes & Noble later today. Kessie?" He held out his hand and they shook. "Thank you for coming. It was a pleasure."

"Thank you," Kessie smiled in return.

And then they cut to commercial. And my mouth was still hanging open.

///// 

MY PHONE BEGAN PINGING with alerts even as I was trying to call Kessie. I kept getting her voicemail, kept leaving messages, which grew more and more terse each time. Tweets and retweets stacked up on my screen faster than I could scroll through them, all gushing with sappy adulation, mostly following the hashtags, *#johntaylordean*, *#jtdean*, *#onwarduntil*, *#comesnowachilles*, and one hashtag that caught me by surprise, *#kessiedeanishot*, but nothing about me or my blog. People were posting on my Facebook page how great Dad had been, how poised Kessie had looked, how proud I must be to be a member of that family.

And then the trolls found me again. It was as if they had just been sleeping through the winter, waiting for something they could chew on to wake them up. The comments were about the same as last time, except now they also went after *Nashville and the Costs of Fame*, and how that was something I would never have so why did I even bother? And how could I stand being so mediocre when my father had been such a great man? And I was still a racist, so I needed to die for that...

My God but there's an angry world out there, bitter, ready to cripple at a word.

Kessie didn't return my calls until after dark, which had left me to stew all day, so I snapped at her.

"Kessie, what are you *doing*?"

"Jop...you sound...is something wrong?"

"Why didn't you call me back?"

"I *am* calling you back."

"I mean this morning."

"*This morning*? Jop, this morning was crazy. Did you see me on TV?"

"Yeah."

"Well, what did you think?"

"You made a book about Dad's *stories*?"

"Well, yeah."

"But...you didn't tell me what you were *doing*."

"I know. I'm sorry, but it was all so crazy. Marcia had this idea and she said we had to do it fast while the *Houston* books were still bestsellers. So that's all I've been thinking about since right after you left. It was more work than I ever thought it would be."

"*But still—*"

And now I had stretched her patience about as far as it would go, because she cut me off and charged in with the voice Mom used whenever Mom put her foot down and wanted to make sure you knew it.

"That's enough, Joplin. Stop yelling at me. You don't check with me about everything *you* do."

"But—" I stopped right there to take a breath, well, a couple of breaths, so when I got back on I was a bit calmer. "But Kessie, this is about Dad, so it's about both of us."

"But you didn't care about any of it, Jop. You said so."

"But what I meant was—"

"And anyway, it was kind of your idea."

"*My* idea?"

"Yeah, you said it that day, that Dad would like it if we published his stories."

"I remember. And you said something like it didn't matter because he wouldn't know."

"*He* wouldn't know, but *we* do. His stories are too good to be forgotten about, Jop. Dad deserves recognition and I'm making sure he gets it."

There was really nothing more I could say to that. There were other things we needed to talk about, financial things. Some I knew at the time, like why hadn't she moved forward with the sale of the condo, and others I didn't know yet, like were we going to share the royalties from this new book. But I didn't have the energy to go on. It was late, Morgane would be home in a few hours, and I really needed to get started on cleaning up the apartment.

"Okay, Kessie," I said tiredly. "Thanks for calling me back."

"It's okay, Jop. I'm sorry this was all a surprise."

"No problem."

"Okay, bye."

"Bye."

/////

GETTING FROM MARTINIQUE to Nashville requires patience, endurance, and the ability to keep track of a lot of details, from taxis to water taxis to island hops to one or two connections with the airline, not to mention a couple of time zones. It takes a while, which is why Morgane didn't arrive until near midnight.

In her place I would have been wiped out, but she came through baggage claim bouncing on her heels and wearing her crooked smile, as bright as a Caribbean beach and as dark as a coconut shell.

"Joplin!"

She opened her arms and grinned, and I stepped into them, caught an exotic scent that I'd never smelled before, like a combination of coconut and cinnamon.

"Morgane!"

She kissed me full on the lips, all the way, and I knew right then that something had changed. Once we came up for air, I held her so that I could look at her. She was a healthy shade of copper, her eyes lighter, less stormy. I said:

"How was it? You look amazing," and I pronounced the z like an s, the way she would, which made her smile.

"And you are looking good too with the winter."

Arms around each other's waists, we waited at the baggage carousel.

"I can't wait to hear all about it," I said.

"And you too," she said. "I saw your blog and the good comments. I am so happy for you."

Later in the car, we skirted through the cold night. Morgane had her phone out, catching up on things. She watched the video of Kessie from this morning, turned to me and smiled as if in congratulations. Her thumb worked at her screen and then she tapped, and another video of Kessie came up. I caught this in quick glances, Kessie in the same clothes from this morning but being interviewed by someone I didn't recognize.

"*These are some of the most extraordinary stories,*" the interviewer said. He had a British accent. "*Can we look forward to more of them in future?*"

"*Yes,*" Kessie answered without hesitation. "*In another couple of weeks, I think they told me.*"

"*So soon? That's marvelous. And can you reveal the title?*"

"*I can.*"

My eyes were on the road, but I could hear Kessie smiling.

"*The title is* The Lives of Clarissa."

## Chapter Twelve

Clarissa did not come to the cafe for the next four days, and since a weekend interceded, it was a full seven days before James saw her in the lunch line again. She had gone to work each day, James had watched her cross the street in the mornings, return in the evenings, but either she had chosen a new place to go at the noon hour or else was taking lunch at her desk.

After a feverish burst of activity in which he filled pages with the ease and satisfaction of a spirited conversation, his productivity tapered to a discomfiting halt, his story teetering at a precipice with no way forward. It was an inconsolable exile. Even the sight of her coming and going wasn't enough to stimulate his imagination, not now that he could imagine so much more.

Still, he went to the cafe every day, sipped coffee, scanned the crowd and waited, and after that week of that watchful waiting she finally returned.

He was seated at a table, facing the door, his coffee cup at his hand. She didn't see him as she crossed to the ordering line, or if she had he couldn't tell. Her back was to him now. His thoughts turned inward while he waited that little bit longer, entire paragraphs assembling in his mind, and when he looked up again she was standing right there at his table, holding her tray, a sandwich and tea.

"Clarissa!" he croaked in surprise, excitement lodging in his throat and forcing him to swallow hard.

"Hello, James." Her smile was tentative. She glanced around as if unsure of herself. "Is it okay if I sit here?"

"Sure it is," he said, standing, a bit of etiquette from his generation that she found simultaneously flattering and awkward.

She sat and looked him over, her exuberance hiding somewhere on that day. He felt a twinge of unease, but worked as hard to sequester that as he had his excitement.

"How are you?" he asked finally, trying to deflect a silence that had become uncomfortable.

"I'm fine. How about you?"

"Never better," and he meant it, although he made it sound casual.

"That's good."

"Were you able to save your dress?"

"No, it's ruined."

"I'm sorry."

"No reason to be. It happens."

There seemed no response to that. The silence resumed, so he lifted his cup to fill the space. Clarissa took a bite of her sandwich and a sip of her tea, and then after dabbing at her lips with a napkin, said as an aside:

"I usually eat by myself."

"You do?" He hoped he sounded sufficiently unaware.

"Yeah. I'm not really good at making conversation."

"That doesn't seem possible."

She looked at him curiously.

"Why not?"

James almost choked on a swallow of coffee. He rushed a napkin over his mouth just in time to keep from dribbling on his shirt. Clarissa watched all of this impassively, waiting for an answer that now felt to James like a test of some kind.

"Well, uh...well because..." Shouldn't he just come out and state the obvious? "I mean, I hope this doesn't offend you, but because you're a beautiful woman."

If she was flattered, offended, or anything else, she didn't show it.

"Do you think so?"

"Yes, I do."

"Do you think everybody thinks so?"

"I don't know how they couldn't."

"So that makes me good at conversation?"

"It can't hurt."

"Are you sure about that?"

"I'm not sure about anything."

That finally earned him the smile he had been missing, although it was a shrewd smile. She took some more bites of her sandwich before she went on.

"I enjoy that," she said.

"Enjoy what?"

"The repartee."

"Do you?"

"Most people you talk to don't like it. Maybe they think it's rude, I don't know."

"But you don't think it's rude?"

"Not unless you're doing it to make yourself feel superior."

"And that's not what you're doing." This wasn't a question, but an observation.

"No. My father and I used to do this when I was little, the back and forth. It was like a game. You remind me of him."

"I'm honored. Where is he now?"

"I'd rather not talk about that."

"I understand."

"How could you?"

James grimaced at his clumsiness.

"I'm sorry. You're right. How could I possibly understand?"

"I don't know. It's possible that you played the same game with your own daughter."

A shadow crossed his face.

"I don't have a daughter."

"That's too bad. So in lieu of a daughter, with whom do you practice your repartee?"

"*With whom*, you say?" He had to grin. "*In lieu of?* Your command of the language is refreshing."

"I read books."

"Fortunate, since I write books."

"That's good to know, but you didn't answer my question."

James felt stimulated, albeit exhausted. He took a breath and slowed his speech to signal the end of his endurance.

"I practice with my characters."

Clarissa caught the lowered tempo, and was kind enough not to clean her verbal knife on his sleeve.

"I see," she said before returning to her sandwich.

The silence was a blessing for some moments, but it wasn't long before James grew weary of it. Clarissa must have noted a change in either his posture or expression because she raised a halting finger while swallowing a bite, and, after she had cleared her throat, said amusingly:

"That's enough, I think."

"Thank you," James said with a long exhale.

"That was fun, though." She hurriedly finished her sandwich, sipped the last of her tea, then stood. "Thanks."

"Are you leaving?" James stood quickly to conceal his disappointment.

"Yesss," Clarissa replied with an arched brow. James laughed.

"I'm sorry," he said. "That was fun for me, too."

"Maybe we can do it again."

"That would be nice."

Clarissa lifted her tray of dirty dishes, flashed him an intriguing smile, then threaded her way through the cafe. James watched her go, following her every move and gesture, feeling so profoundly happy that a tear leaked down his cheek. He didn't wipe it away, he wanted to feel it, to savor it. It had been so long.

## /////

She came to his table the next day without the awkward pretense, her smile beneficent, and the first words she spoke were:

"So what do you write?"

James found himself sputtering again, and again got a napkin to his mouth just in time. That kept him occupied while Clarissa took her seat. Standing for a woman was cute, she thought, but it was just too old-fashioned.

"Clarissa!" James coughed. "That was unexpected."

"I didn't mean to startle you." She arranged her sandwich and tea.

"No, that's not it, just...abrupt."

"All better now?" There was glee in her eyes, a look that James couldn't help but set to memory.

"Yes."

"So then—what do you write?"

James knew the question well, perhaps all writers did, and perhaps they were all as clumsy with the answer. The act of committing words to paper—or nowadays those abominable e-books—never seemed to assuage the questioner. They always sought more, a defining purpose, a narrower niche. James had written essays, stories, even poetry. Presently he wrote fiction, and yet answering, *I write fiction*, was never enough. They always followed up with, *What kind of fiction?*

"I write fiction."

"Oh," she said. "Short fiction or novels?"

She had surprised him yet again.

"Both, actually."

"Have I read you before? Tell me some of your titles."

This was another awkward exchange most writers had to endure because most writers weren't famous. His work was so obscure that he could recite his titles with the sure knowledge that she would never have heard of any of them, and, after he did recite them, she proved this in fact.

"I'm sorry," she said. "I've never heard of any of those."

"Don't be sorry. It's hard these days...for people to find your work, that is."

"But you would think it would be so much easier."

"Why do you say that?"

"Well, you know, because of the internet."

James chuckled ironically.

"Take a cup of water and an ocean," he said, rocking his coffee cup for emphasis. "It's no easier to find a drop of water in the ocean than it is in the cup, but it *is* easier to find a *particular* drop of water in the cup, and just as easy to lose it in the ocean."

"Hmm," she said. "I never thought about it that way."

"And there are so few bookstores anymore."

"You're right." Clarissa frowned in thought. "There's a library I go to. I haven't been to a bookstore in ages."

"Yeah," he grumbled. "That's about how long it's been. It can get lonely. I miss them." He stopped there because he was beginning to sound morose, which was not what he had intended. "But enough of that," he said, trying to laugh it off, and just succeeding because Clarissa brightened and asked:

"Are you writing anything now?"

"Yes," he answered, perhaps hesitantly.

"Can you tell me about it?"

"That would be..." He shifted uncomfortably. "Well, that would be like viewing an unfinished painting."

"Oh. I think I understand."

Did she? She was clearly disappointed, or at least he would have written her that way, but he couldn't reveal his pages to her, it wasn't time. She turned her attention to her lunch. This time the silence was a veil, and he was glad for it.

He couldn't write that night. All the paragraphs that had been assembling in his mind had evaporated like a spot of dew in a desert. He splashed whiskey into his coffee and tried to lure them back. Her lights were out across the way. The darkness that framed his window crept in, edging ever closer, his thoughts circulating through the apparent futility of it all. It wasn't Clarissa. If not for her the darkness would have overtaken him by now. And he wasn't ready for that. Not yet.

*////*

I should have known better than to take James to that place. Now I've cracked that door for myself as well. It's difficult to drive off those thoughts once they get in, without Clarissa as a shield. I have found her though, here and there, in a manner, a look, a turn of phrase, enough to make me smile for Clarissa in her astuteness and for James in his clumsiness. The book is almost finished so this will have to be enough, otherwise the questions will intrude even more deeply. Why suffer the isolation and doubt, the sleepless nights amid a maelstrom of thoughts?

Why agonize over a single word? Why sacrifice so much for a work that will disappear into the unleavened throng?

We writers...once we were lions, respected and even revered. We set the stage of discourse, defined the culture. Our work came at a cost, for sure, but our work was shared, the costs to us distributed along with the truths we described. No more. The ability to separate the language from common vulgarity has been lost. Now the language is vulgar, as inelegant and ineloquent as a drunken riot.

So why?

///// 

*The darkest bells toll in the darkest hours. They tolled beyond the author's window. Time goes by, as it must. He watched the world he had known dissolve little by little into a vapid philosophy that literature could no longer bridge, a philosophy that could never earn greatness, or even recognize it. There is an ebb and flow, these periods come and go. He knew this, but it was different now, voices shouting too loud to hear, a cacophony of ignorance.*

*Why pay the price? To what end?*

*If there was an answer to be found, it had to reside within Clarissa.*

# Chapter Thirteen

MORGANE RETURNED to the pasty white doldrums of winter with a new resolve and a bronze glow from toe to brow and every lovely form and feature in between. It would have been enough to just lie in bed and gaze at her, to savor that Caribbean-tinted skin with my fingertips. What could only have been a fantasy for me bare weeks earlier now made Morgane giggle with ticklish delight. Never before had she responded so enthusiastically to my touch, or offered me such a delicate touch in return. This was such a departure, such a fundamental shift, that I just couldn't let it alone.

We were lying together, quiet for the moment, our sheets damp. The sun shone weakly through the windows, a rusty orb in the chill morning fog. Morgane's bare hip curved gracefully beneath my hand, her lips turned sensually upward, her eyes closed in sated exhaustion.

I did think twice before I opened my mouth, I just didn't think hard enough.

"You're so different since you've gotten back," I whispered. Goose bumps prickled her skin where I traced my fingers. She purred in satisfaction, kept her eyes languidly closed.

"I am no different," she mumbled.

"Yes you are. You're so much more—" She patted my hand, the signal to hush, but I pressed on anyway. "You're being so...I don't know. Just *different.*"

She patted my hand again, this time with a heavier touch, and then she added sleepily, "Do not speak, Joplin. This is nice and I want to keep it."

"But we should talk about it."

"Anon, Joplin—*later*."

"But I want to know *why*."

That did it. Her eyes snapped open and her smile flattened, telling me in both French and English that I should have kept my mouth shut. Her hip disappeared under a wrinkled sheet that somehow found its way around her shoulders at the same time, and all while she drew back like a cobra preparing to strike. Her eyes were a pair of cyclones. I suddenly felt sickly pale and patently exposed, and as foolish as a rooster crowing in a kitchen. She inhaled deeply and firmly through the nose I had just been kissing, and when she let that breath out, an exasperated torrent came with it.

"*Why? You say why?* I say why can you not be happy, Joplin? We are here and it is beautiful and still my passion is not *enough* for you? What is it you want me to say to you, that sometimes you are a little boy and you make me crazy to understand you?"

Her cheeks were red and she was practically trembling, breathing hard and fast, searching for words but not finding them, while I backed away as much as I could, realizing too late how badly I had screwed up. At last she threw up her hands and lapsed into French.

"*Merde...Merde! Mais pourquoi est-ce que je reste avec toi? Ces mecs! Ce mec... Americain en plus! C'est vraiment trop! Mais je t'aime...moi je dois être stupide!*" She slapped her head at that last bit and then leaned back to catch her breath.

That sure was a mouthful. I understood some of it. The *stupide* was obvious, meaning her, not me, or maybe me, too, it's always hard to tell with French. But I also understood something else, something I had never expected to hear, and when I realized she had said it, and was sure I had heard it right, my heart went light and I reached for her. She snapped back with such a hard expression that I wasn't sure if she was about to punch me.

"*Ne me touche pas*," she spat. Don't touch me.

"*Mais je t'aime aussi*," I said in a cracking voice, hoping that I had pronounced it right, then knowing that I must have pronounced it right because she reared back even farther, her next breath frozen between lips gone round in surprise.

"*Mon Dieu,*" she moaned when she found her breath. "So now you speak French?"

"A little."

"A little too much, I think."

I reached for her but she shouldered away from me, crossed her arms and glowered.

"Morgane, if you—"

"Do not say it, Joplin. It will make it too complicated."

"But you said—"

"I said for me, not for you." She pulled at her hair. "*Merde. Qu'est-ce que j'ai fait?*"

I didn't understand that bit at all, and was about to say so when she held up a hand to silence me.

"It is enough for now. Okay?" Her expression said I had better agree, and at least this time I made the right decision.

"Okay, Morgane. It's enough for now."

"*D'accord.*"

And then she rolled up in the sheet, her back to me, but she let me drape an arm over her shoulder. *Mais je t'aime,* she had said—*But I love you.* And just for a little while I didn't think about James Trevor Davidson or Clarissa or Dad or Kessie or any of it. For a little while it was just Morgane and me. For a little while.

*/////*

HEARING KESSIE ANNOUNCE *The Lives of Clarissa* while I was driving Morgane home from the airport that night came as such a shock that I actually swerved onto a curb. It was a struggle to keep my mind off of it, even with Morgane's newfound affection. Up until then I had thought of Clarissa as mine, a kind of literary possession that I could keep locked away in a drawer, unknown by anyone else. But now she was out like a hacked email, as much of an enigma in the real world as she was in James' mind. There was no way to contain it, so now I was going to have to rework all of that, too, although I hadn't got to that point yet.

Kessie mailed me an advance copy, and the first thing I noticed was her name on the jacket as editor, and in letters almost as large as Dad's. She'd even autographed it, for God's sake!

*For Jop with love, Andy*

She probably meant well, but this ate at me in the kind of quiet resentment that sours in your belly. I called Marcia.

"She's listed as the sole owner of the material, Joplin," Marcia told me. Her voice was serious and perhaps a little worried, as if this were a road she'd been down before. "Kessie *did* edit the stories on her own. It took a lot of work. And she registered the copyright. I thought you two were together on this."

"I didn't know anything about it," I growled.

"Joplin—if there's a problem, I'm sorry, I really am. You and Kessie should talk, I think. See if you can work it out."

Marcia wasn't taking sides, this wasn't her doing, and there was no reason for me to call Kessie. It would be the same as last time with *Comes Now, Achilles.* Sure I had given her the stories, but there was no way I could have anticipated *this.* There were so many roiling conflicts going on in my head that I couldn't say which one tore at me the most. There was a lot of money involved, that was for sure. *The Lives of Clarissa* had knocked *Comes Now, Achilles* into second place on the bestsellers lists, with the *Houston* novels (reissued with Dad's full name, by the way) occupying third, fourth, fifth and sixth places. The reviewers were comparing *The Lives of Clarissa* to Virginia Woolf's *Orlando.* I thought that was over the top, but I guess reviewers have to write something.

*The Lives of Clarissa* was an anthology of the stories James had described, of Clarissa in the various guises he had imagined. That Dad had actually gone so far as to write each of the stories and file them in his desk seemed piteously obsessive to me. I read Kessie's introduction. It was full of glowing talk about Dad, about the god-like quality of his prose, the way she had watched him write when she was young, sometimes sitting with her chin propped on his desk while he transferred his greatness into words. The way Kessie told it, Dad's creative world revolved around her, as if there had been no history to him until she had gotten old enough to follow him around like a puppy. What a load of absolute—

And now Kessie was dressing like a sophisticate, glossy black heels and hip-hugging skirts, and jetting from city to city on her book tour, making the rounds of the talk shows and generally carrying on as if *she* were the writer in the family, never mentioning me at all.

I thought it was revealing that she didn't use her introduction to theorize who Clarissa was. I had a pretty good idea, though. Where was Dad when Kessie was born? No wonder Mom left him.

All of this publicity had stirred up the trolls again. I hadn't come up with a new blog post since *Nashville and the Costs of Fame*, but that didn't stop them from migrating back to my site like a herd of carrion eaters, savaging the remains they had left behind last time. If I was angry already, this made it worse.

So I savaged them back, and what a windmill it was.

It's interesting how extremes of emotion can drive the creative process. My next post, *The Trolls Among Us*, popped into my head tinged in red and almost completely written. It had an *Invasion of the Body Snatchers* resonance about it, warning those few whose consciences were clean of this kind of thing that the trolls could even be their friends or loved ones, scary, mind-altered creatures who were digitally subverting the very fabric of civilization. It was past time to act, to purge them from our midst, so check under your beds and in your closets. Look under the kitchen sink and behind the toilet, any dark places where they could hide. Root them out before it was too late.

I also took a shot at Kessie, about the way she was fawning over Dad and riding his work toward fame for herself. It was dying that had made Dad famous, not any inherent greatness, so why weren't the trolls going after her?

I thought the post was witty, I even laughed while I wrote parts of it. Many of my readers thought it was funny, too, with comments like: *Hi-*

*larious; Joplin finally found his funny bone; Remind me to always check behind my toilet:D* Others agreed that internet trolls had to be stopped somehow. A debate started up on how to achieve that, a real debate in measured tones. I felt as if I had really contributed something.

And then all of that was subsumed into hate. Kessie's following had grown larger than Dad's, her hashtags *#kessieanndean* and *#kessiedeanishot* like calls to action. They struck out at me as if I were her creepy, closeted brother, born with a hand coming out of my head or something. It was worse than *The Social Media State*, worse than my perceived racism. Now I was a betrayer of Kessie's innocence, disloyal to my father's legacy, the talentless other child, jealous that I hadn't gotten whichever gene it was that had made Dad and Kessie so great; and added to that were the trolls who hated just for the sake of hating. I had dared to attack them, so here's what they could do in return.

One comment cut deeper than the others: *You are wrong, Jop. You are mean. You break my heart.*

Damn it, Kessie. I shut down Facebook and Twitter. I shut down all of it.

///// 

THE DAFFODILS WERE SPRINKLING the lawn with their yellow blooms when Morgane came home early from the office and approached me with a worried look. I was at the desk, my coffee gone cold, and with little energy to do anything else but watch the daffodils push their way out of the hardened soil. It was a bright day, but that hadn't helped me much.

"I am troubled by you, Joplin," she said. What she meant was that she was *worried* about me, so that meant that this was an intervention.

"I'm okay," I said without conviction.

"No, I do not think so."

She laid a folded newspaper on the desk, then stuck a finger in my coffee and sighed.

"Your *café* is cold," she said flatly.

She took the cup to the kitchen to refill it. When she came back, she set the cup down and then just stood there, probing with her presence.

"Thank you," I said. I took a sip, then moved my hands to the keyboard as if I were about to let loose. Morgane had a way of breathing insistently whenever she thought she was being ignored. It was unmistakable, and it wasn't going to go away unless I acknowledged something, so I added, "You're home early."

"Yes, I have come to speak to you."

"You can speak to me any time."

"This is a good time."

I turned to her then to try to gauge what was up. She was dressed in professional attire, classy clothes for high-class clients. She looked so good that she could have been on tour with Kessie, and then I thought I understood: it was a professional guise for a pragmatic discussion, one that wouldn't descend into kissing and making up and falling into bed.

"Oh-kay," I said warily. "What do you want to talk about?"

"I want to know why you are not working."

"But I *am* working," I whined.

"You are not working, Joplin. There are no words on your screen."

I looked away guiltily.

"I'm still composing it in my head."

"Tell me what you are composing."

"C'mon, Morgane. I can't talk about it ahead of time. You know that."

"I know you are very unhappy, and you are not pleasant to be near when you do this."

"I'm not unhappy, I'm just—"

"And you are very angry. I do not like you this way. You must call your sister and repair the problem."

"What!"

I stood at that, not aggressively, just in surprise. Morgane held her ground, hardening her expression, waiting for me to cave in but I wasn't going to.

"Morgane, you don't understand what this is about."

"I understand it very well. She has hurt your feelings and this has made you unhappy."

"She didn't hurt my damn feelings!"

I said that just loud enough to get her color up, and then she took that breath through her nose that said the French was about to be unleashed, and then I did something I had never done before, I put a finger to her lips to silence her...and she just about bit it off.

"Ow!" I yanked away.

"What is it you think? That I am some child?"

"Morgane? Damn!" I squeezed the teeth marks in my finger. No blood. "That hurt."

"So that is real pain, Joplin, not the kind you make for yourself." She turned in a huff and marched off, warning as she went, "If you are unhappy then I am unhappy. And Joplin—" she turned to face me, "—I want to be happy. *T'as compris?*"

"Yeah, I get it," I said without enthusiasm.

"Good," she said as she went out the front door, back to work or elsewhere.

Morgane was right, I knew she was right, but it's still possible to keep two opposing beliefs in your head at the same time. Religious nuts and partisan zealots couldn't function otherwise; nor, apparently, could I.

A phone call to Kessie wasn't going to help, the issue went beyond her. That's what Morgane didn't understand, and I can't say that I fully understood it at that moment either. I just knew in a deeper place that I had missed out somehow, and that it couldn't have been my fault. Kessie was being feted from coast to coast, a literary heroine in the mold of Clarissa. And she was all over the internet. Anything having to do with her was trending, while I sat at Dad's desk staring at a blank screen and taking abuse as my coffee went cold.

I sat back down and positioned myself in front of my keyboard as if I were about to set a masterpiece into type. I wasn't going to call Kessie, that wasn't going to happen. She had betrayed me. Morgane just didn't understand.

Morgane had left her newspaper on the desk. Something about it caught my eye, and when I looked closer I discovered that there were worse things than internet trolls. It was the literary section from the Sunday *Tennessean*, a quarter-page headline that someone had highlighted in yellow:

*Disgruntled Son Discounts Father's Legacy*. It was an AP story from Houston, carrying the byline of Doreen Ybarra!

I suddenly felt queasy, enough to sprint into the bathroom. Bent over, breathing deeply, nothing came up but bewilderment. Digital media is so dominant that it never would have occurred to me to worry about a story in a newspaper; at the same time though, all writers know—whether or not they're willing to admit it—that their work isn't truly real unless they can see it on paper, which is probably why I always printed out my blog posts and definitely why I was feeling so sick. A thousand ephemeral haters could troll my site, but one story on paper was as solid as eternity.

Doreen's story was a compilation of all that had happened since Dad had died, from our first meeting at the condo, to Kessie's book tour, to my latest blog post. There were no interviews in it, nothing that required comment. The image that came through was clear though, that Kessie was sharing a literary trove with the public while I sat at home and criticized both the quality of her motives and the quality of Dad's work.

But that's not what I was doing. Why couldn't anyone understand? None of them knew Dad the way I did, not even Kessie. I'd always had to live in Dad's shadow, and now, when I should finally be free of all of that, I was suddenly being shoved into *Kessie's* shadow.

That's when it came to me, right then at that moment, bent over the toilet and trying to work it all out. There *was* something I could do to get the recognition I knew I deserved, and it would be all mine, nothing to do with Kessie, and the hell with Doreen Ybarra.

I returned to the desk, my stomach feeling solid with purpose. I opened the middle right drawer, took *The Latter Half of Inglorious Years* from its velveted place, and I didn't hesitate, not for a second:

I scratched out my father's name and wrote mine.

# Chapter Fourteen

BARBER GAPED when he caught on to what I was saying. It took him a few moments. Shelisa had rejoined us after making her rounds. I'm not sure I would have revealed that to Barber if it had just been the two of us, but then maybe it wasn't so bad to confess it to someone whose mind was liable to blink out at just the right moment. From there I could have dissembled on, giving my conscience a rest, if only until the next wretched confession.

Barber took a pull on his Carib, shook himself back into the present and asked, "So, you mean you—?"

"Yeah," I cut in before he could say it out loud.

His eyes glazed as he wrapped his mind around it. Shelisa's expression was inscrutable.

"So this be when you made Evan Usher," she said.

"Yeah," I sighed. "And Hannah."

I searched her face for any hint of disapproval, but her expression remained incorrigibly unreadable.

"But still they are the same as before?" she asked.

"Mostly," I said, rubbing my temples and coveting Barber's beer. Shelisa followed my gaze, smiled, and nudged my coffee cup closer. "It was more work than I thought it would be."

"How so?" Barber asked, back in the moment and seeming interested. I eyed his beer again before going on.

"For one, their names were woven deeply into the prose. There's a kind of rhythm you can get, balancing syllables and sounds. Do you know what I mean?"

Barber went blank again, so that had bounced off of him, but Shelisa understood.

"I get you," she said. "It make the words smooth like poems."

"That's right. And my father was good at it. So I had to go back to all the sentences with Evan or Hannah in them, and rewrite them where they sounded clumsy."

Barber straightened up with a scowl.

"The whole thing sounds clumsy if you ask me," he said.

"Hush, Barber," Shelisa gently scolded; then to me: "And what else did you change?"

"So all that stuff I had to take out? Well, I had to put something back or else it wouldn't have made sense."

Barber drained the last of his beer with an exaggerated gulp, then batted his eyes at Shelisa, who dutifully bent down behind the bar and came up with two Caribs. She popped the tops and handed one to Barber.

"Thank you, Shelly," he said, all but licking his lips in anticipation. She smiled sweetly and passed the other one to me.

"It be time enough for beer now," she said, her smile so genuine that it hurt to look at. I thanked her wordlessly, then took a long, blessedly cold swallow. "So, Joplin," she said after that, "you made a creation too, then, ent it?"

"Huh?"

"Ent it so?"

"Oh. Well, Shelisa...I don't know—"

"Y'ain hear," she cut in with her local dialect, laughing with her eyes. "I know right."

She settled onto her elbows and made herself comfortable. More customers were coming in. A woman named Julie came in to help out behind the bar. Shelisa nodded to her but stayed put. Barber edged his stool closer as others pressed in next to him.

"So now, Joplin," Shelisa said with a fortifying smile, "tell us your tale of Evan Usher and Miss Hannah."

//// 

Evan Usher watched with joy as Hannah crossed the street. It was a morning to match his mood, as promising as the paragraphs he held in his mind. She was wearing white, as he imagined she would, an angelic white that bent beauteous sun and sky into a heavenly aura around her. Today she carried a picnic basket to work, an old-fashioned wicker basket with a hinged top. Even in his deepest imaginings he couldn't have hoped for this, that Hannah would invite him for a picnic lunch by the lake.

He daydreamed through the hours until noon, thinking not of his novel but of the novel experience that awaited him. Today she would reveal her mystery, he was certain of it. She would fuel his imagination with all he needed to finish his work, to lay it to rest, to still his mind and be at peace. From then there would be friendship and fulfillment, a fairer life. From then he would live off the page, reveling in what she could become. From then he would not write again.

They met at a pond that was garrisoned by truculent geese, skirted that with hurried greetings, and made their way onto the path along the lake. Ducks accompanied them, paddling languidly in the still water. Evan took the basket, with its nostalgic smells of peppery cold chicken and warm bread. Hannah's dress caressed her knees in the soughing breeze.

"It's nice here," Evan said. "I like the quiet."

Other picnickers dotted the park greens, but not enough of them to intrude on one another. The sounds of traffic were distant, like a wind rustling far treetops.

"It is nice," Hannah said airily. She clasped her hands behind her back and walked with a carefree sway, turning her cheeks in and out of the sun.

"Do you come here often?" he asked.

"Never have. How about you?"

"The same."

"Then this is a first for both of us. I hope it's not the last." She paused to give him the sincerest smile, which swelled his heart so much that it ached.

"I hope so, too," he said, his eyes glistening like the dance of sun on water.

They went on in silence. Hannah seemed to relish it all, with almost childlike wonder. Dollops on the placid lake betrayed leaping fish, often heard but never seen. Dragonflies clung to reeds, folding and unfolding gossamer wings. Birds chirped and cheeped, and a sweet fragrance lingered in the air.

"What a perfect day," Hannah said dreamily, arms wide and face raised to the sun. "Can you smell them?" she asked. "The flowers?"

"Yes, I can," Evan answered, savoring the scent as well as the scene. Her eyes were closed, her face so tranquil that she could have been a young girl, free of worries and cares, so pure that Evan almost couldn't bear it; but then she turned to him with open eyes and a furrowed brow and said:

"We'd better hurry, though. I only have an hour."

Evan came back to himself with a start, the beautiful spell snatched away with a word.

"Of course," he said. "I'm sorry. I wasn't thinking."

She looked at him curiously, as if she had tripped on something unseen.

"There's no reason for you to be sorry," she said. "I'm the one who has to go back."

He wouldn't hear those words, but made himself smile anyway.

"There's a nice spot," he pointed.

They strolled to a shaded place near the water, the slender limbs of willows swaying gently in the breeze. Hannah spread a red-and-white checkered cloth over the cool grass, kicked out of her shoes and lowered herself onto folded legs. Evan sat stiffly cross-legged, wincing at the twinges he felt in both knees. It took him a moment to find a comfortable position.

"So, what do we have in here?" he asked then, reaching for the basket.

"I'll do it," Hannah said, not sharply but insistent enough to give him pause.

"Uh, okay," he said uncertainly.

"It's just that I kind of pictured it, you know?" She seemed flustered. "I want everything to be just right."

"Just right?" Now he was puzzled.

"I know it sounds silly," she blushed.

"I'm not sure I understand."

"It's just that—" She halted mid-breath and bit her lip as if unsure of herself, an expression that intrigued Evan. "I mean," she continued after those moments, "my father used to take me on picnics when I was little, and he would let me do everything myself, even if I made a mess." She smiled at something. "He made me feel so big, like he couldn't do it without my help. Papa was—" She stopped there and dabbed at an eye. "Anyway," she blushed again, "I just wanted to remember how it felt."

"It's all right, Hannah," Evan said, barely controlling the crack in his voice. "But there must be something I can do."

She cast him a sly look that made him fidget. It was a marvel how quickly her expressions could change.

"You can play a word game with me," she said, grinning now.

"Uh, oh," he moaned, although his own expression defied that.

"Don't worry," she said. "This is a different game, not like last time."

She took out paper plates and napkins, plastic forks and spoons. Evan studied her intently. She went on speaking while she prepared everything.

"So this is another game my father would play with me." She paused with the foil-wrapped chicken in her hands, smiling at some memory. "I was four or five. He would put me on his shoulders and we would go for these long walks in the jungle—"

"Jungle?"

That was a detail that begged for elaboration, but Hannah went on as if it were self-evident.

"Yes. We would just be going along, then out of nowhere he would say a word, and I would have to say the first word that came to my mind that had something to do with his word. He didn't make it too hard for me, but not too easy either..."

She trailed off at that, placed a drumstick on each plate then reached into the basket for the potato salad.

"You and your father must be very close," Evan said.

A shadow fell across her face.

"We were."

Evan's heart skipped. Something had been revealed just then. He wanted to probe further, but this wasn't the time. Hannah finished spooning out the potato salad, and then brought out the bread.

"So do you start?" Evan asked. "Or do I?"

"I'll start," she said. Two bottles of lemonade completed her work. She scanned the area around them, looked out to the lake, grinned and said, "*Duck.*"

"Hmm." Evan stroked his chin.

"You have to say it fast," she complained.

"Fast? How fast?"

"As fast as you can."

"Okay—uh, what was it you said?"

"*Duck*, Evan."

"You mean like a quacking duck?"

"Just *duck*. Come on, you have to be quick."

"Okay, uh, baseball."

"*Baseball?*" Hannah looked incredulous. "How do you get baseball from duck?"

Evan took a bite of chicken before he answered. It was as good as his own picnic memories. He smiled his appreciation, wiped his hands, and then explained: "If you're a batter, and a fastball is coming right at your head, you duck, right?"

"Ooh. You're going to be good at this."

"I hope so. So what's your next word?"

She swallowed a bite, took a sip of lemonade, then said, "That's easy. It's *bat*."

Evan was ready this time. He came right back with, "*Cave*," to which Hannah countered just as quickly, "*Stalagmite*—"

"*Stalactite*," was Evan's easy retort, and from there they took off in rapid succession, not even pausing for breath, their grins growing wider at each word.

"*Water*."

"*Drip*."

"*Faucet*."

"*Bath*."

"*Soap*."

"*Suds*."

"*Beer*."

"*Ballpark*."

"*Baseball*."

"*Duck*—"

They both erupted in laughter, with Evan practically doubled over and momentarily unaware of the ache in his knees. He hadn't laughed so hard in longer than he could remember. What a joy it was, what a simple joy. What had life been without it? Nothing.

Hannah recovered first. Her cheeks and nose were so red from laughing that she looked sunburned.

"We never came back around to the word we started with before," she said through a few lingering chuckles.

"How did we do that?" he asked, deeply pleased to have been a part of something new for her. "It all seemed to fit together so perfectly."

"I don't know." She gave him an amused look. "You've played this before, haven't you?"

"No, never."

"Uh, huh," she said with a mirthful roll of her eyes.

He took a bite of potato salad, but kept her in view over his fork. A sense of simple satisfaction filled a hollow deep within him.

"So how long could you and your father go on like that?" he asked.

"Hours, I think." She screwed up her face in thought. "It seemed like it, anyway."

That brought two comfortable sighs, along with a companionable silence that allowed them to finish eating. Once everything was cleaned up and packed away, Evan stretched out on an elbow and sipped his lemonade.

"I've never had a better picnic," he said.

"Thank you. I hoped you would like it."

Hannah lay on her back and gazed serenely at the weave of blue between the branches above. Evan watched her, her chest rising and falling, legs crossed and her hands clasped loosely on her stomach. She was such a bounty of sensations, such a plenitude of superlatives. Had he brought his notebook he would be scribbling furiously now, desperate to record every nuance. But there was more, there was the mystery.

"Are you staring at me, Evan?" she asked with a wry smile, catching him out the corner of her eye. He looked away in embarrassment.

"No—no, I was just thinking."

"About what? Your book?"

"Yes...well, that and other things."

"Sometimes I see you looking at me, Evan, like you're studying me. Is that what you're doing?"

"No, no," he blanched, caught out in the open like a thief. "It's not like that."

"What if I was a character in your book?" she posed. A pair of goldfinches darted after one another through the limbs. Her eyes flickered as she followed their progress. "If you were writing this, how real could you make me?"

"That's a strange question," he said.

"I don't think it is. Could you write it as perfect as this?"

"I believe I could," he said, trying not to sound boastful.

"So what would you draw from, for my character that is? Would you just have made me up, or would you have copied me from someone?"

"It's—well, it could be both." He couldn't shake the sense that they were playing another word game, a much more elaborate one.

"I see."

She seemed to be considering his words intently, her eyes scanning the limbs above. The finches flittered away, displaced by a mockingbird that perched and studied her with first one eye and then the other. The silence lengthened, to Evan's momentary relief, and then Hannah propped herself on an elbow. They were laying face to face now, a chaste space between them but still close enough to rekindle a long-dormant warmth in Evan's belly.

"How long have you been a writer?" she asked, another spell snatched away.

Evan frowned in thought.

"All my life, but not always writing."

"Is that a riddle?"

"No." He laughed that off. "To be a successful writer you have to be very good, very lucky, or very well connected. I missed out on at least two of those though, maybe all three, so I had to do other things off and on to get by. It took half my life to earn enough to be able to concentrate on my work. It's only in these latter years that I've really been able to dedicate myself to it. The irony is that by the time I got here, everything changed."

Hannah nodded in understanding.

"Maybe they'll appreciate your new novel," she offered hopefully. Evan shrugged.

"Maybe," he said without conviction.

Hannah mulled that for a few moments before changing the subject.

"Have you ever been married?" she asked.

"Once," he answered ruefully. "A long time ago."

"What happened?"

"Everything."

"Oh." Hannah pursed her lips; then: "Do you have children?"

"Only rumors," he answered with a wan laugh, hoping to lighten a mood that had somehow gotten weighty, but drawing only a thoughtful frown from her instead. She sat up and smoothed her dress.

"I've got to go back soon," she said.

"Already?"

"I wish I could stay longer, but it's not up to me."

Evan sat up himself, but with difficulty. His knees throbbed, and no position seemed to offer relief.

"Isn't it my turn now?" he asked while massaging his knees.

"*Your* turn?"

"To ask questions."

"Oh," she mouthed in awareness. "Are you sure you want to?"

"Why wouldn't I?"

"I don't know, you would have to tell me."

Evan sighed away a prick of impatience.

"I'd just like to know you," he said edgily.

"You don't think you know me?"

"I'd like to know more."

"More of what?"

"More of anything."

"Anything will satisfy you?"

"Anything would be better than nothing."

"And nothing would be better than something."

"What does *that* mean?"

"It means, Evan—" She betrayed a little shortness herself, taking a deep breath before going on, "Let me put it this way: when you write a character, do you have everything figured out in the beginning, or do you leave a little mystery and just let things happen on their own?"

"I do that sometimes," he conceded.

"Then leave a little mystery now, and let's see what happens."

"But you're not a character."

"Aren't I?"

"No."

"I feel like a character sometimes."

"Why do you say that?"

"It's...I'm not sure. It's the difference between the things I know and the things I don't know, or maybe things I should know. It's hard to explain. Sometimes it feels as if everything is too perfect."

He leaned back a bit, his mind working through a chaos of contradictions. There was a sadness in her eyes now, a distant melancholy. His conscious need to know more came into conflict with a sudden, instinctive urge to protect her, but from what he couldn't define. There was more here than he knew, as if he really were writing her and wasn't yet sure how deeply to explore her character.

He shook that off. It didn't make sense. She was finally revealing herself, in fond memories and subtle shifts of expression, but there was more, much more, and he needed it.

"Just tell me about your work, then," he pressed on. What kind of mystery could possibly be hiding there? "What do you do?"

"Are you sure, Evan?"

"Yes," he answered, swallowing an undefined dread.

"All right," she acceded reluctantly. "I doubt it will make sense to you, but it's like this: I go to the same place every day and do the same thing. I work alone, and what I do is important, I think."

"Is *that* supposed to be a riddle?" Evan threw in a reassuring smile, but it had no effect.

"No, Evan. I told you it wouldn't make sense."

Where had her smile gone? Why did she look so distressed?

"I'm sorry, Hannah. I've upset you."

"It's not that, it's just sometimes I wonder myself." She flicked a glance at her watch. "I've got to get back."

"Please—not yet," he blurted. "We have time. Tell me more."

Something was wrong, he could feel it in the air. Gray clouds smothered the sun. Cold gusts whipped the willows.

"It's that important to you?" she asked, resigned to something he couldn't fathom. Everything inside him said stop, stop now, but he couldn't. He had to know.

"Yes, yes it is."

"Then what do you want to know?"

"Do you have a boyfriend?" he asked shakily.

"No."

"Do you have any brothers or sisters?"

"No."

"Are your parents still living?"

"N—" Her tongue hung on the *n* of another no, but before she could speak it a cloud of confusion crossed her eyes. Her sight went inward, as if that simple question had no ready answer, as if it were forcing her to plumb deeper. Evan could only stare, swallowing dread. He had gone too far. He should have known. He *did* know.

"It's all right, Hannah," he said too late.

"They're..." Her gaze went off somewhere, to a place so crushingly sad that Evan's lips trembled. "...they're gone."

"They left you?" he asked, tears welling.

"No—yes—maybe...I don't know. One day they just...it was like a bad dream. Papa was there. He was so sad." Tears tracked her cheeks. "Poor Papa."

She looked wretchedly at Evan and he saw her there again, feverish cheeks and fluttering eyes. His own tears spilled.

"No more, Hannah," he cried. "I'm so sorry."

"Don't be sad, Papa."

She stood and straightened her dress.

"No, Hannah. Don't go. *Please...*"

He buried his face in his hands, cried whole tears that ran down his arms to drip off his elbows. When he could bear to take his hands away, Hannah had gone.

He sat alone then, on a red-and-white checkered cloth, an old-fashioned picnic basket giving off its nostalgic smells of peppery cold chicken and warm bread. The sky was perfectly blue, and the willow limbs swayed lightly in the breeze.

It was all so perfect, but there were no words.

*/////*

SHELISA NODDED thoughtfully.

"What happened to the girl?" Barber asked.

"She had to go away, Barber," Shelisa explained.

"Oh."

That seemed to be all the explanation he needed. Suddenly the label on his beer bottle was more interesting.

"You get it, don't you," I said to Shelisa. It wasn't a question.

"Yeh." Her expression was contemplative.

"When I read it the first time," I said, "I thought I had missed something. It's all there though, isn't it? I just couldn't figure it out. It wasn't until a lot later that I finally understood."

"She was his muse," Shelisa said sadly.

"Yes," I acknowledged just as sadly.

"And more, I think," she went on. "The poor girl."

"Yes."

"Well tell *me*, then," Barber said in a huff, probably perturbed that the conversation had gone on without him.

"It is not time yet, Barber," Shelisa told him firmly. "There does be more to this tale. Y'ain hear, Joplin?"

I cupped my chin in my hands and pondered it all.

"Yeah," I said. "A lot more."

# Chapter Fifteen

IT TOOK SEVENTEEN INTENSE DAYS to transcribe it all, to take out what was too revealing, to impose Evan and Hannah where needed. I worked with a focus that startled Morgane. She eyed me incredulously at first, lingering in her morning haste to get out the door to work. After a few mornings of this, and a few matching evenings, she settled into trusting what she was seeing. She softened then, brought me coffee, pecked my cheek on her way out, frisked my shoulders on her way in. It was very domestic, unlike her, but for a while she was content.

Beyond my window, the daffodil blooms had withered away, replaced by the frenetic growth of dandelions and new leaves. Storms piled in and the wind rushed, rustling the hedges and bowing the trees, yielding between fronts to skies of the starkest blue. Only a few crisp mornings remained, and then warmth seeped in. It became easy to see what was on the screen as bold and original, to deflect Morgane's curiosity and take her mounting and mounted affections as reward for hard work.

Mid-afternoon on the seventeenth day, I sat back, sipped hot coffee, and took a breath. The manuscript was no longer pristine, it was dog-eared, blemished with notes and struck passages. I put it back in its place, closed the drawer with my knee, and that was that. James and Clarissa no longer existed. Evan and Hannah had filled those roles so well that James and Clarissa seemed like distant cousins, vague, loosely connected and easy to disregard.

Evan and Hannah had come alive in my mind, especially Hannah, who was so tragically sweet that my heart ached for her as I reworked her scenes. Her mystery remained, but that was Dad's obsession, not mine. He had poured an inordinate amount of energy into it, I thought. To me it was just a thread of tension designed to eke at least a bit of emotion out of stodgy old Evan. I tamped that down where I thought it was necessary, and to make Evan less of a stiff old stick, I added a scene of light affection, questing hands and a brush of lips, not too much considering the differences in their ages, but enough to provide at least some emotional release for the reader.

I emailed the file to Marcia, who was on the phone with me in heaped praise and amazement within the hour.

"Joplin," she gushed. "If the rest of it is as good as the first chapter, I can just about promise you a contract before the end of the week."

I should have been excited, and might have been if I hadn't known since I had first laid eyes on it how good *The Latter Half of Inglorious Years* really was. Of course Marcia would be enthusiastic, of course she would get me a contract quickly, that was a given. But how different would I have felt if the story had been mine from the first seminal thought, if I had built upon it day by day, week by week, laughing with my characters, crying with them, sharing their hope and pain?

True to her prediction, Marcia was back with me in days. Knopf wanted to speed the book to press, to capitalize on all the publicity Kessie had generated with *The Lives of Clarissa*, which was still number one on the best-sellers lists. My book could knock Kessie off her pedestal. Now *that* was something I could get excited about.

I lifted Morgane and spun her in the doorway when she got home that evening. This flustered her in an hilarious way. As passionate as Morgane could be, girlish twirling wasn't part of it. I set her back on her feet, grinning as she blushingly sought to regain her dignity.

"Joplin, this is a surprise," she sputtered, trying to pretend that nothing but a breeze through the door had rustled her hair. "What has happened to you?"

I took her by the shoulders and smiled proudly into stormy green eyes that were still a bit dazed.

"They're publishing me, Morgane. They're publishing my book."

"Book? What book is this?" Her crooked tooth tentatively appeared through a smile that wasn't quite sure of itself.

"The book I've been working on every day," I explained in a rush.

"You wrote a book so fast?"

Now she stepped back from me, her brows scrunched together in puzzlement. She bumped the door closed with her hip, crossed her arms and faced me head-on.

"Yeah, well..." I clambered for an explanation that I should already have thought up. "No, I mean...not that fast. I've been working on it for a long time."

Her look was so dubious that I almost confessed it all right then.

"You have been writing a book for a long time?"

"Uh, yeah. Since before we met."

Her brows lifted at that. I could see that she was reordering the history of the last year and some, questioning her assumptions, her observations, her interpretations.

"Sometimes you cannot write your blog for weeks but you can write a book?" she asked pointedly.

I hesitated. How would Evan have explained it to Hannah, not at the picnic where everything had fallen apart, but earlier, before they had learned too much about one another and words were still spoken with care? I pictured Evan, coffee in hand and sitting across from Hannah and her trim sandwich. I called to mind his nostalgic competence, his command of his own voice, always ready with the right words to counter Hannah's keen wit. It was a settling image, and when I answered Morgane, I answered as I knew Evan would.

"Sometimes I would get so caught up in the book that I wouldn't have anything left for the blog," I explained to her. "Scenes would come to me, and I would go over them in my head, trying to get them just right before I wrote them down. If I let myself think about anything else, I could lose the thread. It happened enough, believe me. And I did a lot of it while you were gone."

She wavered then, searching the air to make the pieces fit.

"Why did you not tell me?" she huffed.

Again I borrowed from Evan.

"It's hard for me to talk about a story while I'm writing it, Morgane. It's...like looking at an unfinished painting."

She wasn't convinced. The evidence of that was as clear as her searching expression, but she had seemed to run out of arguments.

"Okay, Joplin. I understand you." She tipped up to peck me on the cheek. "I am happy for you."

"Are you really?"

"Yes I am really."

I hugged her then, and we kissed, and I could think that I had successfully threaded that needle of dishonesty, had stitched it all together and could now fold it and put it away.

/////

IT'S AMAZING HOW FAST a publisher can move when it thinks it has a goldmine on its hands. A few rounds of editing, almost daily encouragement from Marcia, and within a couple of caffeine-addled weeks UPS showed up at the door with my advance copy.

I knew what it was without even looking at the label, the dense feel of a cardboard envelope wrapped tightly around a hardcover book. I urgently pulled the tape on the envelope, and the book slid out like an effortless birth, into the light, bright with promise. My heart thudded against my breastbone and then seemed to stop, suspending me in a moment of absolute vindication. The proof was in my hands, no longer an idea but a solid reality, that the trolls had been wrong, that Kessie had been wrong—that Dad had been wrong. I have never known such righteous satisfaction.

I rubbed at a smudge with my sleeve. The cover art was clever, sunlight slanting through an open window onto a title page emerging from a typewriter, *The Latter Half of Inglorious Years*, a novel by Evan Usher, but with Evan struck out and my name below it in a larger font.

My name, and the irony passed me by.

I felt transported into the image, into an alternate world as real as this one, sitting at that typewriter, the scents of ink and irises mingling on a warm breeze, whiskey glass sweating a ring on a well-worn desktop, the indistinct figure of a woman on the street below, the mystery.

I sat with the book and thumbed through the pages, as if each page would reveal something new, some detail I hadn't noticed before, page by page, and then once more, each page a life, a revelation. I lingered on the copyright page, the esoteric numbers and disclaimers that had never meant anything until they were mine, the printing history at the bottom, and the words *First Edition*. This book would be the first of many, I was certain of it. In that moment I was so full of my own literary prowess, so invested in my own myth, that I was able to crowd out the bitter frustrations of Dad and James and Evan. Shakespeare couldn't craft such irony. I diverted my conscience as all dissemblers must, rationalizing that my contributions to the book were not insubstantial, and truth be told it was *my* work that had livened up an otherwise moribund story.

When Morgane got home I swooped her up again, held on tight through her protests, let go haughtily, put the book in her hands, then stepped back with a self-satisfied grin.

She studied the book skeptically, as if it were a magic trick, ran her fingers across the cover, across my name, threw me a mysterious look, turned the book over, examined the back, the black & white author photo that had been a hasty selfie but had turned out pretty well, the list of complimentary blurbs that Knopf had generated somehow. She thumbed through the pages, slowing as she came to the end, as if buying time to gather her thoughts.

"It is a nice book, Joplin," she allowed at last, if with little emotion. I didn't take offence. This was Morgane, after all. She needed prodding.

"Nice?" I exclaimed, feigning umbrage. "How about *magnifique, incroyable, superbe*, and maybe *brillant?*"

That drew a smile out of her, not the full-tooth version, but at least an affectionate tilt.

"That is not how we speak," she said with an amused look rather than the usual indignant glower she reserved for misused, misapplied, or mispronounced French. I laughed.

"But you like it, yes?"

"Yes, Joplin. It is very nice and I am happy for you."

"So let's go out and celebrate."

Images took shape in my mind, valet parking for the BMW, Morgane wearing something elegant, a central table but not too crowded, my book laying in plain view—

"I think no, Joplin, not tonight because I must go early tomorrow. *Mais* we can have some wine, yes, and celebrate here?"

She was prepared for my disappointment because she had my face in her soft hands before I could whine anything in return, and she kissed me and she smelled nice despite the cigarettes.

"And I would like to read your book," she added. "This is okay?"

I was more inwardly thrilled than she could have possibly imagined. She was *asking* to read it, I wasn't having to coerce her into it, and for an author that is the greatest compliment of all.

/////

EVENTS TOOK OFF so quickly from there that I didn't have a hope of controlling them. It was the antithesis of the social media storms I had suffered through, but with that same helpless sense of being at the mercy of the current.

*The Latter Half of Inglorious Years* became a bestseller while it was still in pre-order, dethroning *The Lives of Clarissa* from its first-place perch and drawing a profusion of literary largesse even before it arrived in bookstores or for sale online. *Kirkus* called it brave and original. *Publishers Weekly* believed the book had broken new ground in literature. Literary names I had never heard of predicted that it was sure to win the National Book Award in November, while others were convinced I would receive the next Pulitzer Prize for fiction.

Marcia pleaded with me to write some new blog posts. Despite this avalanche of positive publicity, she felt it was crucial that I reach out to my readers. So I sat at Dad's desk, my stomach roiling, my first signing event mere days away, my coffee gone cold, and with Morgane carrying on in an unmalleable mood. I sat there, and all I could do was watch spring advance beyond my window, wordless.

My first signing, billed as the official book launch, was held at Parnassus Books, just about the only traditional bookstore left in Nashville, echoing that long-ago lunch conversation between James and Clarissa. I had been to Parnassus a few times, mostly when I was on the way to The Bluebird Cafe up the street to check out the new music. Otherwise the traffic is awful in that part of town, and I thought the people there had been a little smug with me when I had asked them why they didn't carry Dad's detective books. It's what he had been accustomed to from bookstores, what had made him so bitter. It goes without saying, though, that they loved him now, after the fact. Still, it was a nice store, narrow and deep, with a high-end literary feel.

The signing was set for a Saturday evening. It was a cool and clear evening, but with a stale breeze that was too weak to dissipate the fumes of incessant traffic, scattering the sunset into burnt shades of orange. The store was in a U-shaped strip mall that I crept toward a few cars at a time through a hyperactive traffic light. Morgane was at Vanderbilt auditing one of her classes, but promised to show up later. Marcia had intended to fly in for the event, but her plane had been delayed. She was stuck in Dallas, and I was on my own.

It's what Dad had always wanted but had never experienced, the chance to be feted in a bookstore, to speak with enthusiastic readers, to sign their books and know that his words had affected their thoughts and imaginations. I was terrified. Receiving enthusiasm online would have been enough for me, but this process of meeting the fans in person is such an established tradition that it was impossible for me to avoid it. Knopf would pull the plug if I didn't do personal appearances, Marcia had said so, and I believed her.

I had been told to park in an alley around back, which is why I was unaware of just how many people were waiting in the pungent evening air for my arrival. It seems they had packed the inside and then had trailed out the door in a winding line, the way fans might line up outside The Bluebird for a Tim and Faith appearance. A woman with a subdued look met me at the back door. She gave me her name through a forced smile, and kept flicking glances at her watch as she guided me inside.

"We weren't expecting this many people," she said hurriedly. "We should have done this off site."

"How many people?" I asked, even more apprehensive if that were possible. I rubbed my churning stomach. She stopped and fixed me with a bedazed look.

"A lot of people."

We were in the stockroom. She motioned me to wait amid the stacks and alleys of books while she went out to introduce me. I snuck a glance past her to see people pressed against every wall, while others were seated shoulder to shoulder in folding chairs. Bile fingered the back of my throat. I cast about, looking for a bathroom, and then my phone pinged. It was a text from Kessie:

*Stomach bad at first but goes away. Promise. Dont drink coffee.*

Typical Kessie, short, insightful, and remarkably timed. That was the first I'd heard from her since her comment about *The Trolls Among Us*. Maybe she had calmed down since then. I'm not sure I had. It was presumptuous of her to assume that I needed her advice, but then my sour stomach was proving her prescience even as I was finishing the thought.

I sat back on a box of books, which turned out to be a box of *my* books. This seemed hilarious for some reason. I laughed and shook my head, and took hot breaths until my stomach calmed down. Sooner than I would have wished, the woman returned to lead me out onto the floor.

"We're going to have to cut the Q&A short," she said, still with that subdued look. "There are just too many people waiting to get their books signed."

"That's fine by me," I said. I wouldn't have minded cancelling the Q&A altogether, but didn't have the stomach just then to say so.

"Okay, are you ready?" She blew a wisp of hair out of her eyes.

"I guess so."

"Then here we go."

She swept out of there quicker than I could exhale a last heated breath. People started clapping the moment I stepped through the door. *Clapping.* It was surreal, and had the instant effect of setting my stomach in motion again. The woman cleared a path to a central table and chair, passing a display along the way that was loaded with all the books the Dean family had produced, Dad's detective books, Kessie's two books, and now mine. It looked like more of a monument than a point of sale.

Feeling numb and displaced, I took my seat at the table. The clapping trailed off as the woman gestured everybody to silence. She was speaking but I couldn't hear her, just the numb rush of the blood in my head, my sight tunneled, a hand on my shoulder squeezing and lifting; and then I was on my feet and people were clapping again, and someone handed me a bottle of water. I took a disassociated sip, and then sound snapped back, and color, and the people were quiet and eying me expectantly.

"U-uhm," I stumbled, and they loved it, laughing as if I were the wittiest guy in the room.

I took another sip of water, found one gentle old woman to focus on, then stuttered my name, which sent them laughing again. The woman was still by my side, seemed to know a fiasco in the making when she saw one, so spoke on my behalf in a soothing voice.

"Those of you who have already read the book know that it's a powerhouse of literature, and from a member of what must really be a gifted family. But this is his first public event. I'm sure he's a little nervous, so let's see if we can all help him through this." People chuckled at that. "Now who drew the first question?"

An older woman held up her hand, not the woman I had been focusing on.

"Mr. Dean—" That brought me around. I caught myself looking for Dad in the crowd before I realized the woman meant me. "—Hannah is such a complicated character, but she seems out of her element. As I read her, I couldn't help but think of Alice Liddell. Was that your intention?"

"Huh?" I blundered. "Alice—?"

"*Alice in Wonderland*," my host whispered in my ear.

"Oh, right...uh, no, I don't think so."

That drew a perplexed frown from the questioner, who perhaps was thinking that she had waited in line all that time only to be short-changed. We moved on to the next questioner, another older woman.

"Mr. Dean, in some ways Hannah seems like an innocent child. In other ways she's worldly and experienced. It's obvious Evan was in love with her. Were you trying to show the dichotomous roles women must play? And who did you draw on to write her character?"

*Dichotomous?* I didn't even know what that word meant. And these questions weren't what I had expected. I thought they would only be asking about me, maybe throw in some questions about Dad or Kessie. How could I answer the woman? I had always thought of Hannah—Clarissa, really—as a fixation, a fantasy, someone Dad had borrowed from to balance out Evan.

"Uh, Hannah was just a fixation, a fantasy. She's there to balance out Evan."

That explanation didn't satisfy anyone. A drop of sweat ran a chill track down my temple, under my jaw and into my collar. I felt space closing in again, my vision graying.

"Joplin?"

It was a familiar voice but I couldn't place it. I scanned the seated people, spotted a raised hand clutching a notepad, and then I went cold.

It was Doreen Ybarra. She stood.

"Joplin, your protagonist, Evan Usher, is a writer who struggles all his life for recognition. Did you base this on your father? And if so, did you ever talk with him about it?"

"Uh...uh—" I felt feverish. My stomach lurched loud enough to startle a few who were sitting closest. "—no, uh, it's not Dad. We never talked about it."

A man raised his hand for the next question but Doreen bulled over him as if he were no more than a panhandler at a public rally.

"And it's interesting how the time period is so nebulous," she said, so full of arrogant confidence that I gritted my teeth. "Evan and Hannah discuss the internet, so it must be contemporaneous with the present, and yet the two of them seem dated, like they belong to a different time and place. What's that all about?"

I had wondered about that myself, and had decided that it was just something Dad had done to be enigmatic. It worked, didn't it? It got people's attention. It didn't have to mean anything more than that.

"Uh." That came out as a croak. "Uh, it's nothing. It just happened."

Disgruntled murmurs rose here and there, like fetid bubbles in a stagnant pond. I could see some heads shaking, some arms crossed tightly, outright hostility on a few faces, absolute bewilderment on a few others.

The man who had raised his hand had his mouth open, ready to finally get his question out, but Doreen's dominating demeanor overrode him once more.

"One last question," she said with a glance at her notepad. "You use complicated literary devices, such as the multiple narrative, in a style that is nothing like anything you ever published online. Where and when did you study these techniques?"

"Okay, then," my host stepped in with authority, wiping her hands for some reason. "Let's get the signing going."

I fell into my chair, reprieved but too exhausted to feel relieved. Doreen continued to eye me, casting something more than curiosity. I looked down, around, reached for my water bottle, and prayed it was over.

"Let me ask this please—"

I jerked my head up to another familiar voice, a woman squeezing through across the way.

"When was the time that you begin to write this book, Joplin?" she asked tersely.

It was Morgane.

# Chapter Sixteen

IF I COULD HAVE TALKED to Dad I would have told him that sitting for a big book signing was like being forced naked through an insatiable gauntlet. No detail was too small for the readers to burrow into, no topic too personal to broach, and no time too late in the evening to sign just one more book. They kept coming and coming, some with adoring smiles, some less so; some were shy, some were blunt; some fawned as I scrawled my name, some critiqued my signature as if I were tattooing it on their arms. And always out the corner of my eye, Doreen Ybarra, who didn't line up for a book to be signed, but who must have scribbled enough in her notepad to produce her own book alongside mine.

Morgane was sitting on the couch when I got home, her knees tightly pressed and with a stormy look in her stormy eyes. I didn't want to argue, I wanted to go someplace dark and quiet, curl up and shut it all out; but I had no choice, she was practically barring the way with her glare, so with a sigh of resignation I came right out with it.

"Why did you do that to me?"

I crossed the living room toward her, but a sharp flick of her head advised me to keep a good space between us.

"Because something is not correct, Joplin."

"What are you *talking* about, Morgane?"

"This book does not feel like you."

"What the hell does *that* mean?"

"It means that something is strange and I do not understand it."

I felt rancid from the humid breaths of a hundred strangers, too exhausted to go on with this. I couldn't decide what combination of umbrage, agitation, or carefully chosen words would cut this short. She would launch into French if I took the wrong tack, which would about guarantee that we would be at this all night. Just the thought of it made me weary.

"Morgane," I rubbed at the ache in my temples, "what do you want me to say?"

Her gaze was a roiling tempest, but I could tell that behind it she was still searching for the pieces to a mystery she couldn't define.

"Say when you begin to write this book."

"That again? Why does it matter?"

"Because I know the person you are. I see nothing of this for a year, *et tout d'un coup, voilà*," she made starbursts with her fingers, "you have this famous book."

Morgane knew, somehow she knew, not the particulars, but I hadn't fooled her, not even close, and all I could do was swallow guiltily and repeat that same weak story.

"I told you. I've been working on it for a long time...since before we met."

"You are not telling the truth to me, Joplin."

She said this to her hands, in a tone of regret that wrenched the stomach out of me. Morgane had always been a Gallic force of nature, but now she was wilting right in front of me, as if I had reached inside her and stolen the one thing she believed in. I thought of Evan under the willows forcing Hannah to reveal the truth, his carefully crafted creation coming undone by his own recklessness. But life is not prose. There was no way to rewrite this, no way to rework a few paragraphs to make a happy ending, the way I had done with them.

I left her, feeling sick, went into the dark of our bedroom, but it wasn't dark enough.

/////

I WAS OUT THE NEXT MORNING to sign at the Barnes & Noble in Cool Springs, that dense shopping district south of Nashville. This signing was well attended, although not as overwhelming as the other. The questions weren't as biting either, and to my relief—enough so that my stomach remained mostly calm throughout—Doreen Ybarra wasn't there.

I thumbed through my social media accounts while on the way to Cool Springs. Marcia had hired an administrator to manage them for me, warning me not to look at them anymore. "It'll make you crazy," she had told me. But I had to look, of course, and was gratified if not also relieved to find that this time, except for a trolling few, the tweets and comments were mostly sympathetic: *It was his first signing; He was nervous, wouldn't you be; The book is incredible; Just give him a break.*

So people could be forgiving after all.

Morgane, though—we lay back to back that night, flinching like strangers, and in the morning she went off to work without a word. There had to be something I could say or do to allay her suspicions. Sure she suspected something, but not *the* something, and I wasn't positive her suspicions were going in that direction anyway. I decided it was best to let it rest, to let some time go by. With the hectic schedule the publicists had set up for me, I wouldn't be seeing much of her over the next few weeks anyway. Things would settle down eventually, they had to.

Memorial Day happened out there somewhere, and then June went racing along. The bookstores became a blur of backrooms and long lines, felt-tipped pens that left indelible stains on my fingers, and emotive inscriptions to people I didn't know and never would.

I missed Morgane. I texted her from the hotels late at night, received her replies the next morning. Her texts were always as short as texts tend to be, and usually vaguer than they needed to be. I kept telling myself to call her when I had a moment. She never called me, either.

The pace forced me to admit that my jealousy of Kessie had been misplaced. There was nothing glamorous about being prodded awake before a solstice sunrise, then steered through the day by a procession of harried publicists or studio people, waiting with heavy eyelids while the make-up dried, desperately needing coffee but knowing that my stomach would revolt if I dared. I jetted into cities that I'd always hoped to visit, then jetted out of them having visited nothing but bathrooms and sterile hotel rooms. I felt rumpled all the time. At least the makeup hid the circles under my eyes. I couldn't imagine how Kessie had kept herself looking so good during her tour.

She texted me every few days, asked how I was holding up, and did I know that Dean books now occupied the top seven spots on the fiction bestsellers lists? She had been a guest on a women's talk show, and that appearance had pushed *The Lives of Clarissa* back into first place.

Our books traded back and forth from then on. The media started calling us *The Dueling Deans*, which Kessie thought was laugh-out-loud hilarious. I thought it was cringe-worthy horrible, made worse when *Publishers Weekly* did a cover called *The Dueling Divas*, showing two cartoon heroines in boxing gloves, one dressed in yellow, the other in white, both sporting a black eye. Fans actually took sides, lining up behind their heroine of choice. They loved Hannah for her wholesome innocence, Clarissa for her wholesome worldliness. The two had their own Facebook pages, with minute-by-minute Twitter posts announcing the current *friend* and *like* standings. It was ridiculous, I mean absolutely ridiculous. Knopf loved it, though. So did Marcia. Kessie thought it was cute. You know how I felt.

The irony eventually settled in, though, and then I would laugh or smile whenever I thought of that *Publishers Weekly* cover. If only they knew, what would they think? And what was I thinking for thinking that?

*/////*

MY TOUR FINALLY MADE IT to New York City for a live appearance on a morning show, the same show Kessie had been on with *Comes Now, Achilles*. My stomach wouldn't let me sleep that night, and up until then I'd had no idea how early in the morning people had to get up to be on those shows. My eyes were sticky when I finally rolled out of bed, my body still thinking it was yesterday. I needed coffee and a shower in no particular order, and wound up doing them both at the same time since the coffee maker was in the bathroom.

I shouldn't have had the coffee, and I shouldn't have had to get up that early for anything, so my mood was as sour as my stomach during the drive to the studio. New York passed by in gray light, as gritty as Gotham. It was humid out, and the air smelled like crotch. I fell asleep along the way, was startled awake by my driver, who held the door impassively. Marcia met me on the curb, along with a publicist from Knopf and an intern from the studio.

"How do you feel?" Marcia asked, too chipper for that time of the morning. She received bloodshot eyes in answer. "Poor Joplin," she said with a commiserating look that might have been sincere. "Hang in there, it's almost over...at least until your next book."

She winked at me then, while I swore to my bedraggled self that there would *never* be another book, mine or otherwise. I would be like Harper Lee, one hit book and enough money and fame to live off of forever.

The intern didn't look old enough to be out of high school, and yet she held an air of competence that eclipsed me on my best day.

"Here, drink this," she said. "It'll settle your stomach."

She handed me what looked like a smoothie. The glass was glass, it was cold, and the smoothie tasted undefinable but good just the same. I thanked her with a sigh, and then I was hustled inside.

It was all no-nonsense after that. Marcia and the publicist stayed well back while I was steered through hallways, fussed at by people whose names passed between my ears without catching on anything. They tended to my suit, my hair, and my shoes, brushed powder on my face, and touched up the circles under my eyes, all while we moved toward what was called the *green room*, even though it wasn't green, but some shade of beige.

I sat at last, on a plush couch that at that moment I could have slept on better than the bed back at the hotel. Marcia sat with me. The publicist was elsewhere, and all the studio people along with her.

"I'm really tired," I said to Marcia.

"I know, Jop. When Kessie was here, we almost had to carry her in like a sleeping child."

"But she looked so good," I said in wonder.

"And you will too. It's studio magic, Jop. These people know what they're doing."

"How long until I go out there?"

Marcia checked her phone.

"Not too long."

Nothing so far had made me as nervous as I was now, and I was pretty sure I understood why. Kessie's performance here had been perfect, earning her a following of adoring fans who defended her as if they had known her all their lives. What if I messed up, stammered the way I had at my first signing? It didn't take any effort for Marcia to tell how nervous I was.

"Don't worry, Jop." She patted me on the shoulder. "You'll do fine, plus we have a surprise for you that we think you'll like."

"Surprise? What surprise?"

"Well if I told you that, it wouldn't be a surprise." She said this with a maternal smile.

The intern came in at that moment, wearing a headset, serious and focused. She gestured me up, and that left no time to probe further into the nature of whatever surprise Marcia had in store for me.

And then I was on my own, Marcia concealed by equipment and screens and looped electrical cables that descended from the ceiling like nooses, bright lights glaring beyond a partition that shielded me from the set. I could see the host perched on his chair, the smirk, the tan, the male-pattern baldness, his co-host a beautiful woman with a toothy but pretty smile. The intern held up three fingers, two fingers, one, then waved me ahead with tight lips, all business. I swallowed a painful knot, and then walked out there with a frozen grin and a fixed spine and a foreboding feeling that my fly was open. Kessie had seemed so natural when she had made this walk, smiling easily and waving as she went. I waved like a puppet, shook hands stiffly, then backed up to the offered too-tall chair and kind of hopped onto it, not quite landing both cheeks.

This awkwardness couldn't have gone unnoticed, but the hosts kept their smiles and held their comments until I could get myself adjusted. I could have made a great humanizing joke out of this if I hadn't been so nervous, and if I had thought about it at the time rather than later, when

I was replaying the whole thing and berating myself for the fiasco that was to come.

"Joplin," the host said. Our chairs were arranged in a straight line, he to my left and his co-host to his left, leaning forward a bit to see. "Let me begin by offering my sympathies about your father. He was a brave man."

"Thank you," I croaked while clearing my throat.

"And a great writer too," he went on, "considering the success of your sister's books."

"And so are you," the co-host piped in. "Your book is back in first place this week. You and your sister have been trading that spot all summer. Is it a friendly rivalry between you two? How do you handle the competition?"

"The Dueling Deans," the host just had to add, and with smirk obvious.

"Well, it's not really like that," I said weakly.

"*The Latter Half of Inglorious Years...*" mused the host. "Tell us what it's about, Joplin."

"Well, uh, it's about an unknown author's struggle to write something really great, but—"

"Did you take inspiration from your father?" the co-host interrupted, scattering my thoughts like confetti.

"Huh?"

"Of course John Taylor Dean isn't unknown anymore." That was from the host.

"Uh, what was the question again?" I asked, befuddled.

"Did you take inspiration from your father?"

"Oh, yeah...well, in a way." All of the signings and events I had attended had allowed me to practice a satisfactory response to that question. "He never got the recognition he wanted, much like Evan Usher—"

"Evan Usher is your main character," the co-host interrupted once more. I ground my teeth.

"Yes, that's right."

"I'm really interested in your character, Hannah," said the host. "Who did you base her on?"

"I didn't base her on anybody."

"She reminds me so much of Clarissa, your sister's character." This was from the co-host, who now wore a pair of reading glasses and was holding a copy of my book in her lap. "After all, both women are young, and just a bit mysterious—"

"Except that Hannah is a metaphor." This time I interrupted, with a flush of heat and a barely restrained bark. Clarissa was not Kessie's character, she was Dad's character.

"A metaphor for what?" the co-host asked with a frown.

"An idealized image."

"Uh, huh," said the host with his tongue truly in his cheek. I had never wanted to pop someone in the mouth so bad in my life. "On that note," he continued, "here's an image we can all idealize."

And with that, Kessie rounded the partition, smiling and waving and as comfortable as if *she* were the host of the damn show. My jaw fell, it really did, I saw it in a replay of the show later.

"*Kessie...?*"

She came to me and pecked me on the cheek. She smelled...fresh, and was dressed in hues of hip-hugging yellow.

"You're doing great," she whispered in my ear.

"What are you doing here?" I asked, meaning to keep my voice down but the microphones picked it up anyway. It sounded harsh, harsh enough that I would have heard plenty about it later if not for everything else.

Kessie knitted her brows and whispered, "I came to help you."

I didn't need her damn help, and that was rising from my chest into my throat, ready to erupt but for a reprieve from the hosts, who were up and fawning over Kessie as if she were royalty. She was ushered to a chair on the far end from me, and looked completely poised as she sat and clipped on her microphone. Both hosts were turned her way now. I felt an imaginary distance growing between my chair and theirs.

"What a surprise," the host said, ogling obviously.

"It's *so* good to see you again," the co-host gushed, clasping Kessie's hand as if the two were sisters.

"It's great to be here," Kessie beamed.

"Meet The Dueling Deans, ladies and gentlemen," the host said to the camera.

"It's really not like that," Kessie said with an exuberant smile. Yes it was, I thought.

"But it has to be a competition," stated the host.

"The best kind," said Kessie. "The kind where neither one of us loses."

"How do you feel about that, Joplin?" the host asked without actually turning toward me.

"Yeah, that's the way it is," I muttered.

I spotted Marcia back by the partition. She smiled eagerly and gave me a thumbs-up, and had no idea how angry I was. The conversation was all to my left now. I had become the appetizer, and not particularly palatable. The main course had been served at the other end.

To her credit—and I can acknowledge this to myself now—Kessie wasn't trying to steal my moment. Over and again she tried to turn the attention to me, but at each effort the hosts would steer the conversation back to her. I began to sweat from the heat of it, the lights and my rising anger. I did manage to keep a lid on that anger, fully aware that the trolls would be parsing every nuance, but my demeanor gave me away just the same, my sweaty forehead and clammy hands, and with Kessie as poised as a princess. What a complete disaster.

That interminable segment finally ended at the commercial break. Everyone was up, stretching and congratulating and shaking hands. The host grimaced when he shook mine, and through obvious force of will resisted wiping his hand on his pants. An intern with a bottle of hand sanitizer passed us as Kessie and I left the set.

We paused behind the partition, amid a flurry of activity by the crew, who were getting things ready for the next segment. Marcia was nowhere in sight. Kessie was pensive. I was furious.

"I'm sorry, Jop. I didn't mean for that to happen."

I rounded on her.

"Didn't you?"

"Of course not." She seemed shaken by my tone. "This was your time. It was supposed to be about you."

"Then what are you doing here?"

"The network wanted it, and so did Knopf...to drive sales. Plus I wanted to be here for you."

"Well you were here all right," I hurled at her. "You gave them just what they wanted, their innocent Clarissa. That's who they think you are, you know."

"They do not!"

That had wounded her, I could see it in her trembling lips, and I hate to say it, but it felt good to finally pierce her indomitable composure and expose her to the same plane that I inhabited. That should have been enough, I should have stopped right there, but all of that pent up frustration had my mouth way out ahead of my brain.

"Yes they do," I spat back. "They think you're Clarissa. They think Dad wrote all of that about you—about *you*—like I never really existed, but you know what, they're wrong, all of them, because I know who the real Clarissa was."

"Joplin, please stop being so mean," she begged me.

She looked like a vulnerable child now, a child with sad wet eyes who could draw sympathy from even the worst kind of person. So what did that make me, because I just had to add, "I mean, who do you think Dad was with when you were born?"

Her face screwed up then with the most pitiful pain I had ever seen. She threw a hand over her mouth and ran off, dodging cables and cameras and crew, and then my brain caught back up and I felt like hell. The intern came up to me with such a hateful expression that I actually checked to see if she was holding a knife.

"Nice job, big brother," she said, dripping scorn, and then she reached up and unclipped the microphone from my lapel. "By the way," she added in disgust as she turned on her heel, displaying the microphone as she went, "Live mic, dude."

Every eye was on me as I left the studio, as if I were a pedophile who had beaten the rap. Even my taxi driver seemed to be eying me suspiciously, and was it me, or were the people at the hotel suddenly stiff and abrupt? My stomach was in turmoil. I barely made it to the bathroom in time, and then I went to bed, even though it was mid-morning, and when I woke up it was evening and my phone was ringing and it was Mom.

"Oh, Joplin," she said in a quavering voice. "What have you done?"

# Chapter Seventeen

"YOUR OWN SISTER," Shelisa softly chided me. "You were cruel, Joplin."

"I know," I said guiltily, finding it hard to meet her eyes. I locked eyes with Barber instead, whose expression was more forgiving if not simply disinterested.

"So what did your mum say?" he asked.

"That was it. Then she hung up."

"She took the part of sweet Kessie, and she does be right," said Shelisa.

"Yeah, that's what I thought, too, at the time," I said.

Barber's brow wrinkled in confusion, while Shelisa took a knowing breath, drew back and smiled mysteriously.

"What is it, darlin'?" Barber asked her.

"Joplin opened a box, that what he did."

Shelisa's perception continued to be uncanny.

"Box? What box?" grumbled Barber.

"You keep listen, Barber, and soon you know it, too."

"I'll listen after a pish," he said unsteadily. He rose without further comment and wound his way toward the restroom. Shelisa sighed and scanned about. The Double Deuce was filling up with the lunch crowd, and Julie looked harried trying to keep up.

"I gawn do some more work now," Shelisa told me. She slid two fresh Caribs across the bar. "You keep tellin' your tale to Barber. I ketch you soon enough."

She spun around then, flapping through the swinging doors into the kitchen. I felt so immediately alone that even Barber would have been a comfort, and this despite all the people pressing in around me to put a hand or forearm on the bar to mark their places in the beer queue. You could call it the loneliness of conscience. No crowd is a cure, only talk and more talk and hopefully a sympathetic ear; and in the absence of these, characters on a page who have no choice but to listen, what my father had indulged in so well.

*/////*

*There was nowhere to take them after the picnic. Whiskey and darkness weren't enough to re-conjure that scene in a redemptive light. If you pour enough into your characters, they will inevitably follow their own discerning paths, like children grown into what they might become. As for Evan and Hannah—this Evan and this Hannah? They had been doomed from the beginning. He accepted that now, so he filed his pages away, like friends long past, and with a tear brought out fresh paper.*

*Sometimes you have to find the will to throw out a story and start again. This time he would cast Evan in a different role, integral to the mystery.*

*/////*

"*Rikki-Tikki-Tavi, Rikki-Tikki-Tavi,*" Hannah recited in her sweet sing-song as she marched down the garden path, hands clasped in the small of her back, her shoulders rocking with each syllable, olive shorts, pink T-shirt, bare feet, and golden hair in a pair of pigtails that resembled soft brushes ready to be dipped in paint.

She brightened when she saw her father ahead, sitting on a bench beneath a spreading parrot tree.

"Papa!"

She ran to him, all sinewy and full of energy, leaping into his arms just as he got to his feet.

"Hannah, sweetie," he grinned, gathering her up. She wiggled like a cat until she had her arms around his neck and her knees locked into his sides. Her energy was boundless and he loved it, tiring but never tiresome.

"Papa I saw him! I saw Rikki-Tikki-Tavi!"

"You did, sweetie? Where?"

"Over there in the jungle, Papa." She steered him somehow, until she had turned him enough that she could point toward a thicket back up the path.

"You shouldn't run off like that, baby," Hannah's mother, Sarah, said as she approached the two.

"But Mummy, I saw Rikki-Tikki-Tavi."

"Did you now?"

"Yeh, I did. I want to show Papa."

"Okay," her father said, flipping her over his shoulder like a sack of rice, "show me." Hannah arched up to point the way, and then the three of them set out up the path.

"You know, *Papa*," Sarah said impishly as they went, "you don't look like a papa, you're too young for that. You look more like one of those 50s beatnicks."

"Ah, but I bathe more often," he laughed, slipping an arm around her waist and drawing them all close. Hannah giggled and blew kisses into her mother's ear.

"Did you work today?" Sarah asked with perhaps a note of apprehension.

"Yes," he beamed, and gave Hannah's tummy a tickle with his thinly bearded chin. "This little one inspires me."

"I inspire Papa," Hannah told her mother soberly. Sarah's cheeks quivered just slightly.

Presently they arrived at the edge of the thicket. Hannah slipped backward off her father's shoulder, then raced to the thicket, where she pointed into its depths.

"He's in there, Papa, he's in there!"

"You know," Sarah whispered anxiously to her husband, "if there's a mongoose in there then there's also probably a—"

"Yeah, good point," he said. "Hannah, sweetie, why don't you step back a little."

"But Papa, come see."

"I can see, sweetie. I'm looking hard."

"Okay."

That satisfied her for the moment.

"I don't know why we worry," he said to Sarah, keeping his voice low.

"She runs all over the place."

"But she's only four—"

"And smart enough to be six."

Sarah sighed, and then in a matching low voice said, "Nixon ended the draft more than three months ago. Isn't it time we thought about going home? Even the Beatles only stayed for a few weeks."

"But your lover-boy George," he countered with a rakish grin, taking her gently by the hips, "was here for *six* weeks."

"He was never my lover-boy," she said, blushing, and then with a sigh, "Honey, we've been here for—"

"Four years, five months and some days."

"Are you counting minutes and seconds, too?"

"Only until..." he trailed off, batting his eyes. He wrapped his arms around her and held her tight until she demurred and melded against him. "Soon." He brushed her ear with his bristled lips. "I'll finish the novel soon, and then we can go. Okay?"

"Okay," she exhaled.

"There he is, Papa! There he is!"

Hannah was bouncing up and down and pointing urgently. Sarah smiled wistfully.

"Well, then," she said. "We'd better go have a look, Evan."

## /////

BARBER RETURNED FROM THE RESTROOM, looked around in puzzlement for Shelisa, saw the fresh Carib sitting at his place at the bar, then gave a happy smile and took his seat. He sat there, contemplating his Carib in silence, and then without any prompting from me said, "I took credit for a colleague's work once."

This admission seemed to cause him more pain than he could endure, because he had to cover his eyes and sniff away whatever his memory was bringing forth.

"Mind you, I didn't mean to," he said after a quick recovery and a pull on his Carib. "It was a misunderstanding, but then you get caught up in things, and you might want out but people won't let you. Ent it right?" He patted me on the shoulder as if we were co-commiserators.

"That's right, Barber," I said, which seemed to please him no end.

"Well, get on with it then," he said after another pull on his Carib, vanquishing whatever distress he had been suffering from a moment ago. He smacked his lips and waited expectantly, and Shelisa gave me a fortifying smile as she carried a tray of burgers to a customer's table, so I sighed and resumed.

/////

WHEN MOM HUNG UP on me, I plopped down on the bed in complete disbelief. How bad could it have been that she took Kessie's side in this? And what had I done, really, but call Kessie out? They could all see that. Surely they could all see that. So the mic was still on, that didn't change what Kessie had done.

I was about to call Mom right back, let her know how *I* felt about the whole thing, but then I came to my senses and realized that if I got into it with her while she was still mad, then Kessie would be in and I would be out and Kessie would win, the way she had with Dad. I wasn't going to let that happen with Mom. Instead I called Marcia.

"Joplin," she answered tersely. Our connection was scratchy.

"Where are you?" I asked.

"Houston."

"Already? I thought we were going back together."

"I went with Kessie."

"With Kessie! But—"

"Listen, Joplin," her voice was formal, clipped, distanced, "Knopf is furious. *I'm* furious."

"Why?" was all I could ask.

"How could you say those things to your sister?"

Just like that she had me over her knee, like Mom when I was a boy.

"I didn't know the mic was live," I whined.

"Neither did Reagan when he almost started a war."

"Huh?"

"It doesn't matter that the mic was live. Everybody heard what you said anyway."

"So—?"

"So your behavior affects a few things, Joplin, a very large business arrangement, for one. And you hurt your sister. *Deliberately.* And—"

"Well? It's all true," I sputtered, as if that defense meant anything.

"*And,*" she repeated, "you wrecked our relationship."

"*What?*"

"I'll send you a few names from the office tomorrow. Someone will take you on, I'm sure. I don't want you for a client anymore."

"But *Marcia*—"

"That's it, Joplin. Good bye." And with that she hung up.

I never had a girlfriend who had left me shattered at the break-up. Those relationships came and went, so I had always been puzzled why some of my friends would fall into outright slobbering misery when their relationships ended. I had a sense of that now, if not the loss of an emotional connection then at least the loss of essential support. Marcia was what made this whole thing not insane. Losing her meant I was going to have to figure it out for myself, and just the thought of that made me want to lie down.

I sat down instead, and thought of nothing for the longest time. That might have been a blessing in itself, but then I had to get up to pee, and my mouth was sticky and gross, and it was dark outside, and I thought a drink would help, so I threw on my clothes, which still carried the scents of that morning, including a lingering trace of Kessie, which I inhaled with conflicted breaths, and then I went down to the hotel bar, sat at the dark end and ordered a whiskey.

I was the only one in there. I could tell that the bartender was bored. I gave a thought to talking to him the way they do in the movies, deep confidences, inebriated clarity, but no, that wasn't me, so I downed my whiskey and held the glass up for another. That next drink arrived quietly. The bartender could have engaged with me, I guess, but he didn't want to for whatever reason. If I were a bartender I would probably be him. That was a depressing thought, and then I wished I had just ordered beer instead, a high-gravity microbrew maybe, because I could have made it last longer. The whiskies went too fast, and the bartender was no more talkative at each return, and suddenly I was angry again.

Someone warm slipped onto the stool beside me, little black dress, brown shoulders, tight body, smelled like lavender and musk.

"That was a pretty good performance this morning," she said. "You're getting better at this."

I focused hard through the subdued light and the whiskey buzz, and then my eyes went round.

Doreen Ybarra.

"It's you!" I stammered, and couldn't decide what to say or do next. After a woozy moment I settled for, "What? You followed me all the way from Houston?"

"That's some ego," she smiled condescendingly, "but then you *have* made yourself a millionaire in just a few months, so maybe you deserve it."

"That's not what you really think."

"You're right, it's not."

She crossed her legs and eased back a little, and I tried not to but I had to look down. She had really nice legs. What's worse, she knew it. The bartender came up to her but she waved him off.

"So what are you doing here," I asked, still entranced by her legs so a little less belligerent.

"I'm working on a story."

"So you *did* follow me."

"You're not the story...or at least *this* story."

"What story am I then?"

"I'm not sure, Joplin. I'm still trying to put it together."

"Then what do you think the story is?" Too many whiskies, I was becoming sibilant in my articulation.

"Hmm, I'm not too sure. Let's just say that your writing qualities seem to be...I don't know, *borrowed?*"

I jerked back and eyed her narrowly. There wasn't an honest response I could throw at an accusation like that, only umbrage, an appropriate fit, so I threw one, and as Doreen's lips formed the tight, inside smile that said

I had confirmed her suspicions, I remembered something a friend had told me once, a friend who worked in retail: *The customers who were lying always made the biggest scenes.*

She shook her head, a pitying gesture, pushed back from the bar and stood.

"You're a great writer, Joplin," she said with barely-concealed sarcasm, "a walking National Book Award. It's not often that this much talent turns up in someone with so little to show beforehand."

A guy looking smug in a tux appeared at her side, rested a proprietary hand on her waist.

"Yeah," she went on, "you're a real prodigy. I bet you made your father proud, and your mom, especially when you hurt your sister just because you could."

Then the guy steered her away, and they were long gone before I could think of anything witty to hurl back at her.

///////

MY FLIGHT HOME was from the Newark airport, which meant I had to get up insanely early yet again so that there would be enough time to make that torturous drive from the hotel. It was clammy and dark outside, and there were plenty of people sleeping in the city that never sleeps, except for my taxi driver and me, and all the other taxis, and all that traffic on the bridge, and those people in the tollbooths. It was so early that I was still metabolizing last night's whiskey, and if I had closed my eyes last night trying to think up a satisfactory rebuttal to Doreen, I had opened them this morning at about where I had left off.

I felt wound in gauze, and my stomach was churning in ways that would not enhance my flight experience. It's amazing how quickly word spreads, and how quickly people will abandon you to your fate. I should have been making this drive in a limousine, with Marcia and a publicist and maybe another of those stomach-settling smoothies. Instead I'd had to coordinate it all myself. The coffee in the lobby had tasted like burnt bacon, and my taxi smelled of something that didn't belong on this continent.

Doreen had said that I was a millionaire, and I wondered if that was true. If so, why did I have to fly home in a jouncing commuter plane with props sounding like angry bees just beyond my window? It is possible to feel worse than hungover, and that's the way I felt when we finally bumped onto the runway in Nashville. Millionaire or not, I didn't feel any better for it.

I had texted Morgane from Newark. She wasn't at the airport to meet me, so I waited and wished my stomach would settle down, then after a while I called Morgane and got her voice mail. It seemed unduly bright outside, but it was actually still early. She was probably dealing with traffic, always bad these days, especially coming from West End, so I readjusted my numb butt in that hard chair and willed myself to hold on a little longer.

I had barely made that decision when my phone pinged and a text came in and I figured this was Morgane texting to reassure me, but it wasn't Morgane, it was some woman named Lisa. It turned out that Lisa was my social media administrator and she was texting to say she quit. She had reverted all of the passwords, she said, and she must have done it right then because all of the sudden my phone blew up.

It had never been this bad before. Tweets and posts were coming in on top of one another, with a new hashtag to feed my haters, *#joplinthecreep*. I looked around, certain that I was in the derisive sights of everybody present, or else the ceiling was set to collapse on me at any moment. I couldn't breathe, and if I hadn't already emptied my stomach after that horrible flight, I think I would have been on my knees emptying it right there.

I fled outside, where the air was not fresh but at least it felt freer than what I had been inhaling inside. I silenced my phone, bent over and focused on my breathing. I could see my suitcase through the glass, and I knew that if I didn't go in and get it right now, it would be declared unattended and then I would get the hashtag, *#joplintheterrorist*, so I groaned and went in to retrieve it, and then I came out and hailed a taxi.

The subconscious picks up on things. It tries to phone it in, but all you feel is a vague tugging at the back of your mind until whatever it is becomes obvious, and even then you debate it because it just doesn't fit.

In this case it was Morgane's French aloe plant, which lived in a chartreuse pot to the left of our door during the summer, and below our bedroom window during the winter. She had brought it with her when she moved in, I thought because the plant was French, something to remind her of home, even though the plant is actually from Africa. She kept it because it was something uncomplicated she could look after, and now, as I hesitated at the door, it finally occurred to me that the plant was gone.

I was debating the incongruity of that as I rattled my keys and stepped inside, and dropped those thoughts the moment I saw Morgane, who was just standing there with eyes more steely than stormy. My subconscious was trying to speak up again, urgently this time, but I interrupted it with a typical greeting that sounded desperate for some reason.

"Hey, you're home. I tried to call you."

She said nothing in return. I tried to shrug it off, bent over to roll my suitcase inside and then pushed the door closed. Something was off, something I couldn't quite get a handle on. Morgan was dressed professionally for work, so she was in that guise, and something was different about the apartment, like there was more space, more light. I tried again.

"So what's up?" I asked, and that sounded as lame to me as it must have to Morgane, and then, without comment or inflection, she held out a dog-eared manuscript and dropped it at my feet.

I gawked, or tried to make that face. I knew what it was, she knew that I knew what it was, and I knew that she knew that I knew, and still I asked stupidly, "What's that?"

I could hear her heated exhalation like the rush of a runaway bus.

"You lied to me," she said measuredly. "All this time."

I felt faint.

"Morgane, it's not—"

"You cannot lie to me anymore, Joplin, I will not allow it."

"But I didn't mean—"

"Stop what you are saying." She brushed past me to the door, opened it, then: "My life has too many pieces, Joplin. There is too much to do to make this and to make that. I like you because you are not complicated. I can know what you will do and that is enough to help me with the rest of this life that I want to do. But now that has changed. If you can do this and not tell me, then you are no longer that person. *Au revoir*, Joplin. I hope you can be made happy."

She went through the door. My knees were weak and my stomach was scrambling to keep it together. Morgane was leaving me. I knew she was serious, that there was no turning her back, because she hadn't used French except to say goodbye. But of everything that had passed, from when I first concealed the manuscript until now, I was most ashamed of what I said next.

"You won't tell anyone, will you?"

She snorted derisively, even as her eyes filled.

"No, Joplin, I will not tell. That is for you to suffer. You will tell it yourself because it is too much work to keep the lies, too much work for you. You will see." And then she pulled the door and was gone.

I sat down on the couch, in the quiet of an apartment that suddenly felt empty despite that oversized desk. I couldn't find my feelings, they were so tangled, and then I realized that Morgane would not be with me that night, or the next morning, and then I began to cry and it wouldn't stop, and there was nothing I could do about it.

I didn't want to go out. I didn't want to be seen by people, or see them, the malevolent stares, the pointed whispering. After I had emptied the kitchen of easy food, I got by on pizzas, cracking the door only as much as necessary for the pizza box to be tipped through while avoiding all eye contact with the delivery driver. When I finally went out in the Beemer one hot, sticky morning, it was only because I had run out of coffee and couldn't get anyone to deliver more.

I wound up at the Publix Super Market in Belle Meade, where the self-checkout glitched, forcing me into a short but claustrophobic line at the cashier. I had my coffee and a few other things in my arms, and waited my turn by focusing on the racks of gossip magazines, and a stack of last Sunday's *The New York Times*. A header caught my eye as if it had been placed there just to get my attention, in a sidebar for the *Arts & Leisure* section:

*The Dueling Deans, By DOREEN YBARRA, The fractures within a new literary dynasty.*

I groaned, my stomach going through its motions, plopped a copy of the paper onto the belt with the rest of my things, then hustled through checkout to the Beemer, where I could finally exhale. I left the windows up as I tore through the paper, cocooned in the heat and feeling safer that way. I was sweating by the time I found the story, a full half page above the fold. The story began:

*Best-selling authors Kessie and Joplin Dean, known in popular culture as The Dueling Deans, are also duking it out off the page, sparring over the provenance of Clarissa, the fictional character created by their father, the late John Taylor Dean. But is Clarissa only fiction? That question was inadvertently thrust into the open during a heated exchange between Kessie and Joplin following their appearance on a morning show last week...*

I fell back with a soul-emptying sigh, squeezed my eyes and tried to imagine a time when existence had been predictable, and the biggest threat to my anonymity had been tracking software. Had it really been that long

# Chapter Eighteen

THE FIRST OF THE MONTH came and went, and without an insistent knock on the door, which meant that someone was still paying the bills. I vaguely remembered, like one of Hannah's uncertain memories, the monthly anxiety of scraping together enough money to pay the rent, the knuckle-rap on the door that had its own recognizable authority, the hovering, judgmental presence of the property manager. It was going to take a lot of energy to unravel the financial end of things, more energy than I had. It was easier to lie on the couch, the blinds closed and with the TV flickering soundlessly in the background.

It had been almost a week since Morgane had walked out, leaving me miserable, wallowing in self-pity, and seeking solace from friends who were becoming mysteriously scarce. Nights ran into mornings, then into point-less days and back into night. I stole glances at social media, swearing that each time was the last. I kept my phone on the kitchen counter, silenced, and yet it taunted me anyway. Come see how much they love Kessie and Clarissa, it seemed to say. Just a peek, nothing more. Don't dwell on the hate, they don't even know you—or what you did. Morgane wouldn't tell, she said so.

I called her a few times, left messages, sent texts and even a couple of emails, but she wouldn't reply. I made calls to her office, was deflected by the receptionist each time. The worst was when I tried to post to her Face-book page, only to find that she had blocked me.

ago, that earlier life, when Mom was on my side, Dad was a shadow, Morgane abided me, Clarissa lived in a desk drawer, and I knew Kessie only as much as I needed to?

Doreen went on to describe the success of Kessie's and my books, the highlights and lowlights of both our tours, and how, until recently, Kessie and I had seemed to be close despite having been raised apart. That last bit came from an interview Doreen had done with one of Kessie's co-workers from the Starbucks. The comment made it seem as if Kessie and I had been wrenched apart at birth, like Luke and Leia, when really we had just been raised in different generations.

Doreen's article was not as shattering as I had feared. It was a simple documentary of the events since Dad had died. She didn't speculate at all about Clarissa, despite the teaser, and to her credit didn't seem to be going after me specifically or even particularly. It was a balanced story, concisely written, and more occupied with the effects of sudden fame than anything else. It occurred to me, in an ironic musing in the back of my mind, that this was the way real writers did it.

I started home, feeling light-headed in relief that I didn't appear to be prey for Doreen's prowess. Time could make all of this go away if I just kept to myself, kept quiet, and whoever it was kept paying the bills.

My route home took me past the travel agency where Morgane worked. I stared long and longingly as I went by, and then at the last minute whipped into a parking lot across the way, thinking that if I could just see Morgane, even from a distance, I might not feel so bleakly alone.

I edged the Beemer into a parking place adjacent to a hedge that gave me some cover. Morgane's office was across a busy four-lane road from me, in a building designed to look like a medieval half-timbered house. It was an ugly building, Morgane said so herself, but no uglier than the rest of the crappy architecture that was popping up all over Nashville. I had written about this in *Nashville and the Costs of Fame*. People agreed with me, but were willing to pay premium for the architecturally garbled McMansions and strip malls anyway.

My view wasn't great, but I could see the front door clearly, and even a portion of Morgane's office window, although I was too far away to see inside. There were a lot of people coming and going that morning. I perked up each time the door opened, then deflated when I saw that it wasn't Morgane. As noon closed in, the heat became even more oppressive. I was drying my face on the front of my shirt when Morgane finally came out, trailed close behind by a good-looking guy with perfect hair and a Vanderbilt visage.

My heart sank so abruptly that I could feel it pounding in my stomach, and then jealousy took over and the pounding moved up between my ears. She hadn't wasted any time, had she. She had probably been seeing this guy all along, whispering lyrical French in his ear while he put his hands in places I didn't want to think about.

I was working my way into a confrontational fury when the two shook hands, and then the guy left. All of the jealousy that had been burning in my chest seemed to escape with one breath. I slapped a damp forehead and berated myself for overreacting. The guy was probably just a client, nothing more, making travel arrangements to the Vandy away games, maybe.

Morgane looked nice in a white short-sleeved blouse and navy skirt, cool despite the heat. She seemed to be waiting for someone. After a moment, she reached into her purse and took out her phone, tapped and scrolled. I eyed my phone in its holder on the dash.

"Call Morgane," I said impulsively.

"*Calling Morgane...*"

Across the way, Morgane shielded her phone from the sun, took a good look at it, and then raised her face to the sky. I couldn't make out her expression, but something in her body language told me she was conflicted. On my end, I got her voice mail. Just hearing that familiar greeting was enough to make my heart ache.

One of Morgane's co-workers came out, a woman whose name I didn't remember. They chatted for a bit, and then turned together toward the agency's parking lot, which was on the side of the office and out of my view. They were probably headed to lunch.

"Text Morgane," I hurriedly told my phone. "*I miss you.* Send message."

Morgane looked down at her phone again, but then the hedge was in the way and I couldn't see anything else.

/////

SEEING MORGANE for that brief time was enough to settle my stomach and convince me for some reason that there was still hope for us.

Back at the apartment, I sat down at the desk with a fresh cup of coffee, booted up my laptop and pondered. I had an inkling of something in my mind, the germ of a story hovering around the fringes where I couldn't quite pull it in. Not a blog post, but a fictional story, and I didn't write fiction, so I had to laugh. People thought I wrote fiction; they thought I was one of the greatest fiction writers around. Only Morgane knew the truth.

It was swampy beyond the window, sweaty gardeners nursing the limp landscaping in the broiling heat. The air conditioner hummed, circulating tepid air that smelled slightly of mold. Where had I gotten the stupid idea that I was in charge of my relationship with Morgane? That she could come or go and it wouldn't matter? Man, I wanted her back. And I thought she might want me, too, even if I couldn't imagine why. *Je t'aime*, she had said to me once. I love you. But why? Why did she love me?

A story idea was still diving in and out of my mind. It wasn't a conscious thing, more like a daydream. I could actually *see* it off and on, not the plot, not the characters, but the words themselves, falling into place like magnets, pole to pole, creating the most perfect combinations all on their own.

I wondered what I could do to get Morgane back, what I would *have* to do. Whatever it was, I would do it. I just had to figure out what. Morgane wouldn't fall for flowers or jewelry, she was too self-possessed for that. If I showed up at her office, it wouldn't matter how miserable I looked, she would be furious. And where was she staying, anyway? I had no idea.

It was hopeless, and so was the story that had been playing in my head. A sentence that had seemed brilliantly formed sounded dumb by the time I could get it jotted down. Fiction was too frustrating, so was life. I let it all go, and went to lie down.

/////

MY DREAMS THAT NIGHT involved Morgane and love and long paragraphs, and people I must have invented but who seemed so real that I would have recognized them on the street. By the time I woke up, most of this was gone, just a vague outline remaining, and some enigmatic images.

It was too early to be up, but I drug myself out of bed anyway, made coffee, sat at my laptop and warred with myself. My social media accounts were only a click away. Maybe things had died down. I checked Twitter. They hadn't. I logged into Facebook. Morgane still had me blocked. I checked Gmail. My inbox was full of junk. At least the trolls seemed to have forgotten about my blog, but then I hadn't written a new post in months.

Beyond the window, people were rousing to go to work. I didn't have a job. Did that make me unemployed, even if I was supposed to be a millionaire? No, it just made me useless.

I eyed the clock in the corner of my screen. What the hell was I doing up this early? If Morgane were here she would still be...*in bed*. And that's when it hit me, that if I got moving I could be parked across from her office before she got there!

I was in place beside the hedge with time to spare, sipping lukewarm coffee while I waited. At barely 8:00 a.m. the heat was already coming up. Cars laid clouds of wafting exhaust as they rushed past. My eyes stung as I kept them focused on the front door of the office, hoping to see Morgane more than briefly. She would be approaching from my right, where the view was mostly obscured by the hedge.

Waiting is the worst. I fiddled with the radio, and when I looked up she was there, along with some of the others from her office. I couldn't see much, and then they were all through the door and that was that. I threw up my hands in frustration and drove home, where I had a whole day to kill until Morgane got off work. Then I would be able to find out where she was staying. And after that? I didn't know. I hadn't thought that far ahead.

Morgane's office closed at 5:00 p.m. Sometimes she would stay a little later, but not too often. Regardless, I was parked by the hedge and watching as 5:00 p.m. approached, and had to wait no later than that because she and her friend Terri came out right on time, turning toward their parking lot, where they were soon hidden by the hedge. I hurried out to peer over the hedge for a better view, saw them get into Terri's purple Prius.

I should have guessed that she would be staying with Terri. The two were co-workers, and had been roommates before Morgane and I had gotten together. Terri was younger though, about Kessie's age, tall and angular but in an athletic sort of way. She had an almost smothering optimism, weekend or weekday, either way, in perfect contrast to Morgane's native reserve. I liked Terri well enough, even if her perkiness was sometimes hard to endure.

The two pulled out and turned toward Bellevue. What I hadn't known about Terri was that she drove as aggressively as the taxi drivers had in New York City. I had a hard time keeping up with the Prius, and then lost it completely when I got stuck in that crazy intersection at Highway 100 and Highway 70. I pounded the wheel in frustration, but then figured that they might be going straight to Terri's place. I knew the way, so I settled down and went with the flow.

Terri lived in a newer complex of condos, up a pretty wooded rise off of Highway 100 near the Warner parks. I drove slowly through shaded driveways, weaving between blocks of condo units and files of parked cars until I spotted Terri's unmistakable Prius parked a short walk from the six steps up to her front door. Morgane's French aloe sprouted from its chartreuse pot to the right of the door, confirming that this was where Morgane was staying.

Finding a place to discreetly park a bright red BMW was going to be tough, but then it didn't matter now because the two were already inside and not liable to come out again until they left for work in the morning. I sighed and drove home, but was back early the next morning, parked beneath some pines beyond a lightly wooded greenspace that gave me a good line on the condo and, I hoped, enough cover to be inconspicuous.

They came out at 7:30 a.m., dressed for the office and in no apparent hurry to get there. They stood on the steps, talking as Morgane smoked a cigarette. I could make out the high notes of Terri's voice, cheerful as always. My heart pounded as I watched Morgane, each puff of her lips as intimate to me as a kiss. I could not recall the acrid smell of the tobacco, only the heady scent of her in the mornings. I liked the way that sounded, so made mental notes. I should have brought a notepad, I thought. I could be writing stuff down.

I had always known better than to criticize Morgane for smoking, but still, it was a nasty habit. At that moment, though, it was the sweetest thing I had ever seen her do. I loved every part of it, how she held the cigarette delicately between her fingers, the way she drew it to her lips, gently inhaling, releasing the smoke slowly, savoring it. I would have been happy to watch her smoke one after another if it would keep her there that much longer.

Too soon she finished the thing, kneeling down to thoroughly stub it out. This tightened her skirt around her hips and bunched the shapely muscles in her calves. I couldn't catch my breath for a few beats there, imagining my hands along her curves, her satiny skin. Had I appreciated her like this when we had been together? Had I paused in my own pleasure to put words to the pure sensation of her? The answer was no. I had been too stupid to know any better.

They went to the Prius then, Morgane smiling at something Terri had said. I caught a trace of Morgane's smoke, or maybe it was just my imagination, and then I followed them with my eyes until they were gone.

I started thinking about that story again as I drove home, not as a whole but in words and phrases that kept repeating themselves, forming sentences that were leading me to the story, not the other way around. Traffic was distracting. I was going to lose it all again, damn it, so I began to recite what I had, my lips moving, urgent to get home so I could write it all down.

I banged through my door, lips still forming the words, like a mantra. I kept at it until my laptop booted up and I could open a new document, and then I typed out those words as quickly as I could. I didn't care about spelling or anything else, I just had to get them down, fast, and when I was done I was surprised by how little I saw on the screen, just a couple of ragged paragraphs.

I sat back, rubbed my eyes and blew a breath. I hadn't written much, but what I had written was enough for a beginning. It was going to be a great story, I could feel it. I even had a title. I would call it *The Six Steps*.

# Chapter Nineteen

It was the faintest trace of cigarette smoke that drew his eyes to the top of the wall. People said only six steps lay between this side of the wall and that, six steps that might as well cross an ocean to reach a country he couldn't even imagine.

It was forbidden to peer over the wall, which was imposingly high anyway. What lived on that side was never discussed, at least openly, but the stories held that just one glimpse of whatever it was could seduce a man into utter insensibility. Once or twice in a generation, someone would come up with a clever new scheme to gain, at most, a fleeting look across. Punishment was harsh, or so it was said.

He stood his post as always, so inured in the day-in, day-out sameness of it all that he had long since abandoned even the barest curiosity of why.

Until he caught that pungent scent.

He recognized what it was because of the habits of others, looked lazily this way and that for someone's approach, but none were there. He remained alone with the heat and the concrete, his nearest compatriots standing similar posts at the very edge of perspective, where the wall seemed to flatten toward poles of eternity. And so his eyes went up, to the only place that a trace of cigarette smoke could have come from, and for the first time in a lifetime he was curious...

*/////*

THOSE WHO WERE MORE CHARITABLE asked later what it was *I* had been smoking to come up with a story like this. The answer, which I still can't provide without residual bitterness, is that I wasn't smoking anything—or drinking for that matter. The story just leapt into my head that day. I have no idea where it came from or, if it had to come at all, why it couldn't have been something a little more traditional. We write the stories we have in us, I guess. Maybe some writers—or should I say authors?—can sit down and consciously create a story based on a plot they've hammered out, but that obviously isn't the way it happened for me, or my father either, or at least James, or Evan, depending on how you look at it.

It took me a few days to get this far along, enough time to establish a new routine. In the mornings, I drove over to Terri's condo, sat quietly in the Beemer with a coffee and a breakfast burrito, and watched as Morgane and Terri began their day. I kept a notepad with me now, to write down my ideas while they still sounded brilliant. Afterward I would drive home, sit in front of my laptop and try to make my mind work; and in the afternoons I would go back, park beneath the pines beyond the greenspace and watch the two go inside, Morgane self-contained as always, Terri still chipper despite the burdens of a long day.

Sometimes Morgane would step back out, dressed in her house clothes, shorts and a T-shirt, smoke a cigarette and seem to be deep in thought. At other times Terri would go out, maybe on a date, while Morgane stayed behind. This made me feel even more hopeful, so in that mindset, through fits and starts, I began writing *The Six Steps*.

It wasn't long though, maybe a week, before I began to struggle with both my story and my new existence. The truth that had become too obvious to ignore was that I hadn't really written anything more after those first few days. I had pretty much spent all of the time since then just going over and over what I had already written, changing a word here or there, adding or deleting a comma, and more or less fooling myself into feeling productive. And it was becoming harder to get out of bed so early in the morning, or to fight traffic in the afternoon.

I looked over the notes I had recently scrawled while sitting in the Beemer, looking for something I could get worked up about, but it was mostly uninspiring stuff. I didn't know where to take my story next, not a clue. Frustration just makes it worse. Evan had gone through this. There was a scene...I couldn't remember it exactly, so I took that tattered manuscript out of its drawer and thumbed through it until I found the page.

/////

Hannah rode on her father's shoulders, leaning forward to duck her head as he walked them beneath a low tree limb.

"Whoa, sweetie," he said with a strained smile. "I almost dropped you. You're getting too big to ride on my shoulders."

"I'm not too big, Papa."

"How do you know?"

"Because you're doing it."

"But what if I couldn't?"

"Then you wouldn't."

"What would you do then?"

"Whatever I wanted."

"And what do you think that would be?"

"To ride on your shoulders, silly."

Hannah giggled as her father reached up to tickle her, clenching her knees tighter as she pretended to fend him off.

"You're getting pretty good," he said. "You think fast."

"Not faster than you, Papa."

"Not yet, but someday, maybe."

"You mean when I grow up?"

"Yeah, when you grow up."

He went silent then, trying to contemplate that eventuality, trying to visualize it, set it to story. Nothing came. Impasse. It was the same with his novel, had been for too long. His thoughts turned sullen.

They continued along the footpath, just a trace through the bush, always under siege by the jungle. Something crashed through the canopy above them, probably a bird or a monkey. He dismissed it out of hand while Hannah searched the interlocking branches for the source of the sound, leaning so far back to get a good look that she put a painful strain on his shoulders and neck.

"Stop that, Hannah," he snapped, "or I'll put you down."

She jerked as if stung.

"I'm sorry, Papa. I just wanted to see."

"There's nothing to see. It's too thick up there."

"But I thought maybe—"

"That's enough!"

"I'm sorry, Papa," she repeated in a tone he would write as wounded. He patted her leg reassuringly.

"No, it's okay, sweetie. I didn't mean it. I was just thinking about something else, that's all."

"Were you thinking about your book?"

"Yeah."

"Mummy says you're stuck."

"Does she now?"

"Yeh. What does it mean?"

"What? Being stuck?"

"Yeh."

"What do you think it means?"

"I think it means you need some help."

"Yeah, I could use some of that," he sighed.

"I can help you, Papa," she chirped, so innocently sweet that he had to squeeze his eyes.

"You are helping me," he said, dabbing at one of them.

"I am?" she brightened even further.

"Yep, you sure are, sweetie."

"How?"

"By helping me practice."

She wrinkled her button of a nose in confusion.

"Practice what, Papa?"

"Well..." he made to rub his chin, then used that motion to squeeze her knee, which drew the reassuring giggle he had hoped for; children were so resilient, "...how about, uh, *knee*." He squeezed again for good measure.

"That's too easy, Papa," she chided him through her giggles.

"It's not so easy."

"Yeh, it is."

"Prove it."

"Okay, *cap*."

"*Sunburn*."

"Hmm...I know! *Aloe*."

"*Green*."

"*Eggs and ham!*"

"Very good sweetie. Now, uh, *breakfast*."

"*Mummy*."

"Yep, Mummy makes breakfast. And guess what? There she is."

That last brought them out of the jungle and into the clearing around their bungalow, where they found Sarah wringing out the laundry into a galvanized washtub.

"So there you are," she commented through the sweltering air as they approached.

"Hi, Mummy," Hannah announced. "I'm helping Papa practice."

"Well that's a relief," Sarah said with a backhanded wipe across her forehead.

"The helpers can do that, Sarah," Evan offered hesitantly.

"The *servants*, you mean?"

"I don't think of them that way."

"Of course you don't."

"Sarah—" She fixed him with a damp look that left his next words wisely unspoken, except for, "—uh."

"It's time to go home, Evan," she said as she bent back to her work.

"We are home, Mummy," Hannah explained with self-evident certainty, which brought her mother's eyes up in a bemused glare.

"Hannah, sweetie," Evan lowered his daughter to her feet, then patted her lightly on the behind, "go play for a little while."

"Okay, Papa," she obeyed, oblivious.

The two watched as Hannah skipped across the yard and then into the jungle on the other side.

"It's not safe for her to play in there, Evan."

"She'll be fine."

Evan ventured to meet his wife's gaze, but found he couldn't meet her head-on. He covered his discomfort with the first compliment that came into his mind.

"You look nice today," he said.

Sarah scowled. She wore a paisley sarong below a damp white T-shirt that molded revealingly to her breasts, her faded and fatigued Keds on sockless feet. Her face was flushed from the heat and everything else.

"It's time to go home, Evan," she said again, this time with more bite.

"Honey...we've gone over this."

She stood abruptly. "Then let's go over it again."

"I'm not ready. The novel—"

"*The novel, the novel, the novel*—Evan, you've been working on that novel for *six years*. You'll *never* finish it."

"I *will* finish it."

"*When?* How much did you write today?" He looked away.

"I wrote a little."

"You didn't write anything." Her voice was rising. Across the way, one of the *helpers* paused but then hurried on. "You've been in the bush with Hannah since breakfast. What's the problem? Doesn't she *inspire* you anymore?"

"Don't say that."

They glared at one another, Evan getting his back up, Sarah sensing the futility of it all. Her face fell.

"You used to say *I* was your inspiration," she muttered grayly.

"You still are," said Evan. He moved toward her but she took a step back.

"Hannah should be in school."

"There's no better school than this," he retorted with a wide gesture that took in their surroundings. Sarah rolled her eyes.

"She's a wild little jungle child—"

"Who knows word association, rhetoric, and chess."

Sarah folded to the ground in defeat, as if wilting in the heat. She hugged her knees and delivered her final, futile argument.

"Evan," she wouldn't look at him, "your inheritance is going to run out. You know that, right?" Now she looked up. "We'll be stranded over here, broke. What happens to your inspiration then?"

"I need more time, Sarah." Now it was he who averted his eyes. "I've been blocked, I don't understand it. I can *see* it, Sarah. I can see it right here." He stabbed his temple with a finger. "But it's gone before I can get it down. It's like...it's like typing is too damn slow. *Handwriting* is too slow. Everything is too slow."

"Oh, Evan," she moaned.

"I need a little more time, Sarah. Please. I'll figure it out."

"Of course you will." She wearily hauled herself up, then bent over the washtub. "I need to finish this before the mosquitoes start up."

Evan stood there for a minute while she silently wrung their clothes, and then he trudged into the house, as empty as he had been before.

/////

NOW THIS WAS AN EVAN I could empathize with. Obviously Dad had suffered writer's block at some point, and considering that he put his James through a few *years* of it, Dad's bout must have been bad. Just as obviously, though, he overcame the problem; but if he revealed his solution somewhere in *The Latter Half of Inglorious Years*, he did it too subtly for me to pick up on.

I spent another day watching Morgane repeat her routine, and when I got home found I had no more words than I'd left with. An email came in from one of the local news channels, with a link to *The New York Times* along with a note: *Care to comment?* My impulse was to delete it, but of course I had to know, so I went to the story. It was another piece by Doreen Ybarra:

*Author's Daughter Continues His Legacy*

*Kessie Ann Dean, the daughter of John Taylor Dean, has announced her intention to write a fifth book in her father's series of detective novels. All of the novels are set in Houston, Texas, and follow the adventures of detective and part-time author, Duane Derrick.*

*"It's sort of like a southern-noir Murder She Wrote," said Dean, who has edited two bestselling books of her father's previously unpublished works. "Duane Derrick solves these gritty mysteries and then writes about them, but in fictional settings." Asked if she thought she had the expertise to write a mystery novel, Dean responded, "I was very close to my father when he was writing them, and would often sit with him while he worked, helping him with ideas. I feel that I know Duane Derrick better than my own brother."*

*Kessie and her brother, the bestselling author Joplin Dean, have been estranged recently. When asked to comment on her brother's claim that the character, Clarissa, had in fact been based on her, Ms. Dean said, "That's totally crazy. Those stories were all written before I was born." As for her brother's suggestion that Clarissa might have been someone her father had an affair with, Ms. Dean responded, "Jop just made that up to hurt me."*

*Joplin Dean would not return calls for comment...*

No, I didn't care to comment, to Doreen, the local news or anybody. This just proved that Kessie was an opportunist and always had been, and that Ms. Pulitzer Prize-winning Doreen Ybarra was fixated on us, or else riding our notoriety in the hope of a little opportunism for herself. I closed my browser and went back to my story, and stabbed at keys until I could say I had at least written something.

## /////

ANOTHER MORNING.

I trudged to the Beemer, barely awake, got in and made that much-too-familiar drive to the condo. I sat there and waited, my neck feeling sticky from the humidity, and with temperatures already so warm that my coffee made me sweat. I put the coffee down, sick of it, felt foolish for the first time since I had started this game, reached for the keys and was about to start the engine and go home when Morgane and Terri came out onto the steps. They talked for a moment, then Terri grinned, which was normal, but then Morgane grinned too, which wasn't.

That got my attention. I let go of the keys and sat up closer, watched as the two stood very close, laughing at something. Terri seemed to go solemn, Morgane too, then Terri bent down and kissed Morgane on the mouth.

I sloshed my coffee, I jerked up so sharply. Terri was taller than Morgane, and so Morgane had to stretch a little to get her arms up around Terri's neck. Their lips never parted as Terri's hand came down to give Morgane a squeeze on the ass.

I made a sound in the bottom of my throat, something like *ggru-*

*uuhyakk,* and looked on with sheer incredulity as the two swayed in place. After a suffocating minute, they broke their embrace and walked hand-in-hand to the purple Prius. It rolled silently away, and I sat as stunned as if I had been tased.

Minutes went by, maybe more, who knows? My mouth had fallen open at the beginning of this, and was still hanging open when someone to my left cleared their throat. I turned, startled, slammed my mouth shut and then it dropped open again.

"Morgane! Uh..."

Morgane and Terri stood right there, close enough to slap me through my open window, and they looked like they wanted to. I thought I was about to pee my pants, and since my crotch was already wet from the sloshed coffee, maybe I did.

"You like to see us, Joplin?" Morgane asked in a fury. "You are stalking me now?"

"Perv," Terri said as if she were spitting out spoiled sushi.

"Uh...uh..."

"You hear me, Joplin." Morgane got down right in my face, didn't touch the car or me or anything, but still I winced, as if a fist were about to follow the venom in her voice. "I see you every day here—"

"It's sick," Terri said, still dripping disgust.

"—and you will stop it now or I will ask the police to take you."

With that she spun around, stomping toward that stealthily-silent purple Prius.

"Sick," Terri hocked for good measure, then spun around herself.

I felt as if every curtain in every condo were instantly parted, and a thousand eyes were reducing me to what I had seen a dog leave in the greenspace the day before. I waited until they were long gone before I left, for fear of encountering them on the road. Then I drove home as quickly as I could, ran inside and threw up.

# Chapter Twenty

SHELISA WAS PASSING behind the bar on the way to the kitchen when she caught that bit about Morgane and Terri. She pulled up short, her brows about as high as they could go, rested her elbows on the bar and leaned in confidentially close.

Barber sputtered, "You mean the French girl was a todger dodger?"

"You hush, Barber," Shelisa scolded him. "Those does be bad words."

"Aw, darlin', but—"

"You hush now," she said again, this time with a tilted head and pointed brow. "Joplin will tell it."

Barber, looking as if he had just been rapped on the knuckles by a matronly schoolteacher, redirected his attention to his Carib. I had never heard the phrase he used, but got the gist of it.

"No," I said with an ironic chuckle. "They just did that to freak me out."

"E suit you, too," said Shelisa, with the same tilted head and pointed brow she had previously applied to Barber.

"Huh?"

"I say it serve you right for followin' that poor girl 'round like a crazy man."

"Oh, you heard that part."

"Yeh, and you should be shamed." And with that, she pushed off and carried on to the kitchen.

"Yeah," I winced as she walked away. Shelisa wasn't being judgmental, just candidly honest, and that might have been worse.

"Well, I wouldn't mind hearing more about those girls," Barber said. There were fewer patrons at the bar now, but he kept his voice conspiratorially low just the same. I had no choice but to laugh.

"Barber," I said with a newly appraising eye, "you're a dirty old man."

"Not at all," he said flatly after a swig of his Carib. "And besides, you're the man tellin' the story, ent it?"

"Yeah," I replied wryly, the laugh still on my lips. It felt good.

"For a man without stories, Joplin, you've got some good ones. So go on, then. Tell us some more."

"Hmm." I was starting to get a little tipsy from the Caribs, that familiar creative buzz. "I'll tell you about my story, then."

"*The Six Stairs?*"

I corrected him with a cantankerous look.

"It's *The Six* Steps."

His face truly fell.

"But what about the girls?"

"They're not going anywhere."

///// 

The days, weeks and then months of his post passed with the abject sameness of the featureless landscape. The only sounds were the whisper of the desiccated wind, the brush of dust against the wall, and his own stifling breaths. Even the cloudless sky lacked character, washed out to the color of burnished tin.

Never again had he smelled the smoke. That memory had receded into the formless procession of days, now even less than a misremembered dream. No longer did curiosity arouse him. There was only his nebulous duty, to stand guard against the possible, regardless how improbable.

Here and there a glitter in the limpid light, like twilight stars cast down from the night, the sparkle of gypsum and quartz, and perhaps a remnant fleck of gold. And just there, beckoning brightly, sparkling in his eye...something. He bent to it, picked it up, hefted it in his hand.

It was a rock, oval, it filled his palm and was chipped on one end, as if it had been struck against something. It felt solid, like flint, not the crumbling limestone that lay everywhere.

He resumed his post, the rock weighting his hand with a native synergy that he couldn't define. It felt right to hold it, to wield it, but for what purpose? He worked his fingers over the rough, chipped end, the end that glittered. What could shatter the smooth edge of such a solid rock? Certainly not the limestone, which fell apart in sharp flakes at the slightest touch. And there was nothing else, nothing.

And then, suddenly, he could sense the gravity of the wall behind him, the unyielding hardness of it, and the answer came to him in a burst. He backed against the wall, hiding his movements even though he couldn't be seen—and no one would have spared him the interest anyway—and with a sheltered backhand, tapped the rock against the wall, one tap, two taps, three.

He strained to listen in the dusty heat, and after a time there came a lithic reply, one tap, two taps, three, and his breath quickened because this was something new...

## /////

I DID FINISH MY STORY, my first and, so far, only work of fiction, and it wasn't Morgane that got me through it, but whiskey.

After my bolt to the bathroom when I got home, I did not feel shattered, crushed, or even deeply wounded. Instead I felt numb, detached, and with a strange trembling in my hands. I didn't know yet that Morgane and Terri had been putting on an act, and were at that moment laughing so hard that the whole office was caught up in it. All I could think was that I had driven my girlfriend not to another guy, but to a *girl*. I mean, how do you reconcile something like that?

If I had stopped for even a moment to feel less sorry for myself, I would have known that it must have been an act. Not that Morgane was necessarily incapable of having a relationship with a woman—and that thought did stir a kind of disturbing arousal—it's just that it wouldn't have been with Terri, her friend and co-worker. Pragmatic Morgane could draw that line and stick to it. She didn't fall for frivolous love fantasies, never had.

I sat on the couch and thought of nothing, nothing at all. I sat for a long time in the day-darkness of drawn curtains, and then this gave way to daydreaming, or perhaps actual dreaming, I might have dozed off there. Regardless, *The Six Steps* entered my mind with a clarity I had never known, fleshed-out characters, full-color settings, dialogue, all of it. I don't have an explanation. Maybe it was simply emotion that was pushing me along, a way to transfer what I was feeling onto something else. When I sat down at my laptop, I didn't get up again until I had added over 6000 words to what I had already written.

It was phenomenal, like a high, and also like a high, it didn't last. Just as suddenly as I'd had that leap of inspiration, I fell back into the moment, my mind slogging along like a beaten horse through a slough of mud. The whiskey was a way for me to feel even sorrier for myself, but the buzz, I noticed pretty quickly, distracted me just enough to get some creative thoughts in.

I tottered as the hardcopy came out of my printer, all 11,329 words and 39 pages, but there it was, I could hold it in my hands, my story, *mine*. I would give it to Marcia...well, I didn't have her anymore, but I would give it to someone. The accolades would come swiftly, I was sure of it, overwriting the episode with Kessie and, maybe, providing me enough of a boost to get Morgane back.

That euphoria lasted until the whiskey wore off. I hadn't written a novel, I had written a long short story, too long for anyone to publish, but that didn't matter anyway because I didn't have an agent. There might have been an agent drowning somewhere in my inbox or voicemail box, but the thought of having to sort through all of that made me tired. I needed action *now*, recognition *now*, so I posted *The Six Steps* to my blog, tapped the last key, chewed a fingernail and waited.

/////

By reporting on Kessie and me and the great show we were putting on, Doreen Ybarra had gotten herself in at *The New York Times*. Another one of her stories appeared in the following Sunday's edition:

*Mystery Painting Reveals Possible Connection to Clarissa.*

That flipped past in the subject line of an email as I was scrolling down, caught me like a fishhook in the eyeball, and reeled me back before I could consciously do it myself. There was only one painting I knew of that had anything to do with Clarissa, and Doreen couldn't possibly know about it. Nobody could.

*Jason Spiegel, the New York City publicist and son of the late artist Marc Spiegel, has come forward with a possible clue to the identity of the woman who inspired the fictional character, Clarissa, from the internationally bestselling book* The Lives of Clarissa.

*"My father used to have a photo hanging in his studio," said Spiegel. "I remember seeing it when I was a kid, but my mother made him take it down. I had forgotten about it completely until I found it in his things after he passed away."*

*The photo Spiegel describes is an enlargement of a painting that depicts a nondescript woman in a yellow raincoat and hat hailing a taxi on a dismal day.*

*"Your eye is obviously drawn to the woman," Spiegel explained, "because everything else is so monocolor. The background seems to blend into itself, but if you look closely there is actually an astonishing level of detail."*

*Marc Spiegel signed the work, which is clearly visible in the bottom right corner.*

*"I don't know where the original is," Spiegel said. "The family rumor was that Pop was in love with the woman in the painting, and that's why Mom made him take it down."*

*Maryam Spiegel, Marc Spiegel's widow, refused comment for this story.*

*The connection between Spiegel's painting and John Taylor Dean's peripatetic Clarissa lies in an inscription on the back of the photo that reads, "My darling, The Woman in Yellow, 1968." The Woman in Yellow is also the title of the opening story in* The Lives of Clarissa. *Spiegel affirms that the handwriting belongs to his father. An analysis is pending.*

*When asked about the coincidence of the inscription, Kessie Ann Dean,
editor of* The Lives of Clarissa, *said, "Yeah, Dad had a painting that
sounds like that. I think Joplin took it after...well, Mom was going on about
it before the funeral, but my mind was on other things. I think she said it had
something to do with the Beatles, I don't know. Anyway, I never heard of Mr.
Spiegel before now."*

*Neither Ann Welch-Percy, the former wife of John Taylor Dean, nor
Joplin Dean could be reached for comment...*

Kessie's memory might have been off, but not mine. I remembered
everything Mom said that day. It was the one loose thread between the
manuscript and me, but I had changed all of that so I was in the clear. I was
still in the clear when Kessie published those stories and gave the world *The
Woman in Yellow*. Mom might have questioned that title, but then she and
Dad had probably still been together when he wrote the story. I couldn't
imagine Mom as Clarissa, though. Who knows what Dad was thinking?
Mom and Kessie had probably talked about it, as close as they had become.
Kessie probably thought it was *LOL* hilarious.

### /////

Yes, he thought. Yes! He tapped out five beats, faster this time, threw
away his caution and faced the wall, placed the flat of his hand on
it as if to feel the beats when they came. He couldn't feel them, but
he could imagine feeling them, like a faint pulse, weak perhaps, but
proof of...something.

He tried new combinations every day, short and long raps with
his stone, like that old code that nobody remembered. He tapped in
different places, he tapped in shapes, triangles and rectangles, and
always he received an answer, but never anything new. As the dusty
days passed, what had seemed magical had become mundane. Even
lifting the stone had become a chore. He signaled his frustration with
a single sharp strike of his stone against the wall, hard enough to hurt
his hand. What replied was light, even timid, the wounded response of
a searching soul.

He was immediately regretful, but how could he communicate that? There came some inquisitive taps, soft, like a gentle hand on his shoulder. He leaned his back against the wall, forgetting himself, and tapped softly in return. And so the day passed, with long interludes between the soft strokes of kindred stones, reminders that neither was alone.

///// 

THEY HATED IT. There were a few charitable if noncommittal comments—*interesting allegory; a bold attempt; kinda biblical but ok*—but the majority of the comments left me naked and bleeding from a thousand ragged cuts: *sophomoric drivel; middle school metaphors; talk about purple prose!; doesn't @joplindean know you gotta do the whole 12 steps?; this is the guy who wrote #tlhoiy? Is he slumming now?* And then this smug beauty from @ *literarymonk: I tried to suspend disbelief, but I believe this was unbelievably unbelievable.*

Nothing from Kessie, though, which said more than I was willing to admit.

I've had to move on to other disasters since then, but I still feel those cuts. How do you recover when a creation you have poured yourself into with soul-baring candor is destroyed in real time and there is no one left to console you, no last sliver of compassion? Something important could be written about this, something I could put on my blog if I could only organize the thoughts that were rampaging through my mind. If Dad were still alive we would finally have something to talk about. I could pour it all out, and he would understand.

///// 

"I THOUGHT IT WAS a rather engaging story," Barber offered after a vacant moment. "How does it end?"

My thoughts had turned morose at the memory, and the retelling of it hadn't healed a damn thing. I finished my Carib with a long pull, looked up for another, but both Shelisa and Julie were elsewhere.

"Do you like whiskey?" I asked Barber.

"No, mate," he said with a shake of his shaggy head. "Beer is best, maybe ale if you're feelin' down."

I acknowledged his wisdom with a nod, but then whiskey is a great tradition in literature. Think Hemingway and Steinbeck and a bunch of others. Did anyone ever stop reading to ask why?

Until all of this, I was pretty much like Barber. I liked beer, craft beer mostly, high gravity brews when I needed a better buzz. But whiskey was so much more efficient. If I drank more whiskey, could I write like them, like Hemingway and Steinbeck? Could I plumb the same truths? I drank a lot of whisky, but didn't plumb anything except my stomach.

Barber wasn't going to be led down the lane of my self-loathing.

"But what about your story, mate?" he pressed me. "How does it end?"

His look was uncharacteristically expectant. That had to be worth a nod and a partial smile.

"Okay," I said, nodding. "Okay."

/////

Now he was eager to stand his post each day. From sunrise to sunset, he transmuted the taps and scratches of his rock into subtle tones that carried feeling and yearning, receiving answers in return that were as intimate as the whispers of lovers. They sent their souls through the stone, and met at a place where they could touch everything except one another.

The physical touch lay at the sixth, unattainable step, a step that could as well reside across an ocean as come any closer to his dreams. His thoughts hurried from point to point, the height of the wall, the depth of the wall, the length of the wall... He dreamed of a way over, a way through, a way around, understanding—if not accepting—that his dreams must be crushed.

He tapped all of this onto the wall, unbearable as it was, sensed the vibrations of a similar quest, but accompanied by an unfamiliar note. He stood back, perplexed, and then came a whistle from overhead and a rock plopped into the dust at his feet.

He couldn't see it at first for what it was, but the answering silence made plain in a surge of revelation that this was the lone instrument that had sent an orchestra of feelings and yearnings through the wall to him!

Imagine, he thought wondrously, bending to bring the stone up from the dust. His counterpart had held this very stone in a hand that might be soft or might be rough, looked on with eyes that could be any and every color at once; and maybe, just maybe, it had been held to lips, breathed upon and wished upon before it had been sent sailing over the wall.

He did that now, held it to his lips, and then he hurled it high and waited. He waited until the sun set on that day and the next. No signal sounded through the wall, no soulful susurration. In rending desperation he hurled his own stone over the wall, and as the silence gathered, he wept.

/////

"WHY, THAT'S TERRIBLY SAD," said Barber, physically moved, or perhaps disturbed. "Don't you have any happy stories?"

"None of my own," I answered dourly.

"Well, now," he said in the way of a pep talk. "We'll need to do something about that."

I snorted, caught Shelisa's eye as she went by, and signaled for another Carib.

"I mean," Barber went on. "You've had a terrible run of luck. It'll all work out, though."

Barber seemed to honestly think that there was going to be a happy ending to all of this. I didn't know if I should feel sorrier for him or for myself. Shelisa came up then, wiping her hands with a dishtowel.

"Okay you two, we gawn to my house now."

Barber was up in an instant with a slavering smile on his face.

"What's going on?" I asked.

"Finish your beer, Joplin," said Barber, and that must have reminded him because he reached for his bottle and drained the last of the foam.

"My beer's empty," I said, nonplussed. "So what's going on?"

"We get to eat now," Barber eagerly answered, wiping his lips with the back of a ruddy arm.

"Yeh, mon," said Shelisa with a gleaming smile. "We got salt fish and pork, and papaws for the chutney."

"Oh, uh, that's okay," I stuttered. "I'll eat lunch here."

"Lunch does be over, Joplin. C'mon now."

She headed out, leaving me in confusion, and Barber looking from me to Shelisa and back, seeming to be prodding me along with his famished gaze.

"C'mon, mate, let's go," he urged.

"But I really don't know her—"

"Doesn't matter. Now c'mon."

And so I followed, bewildered, squeezed into the back seat of a chalky blue car while Barber futilely fiddled with the front seat adjuster.

"It's okay," I said, my knees up to my chin.

"Sorry mate," said Barber.

"It does not be far," said Shelisa, slamming her door a few times until it latched.

And then we were off, heading somewhere new on the island of Nevis.

# Chapter Twenty-One

WE CREAKED AND JOUNCED over some ruts under the tropical tree where Shelisa had parked her car, turned onto the asphalt main road, and then made disorienting progress in the left lane. The few taxi rides I'd taken since my arrival hadn't been enough to acclimate me to the way they drove on this former British possession. I winced, ducked, and stamped a phantom brake pedal as we went along, expecting a head-on crash every time another car approached. And for such a small island, there were a lot of cars rattling along that road.

The main road that circles Nevis is barely twenty miles around. We drove clockwise in a northerly direction, past a hodgepodge of building styles and purposes, as if all of the development had been put in a bag, given a good shake, and then poured out. Some of the vacant buildings were being reclaimed by the jungle right where they fronted the road, others were brightly painted and occupied, and all of them, like the villa I was staying in, were made of cement. We passed a site where some new construction was underway, shirtless men with sweat-glazed backs hammering wooden forms into the outlines of future walls and columns, while others positioned rebar and pipes, and still others hauled the cement from the mixer. Many of the houses we passed were incomplete, with pipes protruding like spines from flat cement roofs.

"They'll build the ground floor," Barber explained over his shoulder, "then move in. It might take years, but when they can get enough money they'll go on and build the next floor."

"Hmm."

While the houses were mostly boxy, with small yards under constant threat from relentless weeds and vines, they looked rock-solid, capable of withstanding hurricane and earthquake alike. Nevis is, after all, a volcanic island, and while Nevis Peak might be dormant, Barber emphasized that it was by no means extinct. There was a hot spring in Charlestown, he told me, meaning that there was thermal activity, and the island of Montserrat, which I could see from my villa, had been devastated by an eruption in the 90s.

"Discovery Channel stuff," I hollered through the slap of sultry wind coming through the window.

"Yeh. See the donkeys?"

A pair of donkeys loitered alongside the road ahead of us. I had noticed the donkeys the first day I was on the island. They roamed anywhere they wanted, just like the monkeys and the sheep.

"Yeah, I see them."

"The Brits didn't build this road until the 60s. Before then, people used the donkeys to pull their carts. When the road was finished, people bought cars and trucks and just let their donkeys go."

"Really?"

"Yeh. And they can be a bloody nuisance. It's the same with the monkeys—they get into everything. And they aren't from here. The Europeans brought them over for pets, kinda like rabbits in Australia, you know?"

I nodded, turned my eyes back to the scenery, then laughed when we sped past a "monkey crossing" sign.

Soon we arrived at a neighborhood called Cotton Ground, where Shelisa turned off the main road onto a side street that climbed steadily toward the canopy above. The street was lined with older houses, the lawns littered with children's toys and, occasionally, huddles of patchy brown sheep that I had mistaken for goats.

"If the tail's up it's a goat, down it's a sheep," Barber said. "These are kept mostly for mutton and to eat the overgrowth."

"Uh, huh."

We drove on, then turned onto a narrow track that was no more than two cement strips for the tires to roll on, and now the way ahead became steep. I felt a nauseating nervousness.

"Is this safe?" I asked Barber, but it was Shelisa who answered.

"Yeh, mon. I does it every day."

The track was so steep that I felt myself pressed into the seatback. The engine labored under the load, and I was certain that it would stall at any moment, sending us careening backward. Shelisa downshifted with a grind, kept her foot flat on the gas, and up we sputtered. Suddenly we were in jungle, dense greenery closing in on both sides. Vines, as taut as guitar strings, stretched between the canopy and the ground in places, like the baleen of whales, ready to snare anything that tried to get through.

As suddenly as the jungle had closed in on us, we emerged from it and into a small collection of shanties built of wood and rusting corrugated metal. Kids sat their bikes and stared as we drove by. I smelled meat cooking, and sure enough spotted a barrel that had been converted into a barbecue pit, a thick slab of something sizzling. The aroma made my mouth water.

We were high enough now that the view behind us looked over the jungle to the blue Caribbean, which still seemed close enough to walk to in a matter of minutes. Ahead, the jungle-enclosed Nevis Peak was higher still. Shelisa made another turn, this time onto a fissured cement street that had us circling the peak on a more level course. One more turn onto another steep track brought us to a clearing beneath some broad trees that shaded a cement house painted bright yellow, with blue window frames and shutters, and an exterior stairway to the second floor.

"Here we are, Joplin," Barber said as he unfolded himself from the front seat. He extended a hand and pulled me out with surprising strength.

"Wow," I marveled, stamping the feeling back into my feet. The view was awesome, a curving swath of blue sea buffered by the deepest green. The canopy hid the houses and activity below. We could have been on a deserted island for all I could tell.

"Yeh, it's a lovely place, ent it?" said Barber.

"So what do you think of our island?" Shelisa beamed.

I stumbled for words.

"It feels so...big." I had to remind myself that Nevis was only twenty miles around, if that.

"It does be big for a small place." She gave a quick look around; then: "I will be inside. You two can make chat upstairs."

Barber licked his lips and Shelisa noticed.

"And yeh, Barber," she smiled knowingly. "You know where it is."

With that, Shelisa went inside, leaving me to follow Barber up the stairs to the veranda and its incredible view, but more importantly to him, to where the beer was kept. He waved me toward a wicker chair, then disappeared through a louvered door, returning moments later with a pair of Caribs that were dripping with condensation. He took the chair next to me, propped his feet on the rail, then handed me a Carib. We sat silently and savored those first cold sips.

It was mid-afternoon, bright and steaming. I sipped my Carib, already warming in the tropical heat, and tried to process everything I had seen and said so far. I had been talking to Shelisa and Barber for more than a few hours. It felt like days, and I knew almost nothing about these people.

"Where do you live?" I asked Barber.

"Oh," he came to with a start, "other side of the island. Gingerland. Not too far from you, actually."

"How do you know where I'm staying?" I asked with an edge of suspicion, fretting momentarily that I had fallen for some kind of scam. Barber worked hard to disguise a sigh, as if he had heard that tone before.

"Small islands have big ears," he said forthrightly.

"Oh," I said, feeling like an ungrateful ass. "I'm sorry."

"Not to worry. You've a lot to get used to."

That brought the silence back, which I felt a need to fill, but Barber sat perfectly content with his beer, sliding his sandaled feet over an inch at a time as the sun began to come in beneath the awning.

A car pulled up below, parking next to Shelisa's car, and right behind it a small flatbed truck came up, with two men in the cab and one more hanging on in the bed. Two women got out of the car, and then the group of five walked together toward the house.

"*Inside*," one of the men hollered.

"*Outside*," Barber hollered back. "Shelly's downstairs."

"Okay, mon."

The women went into the lower level, while the men headed toward the stairs.

"What's that all about?" I asked.

"It's how you let people know you're home. If you go to someone's house, shout *inside*, and if they're home they'll shout *outside*."

"Oh. What about doorbells?"

Barber shrugged. "You could be up here, down there, out back...what use is a doorbell?"

He made a good point, I guess, especially in a place where the doors and windows are open year round, and the stairs are outside.

The men topped the stairs and crossed the veranda toward us. "Barber! Good to see you," one of the men said with precise elocution.

"Kevin," said Barber, offering his hand. Kevin was somewhere in his twenties, average build, wearing new jeans and a white *Rush Slowly* T-shirt. "And this is Joplin, from the States."

"Joplin," Kevin said, emphasizing both syllables. "It is good to meet you. How do you like our island?"

"It's great," I said.

"I am glad you like it. This is Thomas, and this is Nelson."

We shook hands all around, firm handshakes with insistent eye contact. Thomas was a hefty guy, around my age, while Nelson was a black version of Barber. We all took chairs. Kevin and Thomas went inside for beers, and came back out with black bottles of Guinness. Nelson didn't drink alcohol, so sat looking on with his hands folded in his lap.

"So why are you on Nevis?" Kevin asked me.

"Uh—"

"Joplin won a contest," Barber cut in. "A right free vacation."

"That is great, man," Kevin said enthusiastically.

Thomas asked me something, but in the local patois and I couldn't understand a word of it.

"He asks where you are staying," Kevin translated for me.

"Oh," I said. "I'm not sure what it's called."

"Where it be?" asked Nelson.

"He's in Harris," said Barber.

"Ahh," the three mouthed at once.

"Harris?" I said. "Is that what it's called?"

"Yeh, mon," said Nelson. "I does work dere time to time."

My villa was a quarter mile up one of those steep cement tracks, with a couple of villas above me and a couple below, all hidden by the canopy, and with nothing to attach a place name to. There were no street signs, street numbers, mailboxes, or anything to derive an address from. When people had asked me where I was staying, I hadn't known what to tell them. Now I did, even if I didn't know what it meant.

"How long will you stay?" asked Kevin.

"I'm not really sure."

Thomas said something to me, fixing me with earnest eyes as if it were assumed that I understood every word.

"He asks what you do," Kevin translated again.

"What I do?"

"Your work."

"Oh, uh, I'm a writer."

"What do you write?"

"Uh, a lot of things...and a little fiction."

As I said that, I realized that it wasn't strictly true. I had a blog, a short story that everybody hated, and nothing else. Thirty-seven years old and that's all I had to show for it except for a pile of money that I hadn't earned. I had never really thought about it that way until just then. Maybe Dad had been right after all.

Thomas said something, still fixing me with his eyes as if we were speaking one-on-one.

"He asks what kind of fiction?" Kevin said.

"Uh, just general fiction, really."

What a pathetic reply.

"Have I read something you have written?"

That was from Kevin, and the answer was a resounding no. And I wasn't going to bring up *The Latter Half of Inglorious Years*, no way.

"I doubt it," I said. "I'm not famous or anything."

And that wasn't strictly true, either. Fortunately, Barber kept what he had learned about me to himself. I still wasn't off the hook, though.

"We read quite a lot on Nevis," said Kevin.

"Dis is true, mon," said Nelson. "We read many books on Nevis."

I had noticed as much. There were stacks of books at the villa, fiction and nonfiction alike, many of them moldy from the humidity. The little island had two libraries, and there were even shelves of dog-eared books at the Double Deuce, which were loaned out to the customers. Bookstores didn't survive long, though. Between shipping and customs, books were too expensive.

"The literacy rate on Nevis is one of the highest in the world," said Barber.

"So perhaps I have read you," said Kevin. "What are some of your titles?"

"Uh."

I couldn't think fast enough to find a way out of this that didn't extend lie after lie, and I was so tired of lying. Kevin's expectant gaze went long, beginning to take on a perplexed aspect.

"Really," I said finally, "I mostly just do nonfiction stories where I live."

"Oh," Kevin said.

And thankfully that put an end to it, confirmed when Barber's stomach growled loud enough for everybody to hear. There must have been an inside joke or story about this because they all erupted in laughter. Come to think of it, my stomach was rumbling a little, too. I hadn't eaten anything except a couple of pieces of toast that morning, and those followed by all the coffee and beer.

Salvation arrived in the form of Shelisa at the top of the stairs.

"Come eat it before the ants do it," she said.

We were all up at once and moving toward the stairs, except for Barber, who ducked back inside for another beer.

Shelisa and the ladies had set up a rough wooden picnic table on the porch below the veranda, crowded with dishes like a Thanksgiving feast. I waited and watched, not knowing how people did things here. Nelson was the first at the food. He took a plate and served himself, mining a little from each dish, and then the others followed behind him, going off to eat wherever they felt most comfortable. Nelson sat beneath a tree. Kevin and Thomas found a couple of patio chairs, while Shelisa and the ladies sat at the table. Barber's beer run had held him up, so his stomach growled even more fiercely as he waited on me.

"It's all good," he said impatiently. I waved him forward.

"Go ahead, Barber, before your stomach explodes."

That drew a laugh from Shelisa and the others, making Barber blush as he dove in and filled his plate.

I recognized some of the dishes, the roast pork and fish, pinto beans and carrots, but the rest of it... My look of confusion got Shelisa's attention, because she asked, "What you been eating on Nevis, Joplin?"

"Uh, mostly sandwiches."

"*Sam witches?*" the lady closest to me said. She pointed to the dishes. "Dis does be good Nevis food, mon. Fried bananas here, an dis be breadfruit puddin'. Dere be papaw chutney, an dat be pig snout soup."

I took a plate and sampled everything except the pig snout soup. I just couldn't get past those gelatinous pig noses bobbing in the broth. Otherwise, the food was delicious. I really liked the breadfruit pudding, which was sweet and had the consistency of mashed potatoes. The pork roast was dripping with juice, and the salt fish cut like a tender steak, I just had to watch out for the bones.

Everybody must have been starving, not just Barber and me, because we were all finished and patting over-full stomachs in minutes. After clearing the table (which had attracted a persistent column of ants), we carried chairs out into the shade of the tree. The heat was oppressive, and the heavy meal made it even worse, but there was a good breeze, and the view was worth the sweat.

"So what do you think of our food?" Shelisa asked.

"It was great," I said. "Do you all do this every day?"

"Oh, no. This does be leftover from the Double Deuce, and some from Yubrenta's, too."

"What's that?"

"A snackette near Oualie," Kevin answered.

I recognized Oualie. There was a bungalow-style hotel there, a beach, and a dock. It's where I came across on the water taxi from St. Kitts, although I had arrived after dark so couldn't see much of it.

"Did you rent a car?" Kevin asked me.

"No." I shook my head, and didn't add that I was terrified to drive on the left.

"Are you afraid to drive on the left?"

Was I that transparent?

"Yeah, a little," I said.

"Not to worry, man. You will get used to it. You should rent one of my scooters. They are better than a car for exploring our island."

"You rent scooters?"

"That is my business."

"I might give it a try," I said.

"Good, then I will be back soon with a scooter for you."

Before I could object, he and Thomas were up and heading for their truck.

"But wait—" I hollered after them.

"Do not worry, man," Kevin said over his shoulder. "I got you."

"Sounds like you're getting a scooter," said Barber.

"But I've never done it before. What if I crash?"

"Don't worry, it's easy. The tourists rent 'em all the time."

Kevin's business must have been pretty close, because he was back with the scooter before Barber could finish another beer. Once I got a look at it, I let go all of my anxiety. I don't know what I had been expecting, but this scooter looked like the ones you see flitting around in movies filmed in Paris and Rome. It was gray with dark gray highlights, and as innocuous and easy to handle as a kid's bike.

Kevin led me through the controls and so on while the others huddled around to watch, rapt, as if this were the most fascinating thing on the island. He had me circle the yard a few times just to be sure, ran my credit card through his cell phone reader, handed me a helmet, and declared me good to go.

It was late afternoon now, but without the lowering light of home. Tropical days blaze, and then descend into inky darkness in a matter of minutes. There was still about an hour and a half of sunlight left, and I was eager to get out on the scooter and do some exploring while I could still see the way. I said my goodbyes to my new friends, then threw a leg over the seat and started the engine. It idled quietly as Shelisa came over.

"Thank you," I told her, a bit of emotion escaping.

"Your story is not finish," she said, "so you gawn to come back, yeh?"

"Yeah," I promised.

"Good."

I fastened my helmet and gave the engine a rev, which sent me lurching forward a foot or so.

"Remember, Joplin, it is an automatic transmission so it goes when you give it the gas," Kevin reminded me as I twisted the throttle and began to pull away.

"And mind the donkeys," added Barber.

And then I was going down that steep track, and the whole island seemed to open ahead of me.

# Chapter Twenty-Two

THERE CAN BE a universe to explore in just twenty miles. Cruise ships might overwhelm the horizon beyond the Charlestown seawall, but they could never be large enough to contain the history and mystery of Nevis.

I went out every day on the scooter, circling clockwise, and then coming around counterclockwise for the different perspective. People often waved as if they knew me, flashing smiles that rivaled the sun. Hidden tracks crisscrossed the flanks of Nevis Peak, intersecting in unmapped webs through jungle so thick that it dripped humidity, only to open unexpectedly at a clean, modern house with an exceptional view. I followed these tracks, often getting tangled in them as if in a net, but always able to find my way back by simply steering downhill.

The windward coast that lay below the sea-view from my villa was a broad plain overgrown with exotic plants, populated by feral donkeys that scattered in small herds at my approach, and dotted with the rusting and crumbling remains of centuries-gone sugar mills, the kinds of sites that Barber had studied before his funding had run out.

Counterclockwise from there were a few quaint villages that looked isolated and out of time. I was told at a snackette where I had stopped for lunch that a few people living in these villages had never been to the other side of the island, the total of their experience lying along a short curving coast. It was (and still is) hard to imagine.

The leeward coast held the developed beaches and the resorts, wealthy expatriates and bounteous views of St. Kitts. All of the beaches were accessible to the public, though, so I never got the sense of disparity on that side of the island, and I never witnessed any kind of racism. Nevisians seemed to take it all in stride.

I especially enjoyed Sundays on Nevis. Nevisians are deeply religious. There must be more churches on their tiny island than in all of Nashville, representing every imaginable denomination. Riding past the evangelical churches, the singing was loud enough for me to hear over the wind, so boisterous at a couple of the churches in Charlestown that I could park a block away and still hear the congregation clearly. I enjoyed parking in the shade to listen to the people sing, then going for walks along streets that often felt preserved in a time when steamships still came to call. On any other day, Charlestown is congested with traffic and bewildered tourists, the air thick with fumes. But on Sundays, the air is clean and the people sing.

Some days during my explorations I could actually forget what it was I had run from, and feel for a while that I was a different person in a different life, even content up to a point. Dad had written these same feelings into James, I could see that now. I had transferred them into Evan without really understanding them, but now that I could I had to wonder again where or when Dad had experienced such things that he could write about them so authentically.

/////

Evan tore along jungle roads that had once held pavement but were now gravel-embedded hardpan in the dry season, muddy sloughs in the wet. This was the dry season, so he only had to contend with the occasional rut that hadn't yet been worn smooth.

He twisted the throttle and banked into a curve, laughing as Hannah grasped him tighter around the waist. She wasn't afraid. If anything, she was begging him on, grinning beneath a leather helmet and oversized goggles while his long brown hair flicked and tickled her cheeks.

"Go faster, Papa," she shouted over the rush of the wind.

"Can't go too fast, sweetie, but maybe just a little more," he shouted back. He loved it too; he relished every moment of it.

The jungle ripped past, walls of verdure as comforting as a daydream. He steered his aged Vespa scooter onto a narrow trail, slowing as a troop of monkeys scattered ahead. He kept a casual pace after that, jouncing along the uneven path, the wind now just a sigh in their ears.

"Hmm," he said.

"What is it, Papa?"

"I'm thinking...*monkey*."

"*Troop*," Hannah came back at once.

"*Soldier*."

"*Battle*."

"*Rifle*."

"*Bullet*."

"*Gunpowder*."

"*Fireworks*."

"*Fourth of July*—"

Hannah paused at that, like a stutter, her mouth trying to form a word that wasn't there. After a quizzical moment she asked, "What's Fourth of July, Papa?"

"You know what that is."

"No, Papa, I don't."

Evan smiled inwardly. His daughter was barely six years old, and yet already so self-possessed.

"It's a holiday in America, sweetie, the day our country got independence from Britain."

Hannah went silent again, her forehead knitting under her leather helmet.

"But *this* is my country, Papa."

"No it isn't, sweetie. We're just visiting here."

Evan could sense her mind working in the silence that held him by the waist; then: "But I was *born* here, Papa."

She said this with a kind of pleading innocence, as if her world were being upended right then.

"Yes, you were," he said, unable to contradict that fact. "You were born here, but your mother and I come from America."

More silence, and then a shuffle on the seat as if she were searching for a firmer position. Finally, in a small voice: "Will I have to go away someday, Papa?"

Evan brought the scooter to a stop, then threw out the kickstand so he could turn to his daughter. She was getting too old to be drawn into his lap for comfort, so instead he pulled her to his side with a sheltering arm.

"Someday, sweetie," he said soothingly, "but not for a long time."

"Only when I grow up?" she asked with wrenching trust.

"Only when you grow up," he said, not quite meeting her goggled eyes.

"Okay," she said, still pensive.

"What do you want to be when you grow up?" he asked her then.

"I don't know, Papa. I'm not big enough yet."

"Well then," he said, pleased to see her demeanor rebounding already. "What are some things you *think* you might want to be?"

"Hmm," she pondered, stroking her chin the way her father often did. "I could be a writer like you."

"Yes you could," he said proudly.

"Or I could be a movie star."

"Okay..."

"Or maybe a doctor. I could be a doctor if I wanted to, couldn't I Papa?"

"Sure, sweetie. You could be a doctor."

"Maybe for animals, though."

"A veterinarian, then."

"Vet-er-i-nar-i-an," she sounded out the unfamiliar word.

"That's right."

"Hmm," she went thoughtful behind her goggles. "Papa," she stated frankly after that moment, "I think I can be anything I want."

"That's right, sweetie," he said, giving her a one-armed hug while blinking back a surge of emotion.

They set off again down the trail, intersecting a road along the river that would take them in the direction of home. Elephants stood in the river, blowing showers of spray over their backs while naked, brown-skinned boys scrubbed them with coarse brushes. Evan kept them going fast enough for the rush of wind to absorb any lingering questions, but that topic had been used up. Hannah was back in the wind and the moment, and everything was perfect.

///// 

I WAS AT MY VILLA, lounging on the veranda with its incredible view, reading *Houston Storm* and sipping a St. Kitts coconut rum. It was late morning, so the mosquitoes were away. The sun was just then beginning to slant across my feet.

"*Inside,*" someone hollered from below.

"*Outside,*" I hollered back.

I peered over the rail to see Nelson just closing the wooden gate at the steep track that served as my road. It had taken quite a few tries before I had been able to run the scooter up that fractured cement incline, but with practice—and tipping over more than once—I had finally gotten the hang of it.

"Nelson," I said, surprised.

"Mornin' mornin'," he said, looking up and shielding his eyes from the sun.

"Come on up."

I didn't have to tell him that the stairs were around the corner, he was as familiar with the place as I had become. Nelson, I had learned, was the landscaper here.

"What's up?" I asked when he had reached the top. "I don't think the yard needs any work."

"I does not come to work today," he said plainly.

"Uh, okay. Sit down. You want a glass of water?"

"Yeh, dat be fine."

The water supply was from a rain cistern under the villa. They said it was clean, nevertheless I kept a filter pitcher on the kitchen counter, standing in a bowl of water to keep the ants out of it. I poured a glass and returned, sat in silence as Nelson drank half of it in measured sips, and then in more silence as he sat back to take in the view. The island had its own speed, and I had learned not to try to rush things along. Eventually he turned to me and began to speak.

"You see Montserrat and Antigua?"

"Yes," I answered, mystified. The two islands were visible from the villa on clear days, and this was one of them.

"And de little one? Dat be Redonda. It be just a rock."

"Okay..."

"Some days you can see Guadeloupe from dis house, and from Guadeloupe you can see Dominica; and from Dominica you can see Martinique and St. Lucia and Barbados; and dey can see Grenada and Trinidad and Tobago."

"Uh, okay," I said.

He twisted in his chair then, as if gazing through the villa and the mountain behind it toward the view to the north.

"Saint-Martin and Anguilla be dat way," he pointed, "den Virgin Islands, den Puerto Rico, den Jamaica. On Jamaica dere was a great slave rebellion at Christmas in 1831 dat lasted to 1832. Sam Sharpe be de leader. De British hanged him and hundreds more, but dey didn't like de killing so dey did away wit slavery, long before America."

Nelson was intent in this recitation, as if he were lecturing at a college. He paused to drink more water while I wondered why he was telling me all of this.

"I want to tell my poem to you," he announced after he had finished the water.

"Okay," I said, still mystified.

"Do you have paper and a pencil?"

"Uh, yeah." He bored into me with his eyes until I realized he meant me to go get these things right then.

When I returned I handed him the paper and a pen, but instead of taking them he nodded at a patio table and said, "You can write it."

"Uh, okay."

I took a sip of rum—the stuff kicked like a hillbilly with a hangover—and scooted up to the table. Nelson prepared himself with deep thought, gazing beyond the rail at an iridescent purple hummingbird flitting from bloom to bloom in the bougainvillea.

"My poem is called *Nevis Peak*," he said suddenly, before I was ready to write.

"Nevis Peak?" I asked, scribbling fast.

"Yeh."

"Okay, I'm ready."

"It go like dis:

*De mountain is very green,*
*And it can be easily seen.*
*Dere are a lot of trees,*
*And under dem we get fresh breeze.*
*On de top it is very cloudy,*
*But still it is very bushy.*
*De name of it is Nevis Peak,*
*And it is very steep.*"

He sat back and smiled with pride while I finished a hasty scrawl and tried to figure out what to say.

"Uh, Nelson, that's pretty good," I offered at last. Nelson seemed pleased by the compliment.

"You can use it in your book," he said, pushing up from his chair.

"But I'm not writing a book."

"Not now, but mebbe some time."

He excused himself with a nod, headed down the stairs, through the gate, and then began the steep slog in the heat down to the main road. I watched as he descended, his head bobbing with each step until he had disappeared beneath that sea of tropical green. Only then did I realize that he had probably made the journey around the island in one of the colorful minivan buses, then hoofed it all the way up here just to tell me a little history and recite a poem that he was deeply proud of. I had no intention of ever writing a book, but I could put his poem in a blog post—that is if I ever chose to write another one.

/////

ANOTHER WHISKEY WEEK, a blog post that made perfect sense at night but never in the morning, and one more story by Doreen Ybarra about the Deans. I had the addled sense not to publish that ridiculous blog post, and resentment enough to think that Doreen should be paying us royalties, considering how much money she had to be making off our name.

That blog post was titled, *Web Whiners and Wankers*. I thought that last word was dope. It's a British insult that I must have picked up from watching *Trainspotting* or maybe *Shaun of the Dead*, I can't remember exactly. It doesn't matter anyway because I re-read that entry one morning while my coffee was still hot, and it was so stupid that I deleted it right then—and I'm glad I did, too. Things were bad enough as it was.

Doreen's story was titled, *I Know a Place: The Creation of Clarissa*. I was too numb from it all by that point to be sent into a panic at the sight of a Doreen Ybarra byline, but that title yanked me out of the haze in an instant. What was it with the woman? With her credentials she should have been reporting on Syria or opioids or Snowden and the NSA, not on us. We weren't news, we were just dysfunctional. Clarissa was nothing more than a manifestation of that. Of course, I was the only one who actually knew it.

Doreen had scored a feature this time, beginning on the front page of the *Arts & Leisure* section then continuing inside. There was an inset photo of Marc Spiegel's copy of *The Woman in Yellow*, in color, although it was too small to make out much detail. The story began with interviews of various friends of the late Marc Spiegel, including a man named Herschel Leonard, whose name didn't register until:

*Herschel Leonard, a Houston attorney, confirms that Marc Spiegel, John Dean, and Ann Welch spent the summer of 1968 together in London.*

*"I stayed with them all for a week before I went off to college," said Leonard. "Marc and Ann were friends of mine from school. London was going to be their year-off adventure, but it turned into more. They met John later, at a place called Joplin's Pub. It was a dark little joint, down some stairs, just like the song."*

*The song Leonard is referring to, I Know a Place, recorded by Petulia Clark, was a Top-ten hit in 1965.*

*"I was more pragmatic than Marc or John," Leonard continued, "or at least more sensible, and Ann was certainly no wallflower, so I didn't get caught up in it the way they did. But you could feel the energy between the three of them. It was an exciting time."*

*Marc Spiegel's painting, which he inscribed to "My darling, The Woman in Yellow, 1968," depicts a rainy street that has been identified as Camden High Street, in the Camden Town area of London. While Joplin's Pub is not specifically visible in the painting, its facade can be inferred in the architecture adjacent to the figure of The Woman in Yellow.*

*Joplin's Pub is still in operation.*

*When asked if her mother, Ann, was the model for the fictional Clarissa, Kessie Ann Dean said, "I don't know how she could be. Mom isn't Clarissa, no way."*

*Ms. Dean had no further comment.*

*Speculation is that John and Ann Dean named their son Joplin, the controversial author of The Latter Half of Inglorious Years, after Joplin's Pub.*

*Joplin Dean continues to be unavailable for comment, as does his mother, Ann Welch-Percy.*

*Marc Spiegel's friends of that era describe him as...*

I didn't know where to find what I was feeling when I finished reading the story. There was nothing vicious or vindictive in it, and yet it upended me. Mom had talked about the painting, but she hadn't mentioned anything about Joplin's Pub. That was obviously where they had gotten my name, not the town in Missouri like they told me when I was a kid, so why hadn't they just said so? I was mulling a call to Mom when my phone rang. It was Kessie.

She launched in as soon as I picked up, as if there had been nothing going on between us.

"Jop, did you read the story by that...*woman?*"

She spit out that last and I wondered why, since she had been giving regular statements to *that woman.* I wanted to say something snotty, but instead found myself holding the phone even closer to my ear.

"Yeah," I said. "Crazy, isn't it?"

"Yeah."

"So how are you doing?" she asked.

I leaned into that question as if I might be able to bring it closer.

"I'm doing okay," I said without bitterness.

"I thought your story was great."

"You did?"

"Yeah. Everybody should have. People suck, you know?"

"Yeah."

Muscles that had been knotted in my neck for months were easing on the spot. I was feeling that maybe it was time to move on from everything that had happened, but then she had to go and ruin it.

"It reminded me of *Comes Now, Achilles* in a way," she said. Maybe she heard the deep breath I let out, or maybe she realized her slip a step too late, because she quickly added, "Only in a way, I mean."

"My story isn't like his at all," I said testily.

She sighed, and I could hear the hurt in it, but it didn't matter now. She tried to change the subject.

"So do you think Mom and Dad really named you after a pub in London?"

"I don't know. Why don't you ask her?"

"Ask who? *Mom?* Why me?"

"Why not, since you all are so tight now."

"*What?* Jop, I haven't talked to Mom since the funeral."

No way. That had to be a lie, but it did take me down a notch.

"What about Christmas, then?" I asked stupidly.

"She sent me a card like she always does. Man, what's the deal?"

"It was something Mom said a while back. I though you two were hitting it off, that's all."

"I don't know if that will ever happen."

I almost leaped to Mom's defense, considering how she had comforted Kessie at the funeral, but there was something else I needed to air out.

"So," I said snidely, "I hear you're writing mysteries now."

She must have missed my tone, because she came right back in that perky way of hers.

"Yeah. There were some outlines in Dad's stories, so I think I can do it."

Just like that, the knots tightened back up in my neck. So yeah, I had *The Latter Half of Inglorious Years*, but she had *Comes Now, Achilles* and *The*

*Lives of Clarissa,* and soon a whole string of mysteries, and all because I hadn't thought it through when I let her have those stories.

"I shouldn't have let you have those stories," I spat.

I heard her breath catch on the other end, and felt a tension that came right through the phone.

"You didn't *let* me have anything," she spat back. "You wanted Dad's desk, I wanted Dad's stories. It was a trade, and that's it."

"It was more than that and you know it," I said accusingly. "You were his pet. You knew what you were doing."

I had gone too far and I knew it. The sniff on her end was like a spasm in my chest.

"Jop," she said wetly after a moment, "you're always so angry. I don't know why you're like this. I just wanted...all I ever wanted—" She took a tremulous breath. "You wrote a beautiful book, you know? And you're successful. I'm proud of you, I really am. Dad would be proud. You should be proud, too, but you're not and I don't understand it. You hurt me, Jop. So much. You hurt me all the time."

And then she hung up.

# Chapter Twenty-Three

"I KNEW IT COULDN'T BE a coincidence," Barber said after I met up with him and Shelisa again at the Double Deuce. "It's a smashin' place, Joplin's. You'll have to get over and see it someday.

"It does be better than Double Deuce Dean," Shelisa added with an infectious laugh.

"Yeah, maybe," I pretended to grumble.

It was not possible to be in a bad mood on that day. Some peculiar weather pattern had washed across the island, driving temperatures down into the 70s and the humidity down into Venezuela. I'd actually had to throw a blanket on my bed the night before. Add to that a blazing blue sky with a few pristine white clouds, and you had what could have been a nice fall day in Nashville.

The lunch rush at the Double Deuce had ended by the time I had made my rounds of the island. I had been exploring the northwest side, the dry side, almost arid in places due to Nevis Peak's rain shadow. Each trail or cement track had led to another and then another, threading between stands of cactus, eighteenth-century foundations, and a few fenced paddocks. Before I knew it, half the day had gone.

This time we sat at a table off to the side, no one else around. I was drinking Guinness instead of Carib, and was snacking on a plate of French fries.

"You were mean to sweet Kessie again," Shelisa said sternly but not judgmentally.

"Yeah," I said, looking down at my hands. I still felt bad about that phone call.

"But you call your mother finally?" she asked. "What does she tell you about this place in London that you are named for?"

"Nothing—or I mean, I tried to call her but I couldn't get through."

///////

IF WE'D STILL BEEN USING landlines instead of cell phones, Kessie's hang-up might have blown out my eardrum. That's something that tech has taken away from us, the satisfying exclamation of slamming a phone down.

I sat in silence for a little while, not numbed but just trying to sort out my head. In one thought I wanted to punish Kessie for being what I wasn't; in the next I would have done anything just to hear her voice. Kessie was wrong about one thing though: I wasn't angry, I was miserable.

I still held my phone in my hand. I looked at it absently, thought there was something I needed to do, then remembered that I had been about to call Mom. I thumbed her number then sat back as her ringtone—a real ring, like an old-fashioned phone—rattled through a few cycles. I was surprised when it was Ted who answered.

"Joplin, how are you?" he asked, trying to add a dash of dutiful affection, but it went hollow. We weren't close that way and never would be.

"I'm doing all right, I guess. I need to talk to Mom."

"Your mother hasn't been feeling well, Joplin. She's lying down right now and I don't want to get her up."

"Just give her the phone, then."

"Let's let her rest, okay?"

There was something weird about this exchange. As husband number three, Ted didn't get between Mom and me. He was outside of that relationship and had seemed to get it from the beginning. He knew when to be transparent, it's why we got along. Something was going on.

"Listen, Ted, I need to talk to Mom, so give her the phone...*please?*"

I put a little edge in my voice. I'd never had to do that with him, and as I thought about it I started to heat up. Who was he to tell me that I couldn't talk to my mother?

"Joplin, I'm sorry," he said firmly. "I know she's your mother, but she's also my wife. I have to think about her. So goodbye."

He hung up on me. *He hung up on me.* I thumbed Mom's number once more, ready to forget nice and snap Ted back in his place, but the phone just rang and rang, not even voicemail.

I hung up, catching myself as I was about to slam my phone to the floor. First Kessie; now *this*? There was nothing I could do but brood, and of course that made it worse. As evening came on and I went for the whiskey, I had a new idea for a blog post, one that would set all of this straight. I called it *The Bitter Pen.*

///// 

I HAVE SINCE GONE BACK to re-read that post, and in the light of a Nevis sunrise it really wasn't that bad. It was overly dramatic and self-serving to be sure, but the points it made were relevant to the inner conflicts that go on between what we know and what we feel; and all of this as applied to the writer who is trying to get those feelings down in the kinds of words that will affect the reader.

The emotional swings can consume you, but without them there isn't anything to write about. Still I asked: Why do we do it? Why do we put ourselves through this, the naked feelings, the merciless vulnerability? I wrote about expression, about creation, about art. I wrote about truth (and that was a laugh), how truth fights to reveal itself.

I stayed up all night writing *The Bitter Pen*. When I finished, the whiskey haze was gone, just a sour stomach and a visceral need to sleep. I thought it was good, though, maybe even really good. During the small hours, while my last whiskey was working its way through, I was certain that I had finally found my voice. For the first time, I thought I was contributing something important. For the first time, I thought of myself as a real writer.

Wary of my previous experiences with the trolls, I didn't post *The Bitter Pen* right away. I slept on it instead, and when I woke up I went over it—without whiskey—changed a few things, had a cup of coffee and read it again.

And then I posted it.

And waited.

#### /////

IT WASN'T LONG BEFORE I started getting alerts. I had been waiting with my phone in my hand, cautiously confident that I had finally scored with *The Bitter Pen*, and desperate for praise. I scrolled through them expectantly, and was so immediately stunned by what I read that I couldn't process any of it. It was like a car wreck that comes out of nowhere: one moment you're going along, and then *bam*, nothing makes sense.

*You write with a pen? Really? No wonder you suck; Have you been weaned? I bet you don't even know what that means; Whine, whine, whine; Poor #joplindean got his feelings hurt; You should let #kessiedean write your blog...*

My phone quieted down after that flurry. I'm not ashamed to say that I dripped a few tears. Oh, not the big sobbing kind, just some tracks on my cheeks that I absently wiped away. I had nothing left, not anger, not hate—nothing. I was so empty that I didn't even need to run for the bathroom. This is what I got for daring to dive into that rarified sea of the talented. I dove, I couldn't swim, and now I was drowning.

I didn't know what to do. Have a coffee? Have a whiskey? Find a real job? Change my name? Leave Nashville?

What did any of it matter?

My phone pinged a lonely alert, probably someone who was late to the frenzy, but when our phones ping we look at them, regardless, so I did, and saw that I had gotten a text. *I thought it was good*, it read. *I can see where you wanted to go with it.* Another compliment from Kessie wouldn't have had an effect this time, but the comment wasn't from her. Of all the people in the world who might have said something nice about my writing, the one person I would never have expected the compliment to come from was Doreen Ybarra.

Her text was like a life preserver pitched off the Titanic, a heated life preserver, too, but still I hesitated before setting my thumbs to work. Doreen Ybarra had been nothing but trouble for me, but she was also a pro who had successfully navigated that rarified sea...

*u really liked it?* I wrote after that inner debate.

*Sure,* she wrote back. *I liked your short story, too. Deep.*

*deep? really? thx.*

*We should get together and talk about it.*

*ur n nville?*

*Yes. Love Nashville. Your blog helps.*

*it does?*

*How about McCabe Pub? I read your review and I want to check it out.*

I couldn't believe this conversation. Doreen Ybarra liked my blog and wanted to get together with me at a *pub*?

*ok. when?*

*Has to be soon. I'm flying out tonight. What about now?*

Unreal. Was I really in the process of setting up a *date* with Doreen Ybarra? I ran my fingers through my hair, sniffed myself and winced.

*see ya there,* I wrote, and then I launched myself at the bathroom for what would probably be the quickest shower I would ever take.

It was only a little after 5:00 p.m., so I took the back way around to avoid the traffic on West End Avenue. I could have taken my time in the shower after all, since Doreen hadn't made it by the time I arrived. I sat at the bar to wait, feeling exposed even though there were few people in at that time of day.

McCabe Pub was done up tavern style, with dark woods, ceiling fans, and glossy square tables. The menu was a mix of burgers and salads, along with traditional southern meat-and-three dishes and a good selection of craft beers. It had more of a family atmosphere, but every once in a while you got an edgy server who could liven things up. The bartender was in Kessie's cohort, though, so we didn't make much conversation, edgy or otherwise.

When Doreen finally walked in, I was half way through a glass of water and needing to pee. That urge shelved itself while I watched her get her bearings. She was in a gray business suit and sensible shoes, her dark hair in a tight braid that left nothing loose. She spotted me and smiled, and my heart did a thump. We didn't shake hands or anything. I thought about giving her a European-style double-cheek kiss, but that idea got kiboshed (probably for the best) when a server materialized to guide us to a table.

"You look...nice," I said to Doreen, feeling like a teenager with pimples and sweaty palms.

"Thank you," she said in return.

We positioned our phones and settled in. Our server reappeared before I had to try to make conversation again. Doreen ordered white wine. I licked my lips for a whiskey, but ordered a local IPA instead.

"So," she said when all of that was done. "Joplin...you look—have you been sick?"

"No, uh, no." I knew I looked pale. I hadn't been outside much since the day Morgane and Terri had dressed me down. The dark circles under my eyes were from staying up all night writing *The Bitter Pen*. "I've been, you know, working."

"Yeah, I know what you mean," she exhaled in empathy. I noticed for the first time that she had soft, dark fuzz on her upper lip.

"I'm going to take a break for a while, I think," I said, wanting nothing more right then than to reach over and stroke that lip.

"Sounds like a good idea."

Our server arrived with the drinks, and then hovered while we grazed our menus. I ordered a bacon cheeseburger and sweet potato fries. Doreen ordered a house salad with vinaigrette.

With that out of the way, we fell into what I thought of as an awkward silence, although Doreen seemed perfectly composed. She took light sips of her wine, and neither met my eyes nor avoided them. I rehearsed lines in my mind, but nothing seemed to work. I was about to blurt something totally stupid when she saved me by speaking up in a measured voice, as if we had been engaged in regular conversation all along.

"As I said earlier, I thought your last post was good. Your blog really shows the evolution of your writing."

"Thanks," I said.

"Have you ever read John Irving? *The World According to Garp*?"

I shook my head. There was a movie when I was a kid, but I didn't remember any of it. Robin Williams, I think.

"Wasn't Robin Williams in the movie?"

"Yes he was." She smiled patiently. "The book deals with the writing life. You made some similar points."

I swelled at that. Was she comparing me to John Irving? I made a note to look him up on Amazon and see what all he'd written.

"Thanks," I said again. I searched my brain for something to add, but I had nothing. She held her eyes on me in expectation while I flailed inwardly, then I latched onto that bit she had texted me about flying out that night. "Oh, didn't you say you're flying out tonight?"

"Yes. It's my first foreign assignment."

That seemed to animate her, and I drew confidence from it.

"Really?" I said. "Where are you going?"

"Well," she fingered the stem of her glass, "we'll be working on multiple stories. In London to begin. I might even stop in at that pub that Herschel Leonard told us about."

That would have startled me if not for the disarming smile that followed. I made a joke out of it by slapping my head.

"You mean *the* pub?" I asked with my own smile.

"The very one. Did they really name you after it?" She leaned in as if we were close confidants.

"I don't know." I leaned in as well. "They said they named me after the town in Missouri."

"Really?"

"Uh, huh."

"So what happened in Joplin, Missouri? Did they ever live there?"

"Not that I know of. They never talked about it, anyway. Maybe they went there on vacation or something."

"What about London, then? They must have told you stories about that."

"No." I shook my head thoughtfully. "They never did—to me or Kessie. We never knew anything about it until after Dad died and Mom told us about the painting."

Her brows went up.

"Marc Spiegel's painting, you mean?"

"Yeah. Mom said he called it *The Woman in Yellow*, like the inscription you wrote about."

"Really? So that's the actual title, then." She was on an elbow now, leaning in close enough that I could smell the wine on her breath.

"Yeah. Mom says she's the one in the painting. I guess she and that artist, Marc, were together before they met Dad."

"So that means—" she seemed to have just made a startling realization, "—that your mother is *Clarissa*?"

I shrugged. "Who knows what Dad was thinking when he made all of that up? Maybe he just liked the way *The Woman in Yellow* sounded, so he used it for the title of that story."

"But that story *is* about a painting."

"It is?"

"Sure. Haven't you read it?" I gave my head a guilty shake. "Oh, well," she sighed, keeping her face close to mine. "So...what happened to the painting? I'd love to see it."

"Mom has it."

"Oh." She seemed disappointed.

"Yeah. She wanted it."

"Too bad. I've tried to get in touch, but she doesn't return my calls."

"Yeah, mine either."

She pulled back at that.

"Your mom isn't talking to you?"

"No, it's not that. Ted—her husband—told me she wasn't feeling good."

"Well I hope she'll be all right."

"Me too."

Our food came out then. While our server arranged our plates, Doreen sat back and took a sip of wine from a glass that was still half full. I ordered another IPA, then bit into my burger. McCabe Pub had great burgers. Doreen went after her salad with fork and knife, like high society.

When we were finished with our food and the check was settled, Doreen glanced at her phone and said, "I'd better get going. I have to meet up with some people at the airport."

"Okay," I said, deflating a little. "How long will you be gone?"

"I'm not sure. It's an open-ended assignment. I'll be posting my stories from over there." She stood then.

"I'll walk you to your car," I said, hurrying a last fry into my mouth while I got up.

"That's okay," she said. "Don't worry about it."

There was a pregnant moment while I wiped the ketchup off my lips and searched for something to say. I finally came up with, "I had a good time."

"I'm glad," she said. She looped her purse over her shoulder and was about to turn.

"Maybe we could do it again when you get back."

She gave me an odd look, then broke it with another glance at her phone.

"I've really got to run."

I watched her cross the restaurant, a purposeful stride. She didn't look back, and it didn't occur to me that we hadn't talked much about my writing, and that she hadn't once mentioned *The Latter Half of Inglorious Years*.

///// 

DOREEN FILED THE NEXT INSTALLMENT of her Clarissa investigation the following Sunday, dateline London, and titled *The World of Clarissa*.

> *...while the character of Camden High Street has changed over the decades, Joplin's Pub still draws a crowd of aging patrons into its dusky basement setting. Once an unobtrusive place to escape the sidewalk bustle, nestled among jewelers and bespoke clothing stores, Joplin's now shares walls with a busy tourist outlet and a halal meat market.*
>
> *Dederick Coe, the current owner of Joplin's Pub, says that there has been an uptick in business, mostly from American tourists, since the revelation that his pub sits at the center of a literary and artistic mystery.*
>
> *"It's like those books from Sweden about that dragon girl," says Coe. "Everybody wants to come see it for themselves. They'll soon have a bloody tour startin' up at this rate."*

*Coe, who bought Joplin's Pub in 2004, does not know the origin of the name.*

*"There were at least three owners before me," he said. "Maybe more. All the old records were tossed."*

*Joplin Dean recently revealed that he believed he had been named after Joplin, Missouri. "They [his parents] said they named me after the town in Missouri," said Dean. When asked why, he replied, "Maybe they went there on vacation or something."*

*Dean also confirmed that his mother, Ann Welch-Percy, is The Woman in Yellow, the central figure in Marc Spiegel's painting, although Dean claimed to have no idea what her connection was to Clarissa.*

*Ann Welch-Percy, reported to be in poor health, remains unavailable for comment.*

*Regardless the provenance of their common names, Joplin Dean continues to draw controversy with his writing, and Joplin's Pub continues to draw speculation about its role in the triumvirate passions that led to both* The Woman in Yellow *and* The Lives of Clarissa...

She set me up. Yeah, I knew she was a reporter—and no, I never asked if our talk was off the record—but still. I wanted to be mad. I wanted to whip up some justifiable righteous indignation and vent it through the walls. In truth though, even if I wouldn't consciously admit it, Doreen was a damn good reporter, chasing sources the way damn good reporters do. And she was on to something, something that my mother and father had been at the center of, something more than just a painting and the title of a story.

And Ted still wouldn't let me talk to Mom.

## Chapter Twenty-Four

"THAT DOREEN, SHE FASS," said Shelisa. Barber had gone into one of his vacant spells.

"What do you mean by that?" I asked.

"It mean she in everybody's business."

It was with irony stranger than fiction that I then found myself coming to Doreen's defense.

"But she's a reporter, Shelisa, a pretty good one too."

"Yeh. You learned something that day, ent it?"

"Yeah. I learned that talent and competence aren't the same thing. It's like you don't realize how *in*competent everybody has gotten, like we all just accept it now. And then you meet someone like Doreen who's got both. You just want to be near that, you know?"

Shelisa nodded in her thoughtful way. "Y'ain hear."

"It's the same with you," I added.

"What you sayin'?"

"That you're like Doreen. People want to be around you. I know I do."

"Oh, stop play, you!" she exclaimed self-consciously.

"No, really. It's like the way you make sure everything is perfect when you set the tables. Nobody else takes the time."

"I does want it to be right."

"And the way you listen," I added soberly. "You really hear what's inside."

"It nothing special," she said in a matching tone.

"I knew that bloke, Coe," Barber interjected out of nowhere. Shelisa and I were so startled that we practically jumped.

"Barber, you does know when the chat get too serious, ent it?" Shelisa said with an affectionate grin.

"Aw, c'mon now, Shelly. It just came to me, that's all."

"You knew Dederick Coe?" I asked, dumbfounded.

"Yeh. Way before he bought the Joplin. He was a right wanker, that one."

I snorted, drawing a cross look from Barber. That word sounded a lot better coming from him.

"Go on," I said, holding back a laugh. Barber looked me up and down before continuing.

"So I'm at the Joplin one day," he explained, "and in staggers Coe, pissed as a priest, and sits his arse right next to me at the bar. First time I ever laid eyes on 'im and here he is rubbin' shoulders with me like we're mates—"

Barber chose that moment to go blank, leaving Shelisa and me hovering on the edge of doing him bodily harm. We nudged him with our eyes instead, until he recovered his train of thought and carried on.

"—I was about to tell him to sod off, but before I could do that he asked me what I was havin'. You found out quick enough that Coe was always good for a pint when he wanted people to listen to him talk. Fancied himself a philosopher, he did. You know what he said to me?"

"What?" Shelisa and I asked simultaneously. Barber was on a roll now.

"So he's totterin' there, smellin' like a few drams of Glen Livet too many, and then he puts his hairy arm around my shoulders and says—all serious now—that he'd rather be a hammer than a nail."

That drew a chuckle from Shelisa, which drew consternation from Barber.

"Don't laugh. The poor bugger really thought he made the thing up. Damned proud of himself, he was. So you know what I told him?"

"What?" Shelisa and I asked simultaneously. Barber caught his breath and stretched it out.

"I told him it didn't make any difference because both get beaten on and neither gets a say in it."

"What a great line," I said in awe.

"So what happen nex?" Shelisa asked.

"Dunno," Barber answered, lacing his fingers behind his head. "I think I ordered a pint of Fullers."

Shelisa and I burst out laughing, while Barber sat back, too pleased with himself.

"That does be a good story, Barber," said Shelisa.

"And this one happens to be true," he winked.

"Did you know who owned the pub back then?" I asked.

"Yeh, bloke named Harry."

"Did he ever tell you any old stories about the place?"

"Naw, not that I recall."

"Too bad," I said.

"Why's that?"

"It's just that Doreen was over there turning over every rock looking for people who knew about what went on back in the 60s. If it worked out that you knew all along—" I stopped to ponder that. "—well, it would have been ironic, that's all."

"Doreen wasn't finish with you, was she?" Shelisa asked with that uncanny insight of hers.

"No, not even close."

And we'd been having such a good time. I hated to spoil it with a story that wasn't going to get any happier, but even Barber looked intent for more. I waved Julie over so that I could order another Guinness. I was going to need it.

//// 

By the end of that week, I still hadn't been able to get in touch with Mom. Something was wrong.

It's the lack of information that drives the imagination into dark corners, and I was beginning to imagine too many things. What did I really know about Ted? I wondered. Was he capable of doing something bad? You saw it in the news feeds all the time, the guy everybody thought was normal until they found his wife wrapped up and stuffed in the freezer in the garage—

What was *that* doing in my head? Awful. I shook off that image and tried to think of something I could do. After pacing a track from the desk to the kitchen and back, coffee gone long cold, I finally concluded that I had to call Kessie.

I doubted she would pick up if I called, so I sent her a text instead: *somethings wrong with mom. call me.*

The reply came faster than I expected: *whats wrong with her?*

*i dont know. ted wont let me talk to her.*

*ted?*

*her husband.*

*oh. dont think i can do anything about ted.*

*just call him...pls.*

*why?*

*he wont pick up for me.*

*were you mean to him too?*

*no!*

*ok. whats the number?*

*moms number.*

*just a minute...*

Just a minute became more like an hour. I didn't want to push my luck by pestering Kessie with another text. She would probably accuse me of bullying her, and then I would be worse off than before. I had just about lost that debate with myself when my phone rang with an unknown number.

"Hello?"

"That was weird."

"Kessie?"

"Yeah. So what's up with Ted?"

"What do you mean?"

"He wouldn't let me talk to Mom."

"You either?"

"Yeah. This isn't a cult thing, is it?"

"A cult? Ted? I don't think so." I wished I could have been sure about that.

"Well anyway, I guess there's nothing I can do. Sorry."

"But—"

"Later, Jop."

She hung up.

Her attitude was the one she'd thrown at Mom at the condo after Dad died, and here I had thought for so long that she and Mom had gotten close. As bitter—or perhaps jealous—as that had made me over the summer, I now wished that the two *had* straightened things out between them. Knowing that they were still strangers to one another made me feel unexpectedly sad.

It was getting late in the day—an hour later where Mom lived—and I couldn't get rid of the idea that I was somehow running out of time. Should I call the police, then? That seemed over the top. Sure Ted was acting strange, but I really couldn't picture him doing anything bad to Mom if for no other reason than, considering her experience with men, Mom wouldn't have married Ted if she hadn't trusted him.

No, it was something else, it had to be—something that would make me feel stupid if I overreacted. It would have been easier if Mom had stayed in Houston where we knew people, instead of moving to Florida where we didn't know anybody...

It was with that thought in my mind that it occurred to me to call Leonard.

He was in his office when I called, a break that I would have known was lucky if I'd had more experience with lawyers. He greeted me pleasantly, even though I wasn't sure if he was on my side anymore. After I described how I couldn't get past Ted to talk to Mom, there was silence on his end. I could hear him breathing, though. I heard him swallow.

"Leonard? Are you there?"

"Yes—I'm here, Joplin."

"So can you help me find out what's wrong with Mom?"

"You don't know?"

"Know what?"

"Oh my God—you really don't, do you."

That was a statement, not a question, and with an ominous tone that tingled in my stomach.

"Leonard—?"

"Joplin—" He exhaled then, a long, sorrowful breath. "—it's not my place to tell you. You and Kessie need to go see your mother."

"What?" I sputtered. "Why? What's wrong? She doesn't have cancer, does she?" I went cold at the thought. It couldn't be. Not *my* mother.

"No, Joplin. She doesn't have cancer." That came out as if whatever was going on was worse.

"Then what is it?"

"Something that should have been done a long time ago. Go see her. She'll tell you now, I think."

That conversation left my stomach feeling more unsettled than after my trolled blog posts. I had to take some deep breaths before I called Kessie, and when I did, to my surprise, she picked up.

"Hey."

"Hey."

"I talked to Leonard."

"How is he?"

"Fine—I guess. He says we need to go see Mom."

"Mom? Why?"

"That's what I asked him. He wouldn't tell me."

"She doesn't have cancer, does she?"

"No, he says that's not it."

"So are you going to go?"

"We both should. Leonard said so."

"Leonard's not the one who's had to deal with you."

"C'mon, Kessie—"

"No, Joplin. I can tell that you're really worried about Mom and not thinking about yourself for a change, but that doesn't mean I have to go with you. If there's something I need to know about, call."

"Kessie?"

"Goodbye, Joplin."

That seemed to be the end of it. There was nothing else I could say, so I went online and booked a flight, which brought into focus that other recent ending of mine because normally Morgane would have done this for me. I put that out of my mind, hell-bent on doing something proactive for a change.

It turned out that while I had been making my arrangements, Kessie had been on the phone with Leonard. Whether she had called him or he had called her she wouldn't say, nor would she fill me in on how he had convinced her to go. She had a couple of signings to do before she could take off, she said, so we agreed to meet at the Fort Lauderdale airport on Sunday, rent a car, and then drive up to Mom's house together.

I felt strangely empowered during the taxi ride to the airport. Here I was, finally out of my apartment and on the way to stand up for myself. Sure Leonard thought Kessie should be there too, but I had been prepared to go one way or the other. I could visualize the knock at the door, Ted answering, and me stepping in to take charge. I could do it; I was going to do it. I was ready for anything.

I couldn't have been more wrong.

/////

WE COORDINATED as closely as we could, but Kessie's flight from Houston had arrived almost two hours earlier than my flight from Nashville. She was waiting in baggage claim when I came through with the crowd from my plane, squatting in a corner out of the way, an olive backpack at her feet and a Starbucks coffee in her hand. She was dressed like the Kessie of not even a year ago, camo cargo pants, black T-shirt and a Texans ball cap, her hair in a ponytail. The elegant Kessie from the morning shows would have had people stopping to gawk, but in this guise, which I found oddly comforting, she was practically invisible.

She was scanning the crowd, and seemed to go rigid when she spotted me. She stood nimbly as I approached. Her expression was wary.

"I've already checked out the car," she said, "so let's get going."

"My suitcase isn't here yet."

"You brought a *suitcase*? I thought this was a kind of last-minute thing."

"It is."

She just shook her head, took out her phone, and squatted back into her corner to wait. Her attitude hadn't improved once I had claimed my suitcase and we were heading for the rental area. She tossed me the keys when we found the car.

"You can drive if you want to," I said, hoping that concession would get her to lighten up a little.

"You know I don't drive," she huffed.

"Still?" I asked incredulously. "But...you could afford a Ferrari if you wanted one."

"So?" she fired back in a simmering voice. "I could afford a luxury yacht, too."

"Okay, okay..."

I loaded my suitcase into the back, and then went around to the driver's door. Kessie was already inside, seated and belted and thumbing her phone. She put the phone down when I got in, fixed me with a fierce look and said, "Joplin, I'm doing this because Leonard thinks I should and I trust him, but if you rag on me just once I'm getting out. You understand me?"

That really stung.

"Yeah, Kessie, I get it. Look, I'm sorry. I really am."

I had hoped to see a softening in her expression, but there wasn't one. I lingered until she looked down at her phone, and then I gave it up.

"I've got the directions in my phone," she went on without looking at me. "So let's go."

I sighed, not in exasperation but in remorse. It was my fault; I had created this bitter version of Kessie. You could rack up all of my mistakes like pool balls, and this would be the eight ball in the middle of it all.

/////

IT WAS A WARM AFTERNOON, mostly sunny. People must have been heading to beaches up and down the coast because the traffic was pretty bad.

Mom lived in Vero Beach, a couple of hours up the interstate from Fort Lauderdale. We did the first of those hours mostly in silence, with me probing now and then in the hope that Kessie would come around.

"You know what I hate?" I asked at one point.

"Everything?"

That comment was impossible to ignore, but I managed to keep my voice even.

"No, not everything. I hate it when they say *deplane* instead of *disembark*. Deplane* sounds so stupid."

"Yeah, Dad thought so too."

"Hmm. Still living in the condo?"

"Yep," she answered without looking up from her phone.

"So...do you have a boyfriend?"

"Still don't need one."

Man, this wasn't like pulling teeth, it was like pulling tusks.

"Well," I said, "I thought you would have one now, since things are different."

"Nope." Then she looked at me. "I hear Morgane broke up with you."

That caught me by surprise. How could she know?

"Maybe I broke up with her," I grumbled.

"Yeah, right," she said sarcastically.

I almost shot something sarcastic back at her, but caught myself in time. She was watching me now, like she was waiting for me to slip up. I swallowed it all grudgingly, grateful for the silence that followed.

We went on that way for a long time, with me focusing on traffic and Kessie messing with her phone. I had put it all out of my mind, just wanting to get to Mom's house and find out what was going on. It didn't matter what Kessie thought.

We were getting pretty close, Kessie informed me, and then she added, "Congratulations, by the way."

"What? Oh, yeah." *The Latter Half of Inglorious Years* had been nominated for the National Book Award. "You too." So had *The Lives of Clarissa*.

"Thanks. I really mean it about your book, though," she said with more sincerity than anything she had said to me since I had gotten off the plane. "I mean...*The Lives of Clarissa*, that's really Dad's deal. But *The Latter Half of Inglorious Years* is all you."

I covered my wince with a quick glance at the side mirror. I'd felt a lot of emotions since I'd found that damn manuscript, but I hadn't felt shame.

"Get off up here," she said next. "Then turn right."

Mom and Ted lived a few blocks from the beach, in a cozy white stucco house with a Spanish tile roof. They didn't have much of a yard, but what they did have was full of different kinds of roses. Mom loved roses.

I parked on the street, right in front of the house, looked through the window past Kessie and swallowed hard. It had all made sense on the way, but now that we were here...

"Why be nervous?" Kessie asked.

"I don't know," I answered unevenly.

"Well, I'm nervous, too."

"You are? Why?"

"Because I don't know Mom the way you do, and I don't know Ted at all."

"It'll be all right," I said without conviction.

"Will it?"

There it was, in that brief flutter of her lashes, the Kessie from last fall, as earnest as Clarissa, as innocent as Hannah.

"I promise," I said, and this time I meant it, even though it wasn't up to me.

We went up the walkway together, not holding hands but I think she might have if I'd tried. The air smelled like roses, musty and sweet at the same time. We stood in the doorway, said nothing. Kessie looked up at me. I nodded, then knocked on the door. We heard footsteps inside, the squeak of a deadbolt that needed to be oiled, and then the door swung open and it was Ted.

I don't know what I expected, anger maybe, but what I got from Ted wasn't anywhere near that. His shoulders seemed to slump and his expression was resigned, as if a storm surge were rushing in and all he could do was stand numbly and watch it come. I found my voice after a swallow that would have been a gulp if Kessie hadn't been there to kind of shore me up.

"Ted," I said, trying to be firm. "I want to see Mom."

I braced myself, but Ted just nodded darkly and stood aside without a word. We entered the unfamiliar house, pausing at *The Woman in Yellow*, which hung in the main hallway. Even though the painting had been in plain sight for most of her life, Kessie seemed particularly intrigued, as if viewing it for the first time. She raised a hand to touch it, but caught herself at the last moment.

"This way," Ted said.

He padded listlessly down the hall, which opened into an airy sunroom. Mom was sitting on the couch, propped against pillows and with a newspaper in her lap. Her face was lined, her hair lifeless. She had aged since the funeral, years instead of months. My stomach lurched.

"Mom?"

"Oh, Joplin. What have you done?"

She held up the newspaper, her eyes averted as if she couldn't bear to see what was printed on it. It was *The New York Times* for that Sunday, folded open at Doreen's latest story. I took it, scanned it in confusion, then felt ice in every vein.

"But—" Suddenly it was hard to breathe. "But...you mean it was *real*?"

## Chapter Twenty-Five

*His prose could guide him toward the very presence of life, the laughter and love, the sweat and tears, the unwashed reek of loss; and left to wander, his characters could amble into side paths, bend to pluck new qualities, like flowers, and then portray them on the page. But even still they remained mannequins of the imagination. They could not be what they were never meant to be, or else they would not be what they were.*

*There is a mystery at the center of the universe that cannot be known. She was the mystery at the center of his universe, just as unobtainable and always would be. He understood now that he would never find the language to reconcile what might have been. He accepted that she would never step from the lines of his prose into lives she couldn't know. There was only her in the jungle, fearless, clever, called precocious by some, and how he loved that word.*

*The sun rose to slant through his window, casting dark shadows on darker eyes. There was no imagination left in him, no buoyant words, only memory.*

*The story had its ending. He would have to send them there.*

*/////*

OF COURSE I CHANGED the ending. Who would have been satisfied with Dad's depressing finale? It was as if he had written every regret of his life into those last lines, some kind of personal therapy to get him through his days. It ruined the story, made it too raw. Readers would have dropped the book in disgust, so I gave Evan and Hannah the happy ending they deserved. The success of my version proved me right, too. It vindicated me. I didn't just copy Dad's story, I created a story of my own, a good story, a satisfying story. A lot of the book *is* all mine—

—except for the truth.

That truth ripped the heart out of me as I stood there, dizzy and short of breath. Kessie was gawking as if a train were derailing right in front of her, or as if a plane were falling out of the sky. She reached for the newspaper but I held it away, an instinctive move that made no sense. She stepped in like bold Clarissa and snatched it out of my hand, stepped back a few paces to read. She gasped, followed by an abated breath that lengthened until her face flushed.

She had to sit, and wipe back tears, and breathe. She let the paper slip to the floor.

"*Daddy,*" she wept; and then: "*Mom, why?*"

She grabbed her phone and rushed out of the room.

I slumped into a chair, dazed as the ramifications of it all began to creep past my shock. People would figure it out. Mom already knew, had probably known from the beginning. Kessie would put it all together pretty soon. My ending belonged to Evan and Hannah, Dad's ending belonged to James and Clarissa. The two were different, but undeniably the same.

*/////*

They set off again down the trail, intersecting a road along the river that would take them in the direction of home. Elephants stood in the river, blowing showers of spray over their backs while naked, brown-skinned boys scrubbed them with coarse brushes. James kept them going fast enough for the rush of wind to absorb any lingering questions, but that topic had been used up. Clarissa was back in the wind and the moment, and everything was perfect.

They followed the familiar path into the clearing at the bungalow, where Sarah was kneeling to tend her roses. Her clippers were rusty and made a poor cut. She cursed quietly as another stem was ruined, and still had that curse on her lips when she looked up at the approaching scooter.

"Mummy, Mummy," Clarissa announced eagerly as she clambered from the scooter. She got her leather helmet off as she ran to her mother, but her goggles were still in place, lending her not a comic look but a precocious presence. "Mummy, Papa says I don't have to go away until I grow up."

Sarah glared past her daughter at James, held that gaze firm as she stood. "Go play, Clarissa," she said in a tightly controlled voice.

"Okay, Mummy."

Clarissa snatched off her goggles then raced away like a sprite, leaving in her wake a tension that had reached its peak. James dismounted and came forward haltingly. Sarah snipped a perfect bloom right at the head and then threw everything into the grass.

"Why would you tell her something like that?" she demanded, barely in control.

James held his palms open in contrition. "Sarah, honey—"

"Do not—" Sarah stopped to take a calming breath. "Do not patronize me James."

"I'm not, Sarah." He tried to hold her but she pushed him away.

"I want to go home, James." It took all her will to control the tremble in her lips.

"We will, honey, when the novel is finished. I promise." He reached for her again but she twisted away with a flush of anger.

"Your novel will never be finished," she hissed. "It's been years, James. Years."

There was no counterargument to that. James scrambled for something else, found it, as weak as it was.

"What about Clarissa, then? She was born here. It's the only world she knows."

"Well," Sarah spat in disgust, "her world will just have to get bigger. And—" She demurred and turned away.

"And what?" James asked harshly. She rounded on him.

"And I'm pregnant."

"What? But this isn't a good time."

That ripped out of her any reserve that remained. She let it all go, venting every frustration, every damp, sodden morning and sleepless night, every mosquito bite, bout of dysentery and broken promise.

"It will never be a good time as long as we're here!"

James quailed in the face of her fury, licked his lips and searched for words that didn't exist. Her hands were on her hips, the cords in her neck standing out from the strain. Their eyes remained locked. There would be no compromise this time, he saw. No flippant charm would quell the tempest roiling in front of him—

The primal cry from the jungle sounded a parent's most visceral fear. James hesitated for only an instant—locked eyes turning to alarm— before he bolted toward the tree line. He plunged into the dense growth, swimming his arms through the limbs and tangles.

"Clarissa!" he shouted.

"Papa," was the disembodied reply.

"Where are you sweetie?"

"Papa, it hurts."

That was almost more than he could bear.

"I'm coming, baby! I'm coming!"

He bulled through the bush in a panic, prickly vines stitching wounds on his arms and face. Clarissa could somehow move effortlessly through this, but for him it was all but impenetrable. Something was crawling on his chest beneath his shirt. He crushed it against his skin with a slap, tripped and came down on his elbows.

"Clarissa, where are you?"

No answer.

"James?" he heard Sarah call from far behind.

"I'm here!"

He inched forward on knees and elbows, vines catching around his throat like garrotes. Seemingly bound in place by the cloying growth, he pushed his face a last few inches through some low-growing leaves, and then his heart shattered and he gulped a cry.

She was convulsing when he reached her, and all helpless James could do was gather her to him and drip tears into the duff. Her eyelids fluttered as the convulsions eased.

"Don't be sad, Papa," she mumbled with her last sweet breath.
James held on as his precious daughter stiffened in his arms.

/////

*Dateline New Delhi, The Tragic Trail of Clarissa, by Doreen Ybarra*

*...a solitary cement marker surrounded by roses stands witness to the short but inspiring life of Clarissa Jane Dean, whom John Taylor Dean memorialized in the collection of stories published posthumously as* The Lives of Clarissa.

*Born in Uttarakhand State, India on the auspicious Buddha Purnima, or Buddha's birthday, May 2, 1969, she was the first child of Ann and John Dean. The Deans, who met at Joplin's Pub in London during the summer of 1968, traveled to Rishikesh, India later that year, where they were married. Clarissa spent the entirety of her abbreviated life in a forested area just outside that city.*

*A local woman, Asha Mamgai, who speaks fluent English, remembers Clarissa.*

*"I worked for them at their bungalow," said Mamgai, "so I saw her every day. I saw her grow from an infant. She was a beautiful child, very special."*

*Mamgai, along with other women from the region, still tend the roses that adorn Clarissa's grave.*

*"She has nobody else," Mamgai said somberly as we sat on a nearby bench beneath a parrot tree. "We don't want her to be forgotten."*

*Clarissa died after being bitten by a cobra on June 9, 1975, a month and a week after her sixth birthday...*

/////

AT A GESTURE FROM MOM, Ted followed Kessie out of the room. Once she was sure we were alone, Mom looked at me with more anger than anguish.

"How could you do it, Joplin?" she asked pointedly. I opened my mouth to speak, but then realized by her disapproving glare that the question had been rhetorical. "Does Kessie know about this?"

"No," I muttered. "I don't think so."

"Well she will soon enough."

Mom seemed to have become suddenly aware of her hair. She primped it with her fingers, then dropped her hands at the futility of it.

"I look awful," she said.

"No you don't."

"Flattery might have worked before you and your sister let all of this get out." She wrung her hands. "You don't look well."

"I've been having a hard time," I said without elaboration.

"I can imagine. I don't know *how* that reporter managed to dig all of this up."

"She's good, that's all."

"Maybe, but she got one thing wrong. It wasn't called Joplin's Pub back then, just Joplin's."

"Does it really make a difference?"

"It does to me." She mulled that. "I was pregnant with you, by the way...in the story. In case you were wondering."

I had figured as much by then, but it was still jarring to hear. I had been conceived in *India*? That meant I had been a part of it, a part of that day, and that I had unwittingly written myself out of my version.

"Why didn't you tell me?" I asked, more like a hurt child.

"Because I didn't *need* to, Joplin," she replied defensively. "And I *still* wouldn't need to if you hadn't published that damned book. When I first saw the title I knew it had to be John's. Who else would come up with something so maudlin? And then when I tried to read it I was certain. I spent enough years with him...you didn't think I would *know*?"

I couldn't look my mother in the eyes.

"How could I?" I whined. "You never told me anything. How was *I* supposed to know it was true?"

"Doesn't matter, it still belonged to John. Where did you *get* it?"

"I found it in his desk—it was like he was keeping it secret, even from Kessie."

"Especially from Kessie, I bet."

"What's that supposed to mean?" Kessie barked from the hallway. She was standing with Ted, her arms crossed tightly, her lips pursed.

Mom groaned and glanced at Ted, who seemed to shrug without moving a muscle. She waved them in. Kessie hesitated but then complied, as if she couldn't think of an excuse not to.

"Please sit down," Mom said to Kessie, but Kessie just stood there in a combative posture. Mom sighed and ground her teeth. "*Sit down!*"

Kessie's eyes went round. I knew that commanding tone of voice well, but I don't think Kessie had ever heard it before. I would have snickered in other circumstances. Kessie sat grudgingly, but then, as if to even the score, came back with a sharp, "Why didn't you tell us the truth?"

Mom managed to force a smile, which seemed to erase some of the lines she had accumulated recently. "Would you talk to your father that way?" she asked levelly.

"I'm not talking to Dad, I'm talking to you."

"You didn't answer my question."

"Your question doesn't matter."

"Why do you say that?"

"Because Dad's not here anymore."

"So that gives you permission to be rude?"

"I don't need permission, I need answers."

"And you think this is the best way to get them?"

"I think it's the only way I'll *ever* get them."

"I thought so."

"Thought what?"

"It doesn't matter," Mom said, her smile turning down. Kessie's mouth hung open with nothing to add.

I watched in confusion as the tension defrosted, then I understood what Mom was doing. After all, Dad must have practiced on *someone* before he wrote those scenes for James and Clarissa.

"The first story in your book, *The Woman in Yellow*," Mom said to Kessie after those moments, "he wrote that about me."

"No he didn't," said Kessie. "You're not Clarissa."

"No, Kessie, I'm not. Clarissa was my daughter, not a character in your father's stories. You think just because you've paraded those stories everywhere that you're now *an expert on my firstborn child?*"

It's not that I had been in denial about what I had learned from Doreen's story, it's just that it had seemed unreal until the vehemence of those last words nailed the truth to the church door where it couldn't be ignored. Kessie's self-righteous resolve slipped right then.

"Think about it," Mom continued in a calmer voice. If not for the emotional assault she had endured, I would have pictured her with a catty smile. "That story is abstract. There's a painting, a mysterious woman in yellow, and no proper names—just what a young author would write if he was trying to impress a girl. You thought it was part of the same material so you included it, but I was *there*, Kessie. Your father and Marc...it was a magic time." She smiled at something we couldn't see. "I was in London and I had these two smart, good-looking guys chasing after me...I could barely catch my breath. Marc put me in a painting and your father put me in a story." Mom chuckled. "Your name could have been Spiegel, but I chose your father. It was a decision, Kessie. Do you understand? When you make a decision, it's done. You move on."

Kessie's brow wrinkled at that, and mine probably did too. I had no idea what Mom was talking about, and after looking from Kessie to me and back, Mom realized it herself.

"You had to live with your decisions," she explained with an edge of impatience. "It's not like today where you get do-overs and people patting you on the back and calling you brave for surviving your own stupidity. I loved your father and your father loved to write. I wasn't fooling myself. But I couldn't keep him focused. He always needed something new."

She frowned at some memory before going on.

"He got the idea for India from me. I loved George Harrison, and George had gotten the Beatles to go over there. John latched onto that. We were supposed to start college that fall, but he said we could skip a semester. What would it hurt? And he was worried about the draft. You two can't understand what that was like. He thought India would be so cool, so different. He was so full of ideas, he couldn't write them down fast enough. And I was a part of that, like his Marianne Faithful."

"*Who?*" we both asked at once.

Mom rolled her eyes. "Look it up on your phones," and then she pointedly added, "later."

"So you went to India," Kessie stated.

"Yes," Mom said like a confession. "I found out I was pregnant. John didn't know, but I think we would have gone anyway. When I got too big to hide it, I was afraid John would get mad, but he didn't. He was so excited, and that made me excited, too. We got married, and Clarissa was born."

"And then what?" Kessie asked unkindly.

"Didn't you read your brother's book?"

"It's not his book! Obviously he stole it from Dad."

"I did not!" I countered indignantly even though it was true.

Ted exhaled, the first utterance I had heard from him since this had begun. He slid up next to Mom, held her hand, and bored into Kessie and me disapprovingly.

"Kessie," Mom said. "Joplin didn't steal John's work any more than you did."

"I didn't steal anything," Kessie objected. "They were Dad's stories. I always said that."

"Even so," Mom shook her head slowly, "I've had to watch you prance from camera to camera like a diva, telling stories you don't know anything about...you should *both* be ashamed."

"*You* should be ashamed for not telling us!" Kessie hit back.

"Parents aren't required to tell their kids everything, Kessie, that's why they're the parents. If I had known that John had written those stories... maybe then. No one except Leonard knew what happened over there, and they wouldn't know unless we told them. John and I—it hurt too much. We thought we could start over, like it was 1968 again, but when we got home...well, there wasn't any money left. We couldn't afford to go to college, and all our friends had already graduated. We were so busy, working at whatever jobs we could get."

She paused to dab at her eyes. Ted put an arm around her.

"Then we had you, Joplin, and you grew up so fast. More years went by than our whole time overseas. London and India didn't even seem real anymore. I thought we were okay. Obviously John wasn't."

I didn't know how much more of this I could take. Mom was right, there are some things the kids just don't need to know. Kessie had her own inner struggle going on, it was as apparent as her reddening eyes. It must be hard to watch your hero fall.

"Why did you have me, Mom?" Kessie asked, almost a squeak. "Was I supposed to be...her?"

"No!" Mom said adamantly, then she looked up at the ceiling and kept her focus there for quite a while. Finally: "We were doing all right but we weren't happy. Anyone could see that. Your father—" She looked away again, kept her eyes averted as she continued. "—he wanted to write but he couldn't. It was killing him. He wasn't who he was supposed to be and there was no way he could hide from it. I thought if I could give him another child—"

She stopped there, thank God. My stomach was about to erupt. Kessie gasped into her hands. *"Oh, God."*

Kessie's face was streaked when she pulled her hands away, her eyes puffy. Mom was tracking tears herself, shifting and trying to get up while Ted held onto her. I was conflicted, wanting in the pit of my stomach to run from all of this but drawn to it just the same. When Kessie spoke again, her voice was brittle.

"So I *was* Dad's new Clarissa."

"No, Inca," Mom said with a sob. "Your father loved you for who you were."

That could have echoed, things had become so still.

"So why wasn't he there when I was born, then?" Kessie asked.

Mom shot me a reproving look. "Really, Joplin?" I was the only one who could have told Kessie. She knew it and I knew it, and I felt like crap because of it. She reached for Kessie's hand, took it and Kessie let her. "Oh honey, he wanted to be there," she said softly. "John had been tagging along with the Houston police for a while. He said it was research. He went with them right after he got off work, and sometimes he would be out all night. We argued about it a lot."

She paused then, her cheeks twitching. When she continued she looked as if she were speaking to the air. "It's where he got the ideas for his detective novels, I know that now." She shook her head in regret. "If he only could have found a publisher..."

"So that's how—" I interjected with a breath of realization. I had never known about this. Mom nodded, then looked Kessie in the eyes.

"We didn't have cell phones then," Mom said to her. "John knew my time was close. He called me all night from pay phones to see how I was. I thought I still had a few days, so I told him I was fine. Then they got sent to a murder scene. It was pretty awful. He couldn't get to a phone and I couldn't reach him, so Leonard took me to the hospital. You came before John could get there."

Kessie pondered Mom's explanation, betraying nothing in her expression. "Am I like her?" she eventually asked, sounding fragile.

She meant Clarissa, of course. Mom's nose reddened even further.

"Only as much as you're like your father and me."

"I had a sister," Kessie said numbly.

"You still do," said Mom.

It only hit me then that Clarissa was my sister. The revelations in Doreen's story had still felt like fiction to me because they matched so closely with the novel. Clarissa really was my sister, not just a precocious character. What would it have been like to have had an older sister when the storm was gathering and the foundation was breaking? I spoke up then, which seemed to startle everybody except Ted, who had become as stoic as granite.

"Why did you all get divorced, then—when Kessie was so little?"

Mom looked at me in surprise, as if she had expected that question to come from Kessie. She inhaled deeply before answering.

"John started writing again, but he never finished anything. Money was tight, Joplin. We were younger than you are now but I felt so old. I was afraid if I didn't do something, I would get too old and it would be too late. I thought—" she squeezed her eyes shut, "—I thought John might find what he needed with someone else."

*/////*

MOM WANTED US to stay over but Kessie begged out convincingly, which got me off the hook since I was driving. What a relief. It was as if we had been holding our breaths during the good-byes. When we got into the car, windows up and with Ted waving from the front door, we both exhaled at the same time.

"Damn, Kessie."

"I'm glad we found out."

"I'm glad you're glad."

"What?" She turned to me. Ted was still waving. I flashed him a pat smile and waved back. "You mean you wouldn't want to know?"

"I think Mom was right. There are some things the kids don't need to know."

"Well I don't agree with that." She didn't say this in a huff, just as a statement.

Our drive back to the airport went quicker and mostly in silence. The sun set on the way. I felt as if I were fleeing something. Kessie was deep in thought, didn't even have her phone out. I couldn't begin to guess what she was feeling.

Once we were through all the hassle at the airport and into the lounge with the least people, I didn't debate with myself whether I had been drinking too much lately, I went straight for the Maker's. Double. Neat. Kessie held up a finger to the bartender.

"Same here," she said.

I pulled back in complete shock. "Really?"

"Yeah. Good call."

"I can't picture you drinking whiskey."

"Well, in a minute you won't have to. I could've used a few of these at Mom's place. Man, I need to catch up."

"*Kessie.*"

"Hey, so maybe this proves I'm not Clarissa after all." Her lip was trembling.

"C'mon Kessie. Mom said that wasn't it."

"And you believe her? It was nice that she covered for him, but I know better. I read your book—or Dad's book—whatever. Now that I know the truth, it all makes sense."

"What makes sense?"

She looked at me frankly, no trembling lips now.

"Don't you get it, Jop? All his life Dad just went from one thing to another."

"Well, how else do you get ideas?"

"*Ideas?* Look...the way Evan was with Hannah? That's the way Dad was with *me*. When I read your—*the*—book, I didn't see it because I didn't know what I was looking at. But now it all fits."

The drinks arrived then. Kessie knocked hers back in one long swallow, then held up a finger for another.

"You'd better take it slow, Kessie," I said in the calmest brotherly voice I could come up with.

"I'll take it any way I want."

"Okay, okay," I said quickly, fully aware what would happen if she got too wound up. "But really, Kessie—it doesn't mean that Dad wanted you to be Clarissa. Maybe Dad was just being Dad."

"Maybe." Her second drink arrived. This time she sipped, resting her chin in her palm. "Oh Joplin, what're we going to do?"

"Why do we have to do anything?"

She looked at me and scrunched her brows. "Because *that woman* is too good and this is big money now. It's going to come out, Jop. Do you still have Dad's manuscript?" I nodded ambivalently as I raised my glass. "Then you should give it to me."

I had just swallowed that sip, and had not seen that coming.

"What? *Why?*" I croaked.

"Because it's all going to run together, everything from Dad to Clarissa being real, to you and me...and what you did. Man, it's going to be bad."

"How do you know?"

"Because I had more time to see how this works than you did. The story feeds itself, Jop, and it won't stop unless something bigger gets in the way. You think they gave you a hard time about your *blog*?" She laughed darkly and took a sip, swallowed that and gritted her teeth. "Well, you haven't seen anything. Give me Dad's manuscript and I can be ready for them."

"What would you do with it?"

"I'll give it to Marcia. She could get it published. Fast, I bet. We do it in Dad's name. Once it's out that's all they'll want to talk about."

She was being honest with me, and what she said made sense, but giving up the manuscript would leave me with nothing, *nothing*, while she would have *everything*. And then what? Back to my blog while Kessie made the rounds again?

"I want to hold onto it," I said unsteadily.

"It's your deal," she said flatly. She finished her drink, then stood. "I'd better get to my flight. Be careful, Jop."

She leaned down and gave me a hug, which I also didn't see coming, and then she shouldered her backpack and headed out.

I had time for one more drink before my own departure, so I sat and sipped and tried to empty my head but I couldn't. The damn thing about truth is how hard it fights to reveal itself. Dad should have known, Mom should have known, and I should have known.

Soon everybody would.

## Chapter Twenty-Six

"Now I know why you're so fond of whiskey," Barber said with an expression that was unreadable behind his scruffy beard.

"Yeah," I sighed, "but this Guinness works pretty well, too."

"The men say Guinness be good for the heart, but it be too harsh for me," said Shelisa.

"Good for the heart, huh?" I pondered my bottle. "A good excuse to order another one, then."

"Like you of all people needs an excuse," said Barber. He pushed back from the table and drained the last of his Carib. "I wish I could stay for one more, but I must be off."

"What's up?" I asked. Barber gave me a mischievous, yellow grin.

"Met a dolly who lives on Montserrat. She's sailing over in a bit an' invited me along."

"Barber, you are terrible," Shelisa laughed.

"And a terror, Miss Shelly," Barber laughed in return. He held out his hand to me. "Joplin, sorry I don't get to hear the end of your story."

"I think Joplin's tale be almost finish, ent it?" said Shelisa.

"Just about," I said. "But it'll still be here when you get back."

"Maybe not too soon," he said. "But if you're still around I'll be pleased to sit with you and drink a few."

We shook hands, and then with a short bow to Shelisa, Barber took off.

"I miss him already," I sad sadly.

"Everybody miss Barber," Shelisa said, watching him go. She turned to me. "So where will you go nex today?"

"I don't know. This weather is so nice I thought I might hike up to the Source."

The Source was a spring on the windward flank of Nevis Peak, one of only two freshwater springs on the island.

"Yeh," Shelisa nodded. "I think you will like it there."

We fell into an odd silence after that, as if Barber had taken the rest of the story with him. I studied my Guinness bottle intently. Shelisa studied the flags hanging from the ceiling.

Finally, I had to ask, "Did you figure it out before I told you?"

Shelisa nodded in understanding. "About sweet Clarissa? Yeh. I could see what was happening."

"You amaze me, Shelisa."

"Oh, you stop."

"No, really. You should be the writer. You see things."

"You listen close and you see things too, ent it?"

I chuckled. "Maybe with a lot of practice."

"You tell the tale very well, Joplin," she said in a more serious tone. "Maybe you have your nex book right here."

"My next book?"

She smiled and got up.

"I have to go now too," she said. "Where you be for Christmas?"

"Uh, I don't know. I guess at the villa."

"No," she said. "You come to my house. There will be other friends like you there."

"Really?"

"Yeh."

She threw me that knowing smile of hers and then disappeared through the kitchen doors. Julie brought me another Guinness, and I pondered the things Shelisa had said. That she thought of me as a friend tugged at something I hadn't felt in a while, but that other, my own book? The idea seemed crazy, but it settled in to stay anyway, elbowing into everything else going on in my head. Could I really do it? Maybe, but not unless I could fix the mess I was in.

/////

I HAD DREAMS about Clarissa, disturbing dreams that would wake me up, not in a sweat, not in a panic, but confused and perplexed. Afterward, in those early, formless hours between yesterday and tomorrow, I would lie awake puzzling in the dark. The dreams were like scenes flowing in and out of one another, elastic, stretching, contracting, merging. They made no sense.

They started with Dad carrying Clarissa on his shoulders, not in the jungle but on the sidewalk in front of our old Bellaire house. As they went along, Dad recited passages from the novel he was writing, passages that were so brilliant that my heart raced, and yet I could never recall a single word. Then Dad would be at his typewriter, Clarissa in his lap, both of them pecking away, an exaggerated stack of pages rising on the sideboard. And finally, Clarissa would be running from a snake, with me watching from across the way, only able to move with syrupy steps. The snake had a chilling smile. It seemed to laugh whenever its eyes crossed mine, laughing at my impotence. Clarissa would run toward me, inexplicably becoming Kessie, and she would cry out, *Why did you leave me*; and when that startled me out of my sleep, I would be as sure as sunrise that it was Hannah who had spoken.

Now just try to make sense out of that.

Otherwise, there was nothing else going on to make things any different now than before. My apartment was still messy, my friends were still elsewhere, someone was still paying the bills, and if I sat down to write, my coffee still went cold.

Kessie called later in the week.

"Hey," she said.

"Hey."

"How are you doing?"

"Okay, I guess. I haven't been sleeping good."

"Me either."

"Really?"

"Yeah."

"Hmm. So what's up?"

"Nothing. It's weird. There's nothing on the calendar, no signings—nothing. I don't have anything to do. It's crazy."

"Where are you?"

"At home."

"What about your friends?"

"They're all working."

"Yeah, same here."

We might as well have been texting for all that we were saying to one another, but I couldn't think of anything else, and there was no way I was going tell her about my weird dreams.

"Joplin?" she said after a brittle silence.

"Yeah."

"Have you been thinking about her?"

"Yeah."

"I can't get her out of my head."

"Me either."

"I wish we had a picture or—*something*. It's like Dad only made her up and Mom is just going along."

"Except that Doreen has pretty much proved it."

"Yeah. I wish Dad was here so I could ask him."

"Ask him what?"

"Why he left her."

"You could ask Mom that."

"She told us why, but I really think this is on Dad."

"Hmm. Anyway, it'll be a year pretty soon. Are you going to do anything?"

"I don't know. The way I'm feeling right now, I doubt it. I think Eugenia and her family are going to have a service, though."

"They would probably want you to be there."

"Probably, but they're fine anyway. I mean, no secret is going to come out that can change what he did for them. They're lucky that way, don't you think?"

"Yeah, I guess."

"Well, I'd better get going."

"Okay. See you later."

"You, too."

I was troubled when I hung up the phone. In less than a year I had seen Kessie go through so many guises, from idealistic girl to business woman to debutant to bitter sibling, and now to disillusioned daughter. Which Kessie was my sister? The first, I hoped. That's the one I missed the most.

/////

I CHECKED OUT the following Sunday's *The New York Times* anxiously, dreading what I might find, but Doreen didn't have a story in the paper that week. I exhaled the breath I hadn't known I was holding, then laughed at my misplaced apprehension. The story was over, Doreen had finished it. Now she could go back to real news, something that might win her another award.

That euphoria lasted until the next morning, when my phone rang and it was her.

"Hello, Joplin."

Her voice was as matter-of-fact as a business deal, with no inflection whatsoever toward the existential calamity she had created.

"Doreen."

I might have said more by way of greeting, but the apprehension was back and already crowding out any other thoughts. Doreen must not have noticed because her next words were just as pat and just as to the point.

"We need to meet."

"Why?"

"I think you know why."

My stomach fluttered.

"Well I don't."

She let out an impatient breath. "Yes you do."

"Listen, Doreen—" I scrambled for words while my stomach heaved, "—you got your story. So it's over, okay?"

"The story's not finished, Joplin."

Those were the words I was most afraid to hear. She didn't utter them accusingly or judgmentally, but as plainly as established fact. I groaned, squeezed my eyes and tried to think of some excuse, some rebuttal, some way to dissuade her, but I might as well have been trying to write a new blog post. I had nothing.

"When?" I asked, resigned to the inevitable.

"Now."

"Where?"

"I'm out front."

"*What*? How did you know where I live?" Her professional silence provided me with the obvious answer. "Oh, yeah...right."

She was there when I opened the door, dropping her phone into her purse, and alone except for a notepad and a pen. I had a detached moment of appreciation for the exuding competence of everything about her, from what she wore to the expression on her face, and then I looked past that to notice the circles under her eyes and the rough texture of her hair.

"Are you all right?" I asked, and to my surprise I really was concerned.

"I'm fine, just lagged as hell."

"Really? When did you get back?"

"About an hour ago. May I come in?"

"Uh, yeah—sure."

I stood aside and she trod in, had a look around, wrinkled her nose, raised an eyebrow at the overwhelming size of the desk, then pointed at the couch.

"May I sit?"

"Yeah, go ahead."

She checked the couch before she sat, wiped at something, then betrayed her fatigue for the first time when she just plopped down.

"Do you need anything?" I asked. "Coffee or something?"

"No, I'm fine." She scanned her notepad and then gave me a probing look. "So do you want to tell me about it, Joplin?"

"Tell you what?"

She surrendered a sharp sigh, another symptom of her long flight.

"Look, Joplin. I'm going to press with the story. This is your chance to tell your side. This doesn't have to be bad. It's up to you."

It was pointless to play stupid. I sunk into a chair.

"I wouldn't know where to begin."

"People say that, but the beginning always starts in the same place."

Bile burned the back of my throat, made me hoarse as I spoke. I told her. I didn't hold anything back. I even brought out the original manuscript, which she flipped through in fascination. Doreen handled me gently, as if she regretted having had to go this far. My stomach settled down and I felt calm. Briefly, I felt at peace.

///// 

SUNDAY APPROACHED with the slow eventuality of a miles-long train at a midnight crossing in the middle of the desert. I could look left or right and count the cars, but there was nothing straight ahead but rattle and roar and the blur of passage.

During the days I watched the leaves turn, gathering themselves for the fall. During the nights I dreamed. Sometimes Hannah took Clarissa's place on Dad's shoulders. I didn't get it. Clarissa and Hannah were not interchangeable. Even though they had been drawn from the same place, they were as different as siblings raised on different continents. Clarissa died; Hannah didn't. Clarissa was what could have been; Hannah was what could be.

And still the snake, except now it wore Doreen's face, coming toward me steadily, dispassionately, inevitably. That I did get.

///// 

I THOUGHT THE HEADLINE would have Clarissa in it, like a continuation of her story, but it didn't. Clarissa's story had ended at a nondescript marker in India. It was my turn now. If I'd had any room left for rationalization I might have consoled myself that at least this would be the last of them, the last chapter in Doreen's dogged saga. After all, there wasn't anything left to reveal unless Doreen wanted to describe all of the pieces as they fell.

*Son Plagiarizes Hero-Father's Novel, By DOREEN YBARRA, Joplin Dean admits he is not the author of* The Latter Half of Inglorious Years.

My phone blew up before I could even finish the story. I had silenced it and left it on the kitchen counter, but the LED alerts were flashing like an ambulance at a car crash. I could see them winking out the corner of my eye.

I give Doreen credit for unbiased accuracy, and for—I'm certain of it— softening the edges here and there to spare me as much as possible. She wrote in summary that my contribution to the novel was not insubstantial. Coming from her, that was practically exoneration.

Social-media indignation rolled across me like a Chinese mudslide. Some of them might have actually read the book, but I bet most were just retweeting and sharing posts to make themselves feel important. The people leaving the nasty comments on my blog had to be bored with life. Why else would they do it? I shut my accounts down once again, my email account too. By the time I went to bed that night the LEDs had dimmed to a less distressing rate.

I woke up the next morning with the energy of an old mop. I lay in bed in exhausting loneliness trying to think of what I should do if anything, and didn't get up even to pee until I could no longer ignore a weird jangle and clatter coming from outside.

I padded to the window, looked out to the morning gray, and then snapped back as if Clarissa's snake was there and rearing to strike. News crews were encamped outside, not as many as at Dad's condo that night but enough to make it impossible to go out without being accosted. Someone saw me peeking through the blinds, and then it was instant pandemonium as they tripped over each other to be the first up front with a camera.

"Joplin?"

"Joplin?"

"Joplin, why did you do it?"

"Joplin, tell us how you feel."

They chanted my name as if I were a cult leader and they were my insatiable throng. Someone pounded on my door. I tried to make coffee in the chaos of all that, but I couldn't take the noise. It was no better in my bedroom, where someone must have hopped a fence so that they could rap a ringed knuckle on my window. I closed myself in the bathroom, nowhere else to go, turned out the light, sat in a corner and hugged my knees until the muffled pounding tapered into an impalpable silence.

Midafternoon. There was still someone out there, a girl from one of the TV stations sitting on the step of her van and looking bored. I hung a blanket over the big window above the desk, made coffee and ate a bag of chips. My phone vibrated, which meant it was either Kessie or Mom. It was Kessie.

"How bad is it?" she asked.

"Really bad."

"I told you."

"I know."

"You blocked your Facebook page?"

"Yeah, Twitter too."

"What about your blog?"

"I'm still getting ad clicks."

"Figures. You're not reading any of that crap though, are you?"

"No, not anymore."

"Good. So what are you going to do now?"

"I don't know. I hope if I stay inside they'll forget about me and leave."

"They won't forget, Jop. It's like Dad, it's too big. I could help you if you'd let me."

"How?"

"Give me Dad's manuscript."

"Kessie, I told you—"

"You didn't tell me anything. What's the deal with you?"

"It's just that...it's just—" If I admitted it to her then I would have to admit it to myself at the same time: that Dad had groomed her instead of me; that the manuscript was all that I had ever been able to wrench out of him; that without it I would be exactly what he said I was.

"Jop, what's wrong?"

"Nothing. Nothing." I squeezed my eyes and took a breath. "Kessie, you have all his other stuff. I only have this."

"Oh, Jop," she said sadly. "Is that what it's all been about? I thought you hated him."

"It's not that. He was different with you."

"Yeah, sure. He needed me like he needed Clarissa." She said that with a hurt she couldn't disguise.

"Kessie, I really don't think Dad wanted you to be Clarissa. I think it's just the way he was."

"Well, we'll never know, will we? But anyway, look—just email it to me. We can get it published, and none of this will matter a year from now."

"I *can't* email it. I only have a paper copy."

"Seriously?"

"Yeah." I felt like a Neanderthal, or else Dad with a typewriter.

"Oh, man...you'll have to snail it to me then."

"I can't go out there, you know what it's like."

"Hmm—what if I send a UPS guy?"

Somewhere in there I had gone from denial to acceptance, and I'm still not sure exactly when that was.

"Do you really think it'll help if I do this?"

"I really do."

The UPS guy showed up about an hour later. It was starting to get dusky out, but the TV girl was still there. She jumped up when she saw the guy heading for my door, and was in my face with a microphone before I could close the door on her. The UPS guy looked around, blinked a few times but otherwise kept a passive look. Maybe he knew what was going on, maybe not.

I had put the manuscript in a big manila envelope. He slapped on the label and scanned it, but I held on when he tried to take it, putting us in a weird tug of war.

"Can I have it, please?" he asked with a trace of annoyance.

My stomach was coming undone as reality pressed ahead, like I was giving up an organ that I couldn't live without. I saw each page in those last moments, the cross-outs, my notes and additions. All that work. It was like I was leaving her, leaving Hannah.

A sharp tug and he had it. "Thank you, sir. Have a good day."

He shouldered past the reporter in a harried pace to his van while she dogged his heels, her microphone bobbing at the back of his head.

*"What is that, sir? Can you tell us?"*

He gave her a contemptuous look as he climbed into his van. I stood in my doorway watching them, beyond notice for the moment. Maybe Kessie was right after all, but Hannah was the price.

# Chapter Twenty-Seven

THE KNUCKLE-RAP on the door had the insistent sound of authority, but of someone other than the property manager. I took a look through the peephole, expecting one of the reporters to have come up with a new scheme. The national news people had joined the frenzy now, so everyone had upped their game.

Doreen wasn't out there, though. She had scored her story, so she didn't have to troll with the rest of them anymore. And it wasn't a reporter at the door, but some kind of cop. I opened the door warily, remembering my manners when dealing with the law.

"Yes sir?"

"Are you Joplin Dean?" he asked in an intimidating tone that had me inwardly shouting no.

"Uh, yeah."

"Sign here please."

He handed me a clipboard and a pen, which I accepted clumsily.

"What's this all about?"

"Just sign please."

I wanted to read it first, but his impatience moved in time with the tapping of his patent-leather toe. The reporters were hovering over his shoulder, pushing that boundary as far as they dared in the hope of getting a better look. I gulped and signed, and when I did he pulled out some papers and handed them to me.

"Have a good day, Mr. Dean," he said, and then he snapped around to leave, just about impaling a reporter with his chin.

I stood there dumbly, trying to make sense of the scene, but the moment the cop shouldered through the first layer of reporters, the cacophony began.

*"Joplin?"*

*"Joplin?"*

*"Joplin, look over here."*

*"What's that, Joplin?"*

I got the door closed, pushing against it with my back, and realized that my heart was pumping fast enough to fill a swimming pool. I concentrated on my breathing as the shouting outside died down. Eventually I was able to take a look at the papers.

They were from Knopf. I was being sued.

I raced for the bathroom and gave up breakfast. I would have felt better if I'd had the flu.

It took a few tries, but I got a call in to Leonard. I was so rattled that I was practically incoherent, talking so fast that I couldn't even understand myself.

"Calm down, Joplin. Just tell me what it says."

*Calm down? When the ceiling was about to fall on me?*

I took deep breaths, pressed my hand against my chest and read him the first page. I could hear him jotting heavily as I read, and he went on jotting after I finished. He must have laid down paragraphs in that otherwise silent minute. Then he cleared his throat.

"Okay, so you're in trouble, that's for sure." He cleared his throat again. "But this isn't my field. I'll find someone I can refer you to. Don't worry, you have plenty of time."

"But why are they suing me?"

"It's a breach of faith, Joplin. They're suing for compensation."

"But...but..." *Compensation? For what?* "But they made...I don't know, maybe millions from the book."

"Yes they did, but from their perspective they could have made millions more. They say they have to pull the book, and they just finished—uhm—they say a twelfth printing. They have to destroy all those copies, and there's an expense for that."

Even as addled as I was, it made sense.

"Oh, no," I moaned. "What am I going to do?" I sank to the floor, my back in a corner and gray fog closing in all around.

"Just go about your business, Joplin. No matter what happens, it's going to take a long time to get there."

It all raced through my mind, leaving a trace of anger behind. Doreen's story had led to this, and Leonard had fed her the clues.

"Leonard?" I asked, working to amp up some indignation. "Why did you tell Doreen about London?"

He kind of half sighed, half groaned. I could picture him wincing and rubbing his temples.

"She had it figured it out, Joplin...about Marc and your father. But she thought it was something sordid, and it wasn't. I wanted to make sure she had the story right—to spare your mother. It might have been a mistake, I don't know."

He trailed off at that. I got the sense that he was wrestling with his conscience.

"Aren't you supposed to keep it confidential, Leonard?" I asked, and this time I thought I put enough emphasis into my voice to sound reasonably upset. When he replied he sounded a little testy himself.

"Yes, Joplin, that's true. But Ann is not my client and it wasn't a case. And what did I really tell that reporter, anyway? That we were in London in the sixties? Anyone would know that."

"But Leonard, *we* didn't know."

He knew I meant Kessie and me.

"I was afraid of that."

That settled in heavily. I swallowed hard before I went on.

"Did you know about Clarissa?"

Silence; then: "Yes, but I never saw her. Ann wrote me letters."

"Why didn't you say something?"

"Joplin...it wasn't my place. I thought your mother would tell you, especially after John died. But—" There was a tremor in his voice now that gave up his deeper feelings about all of this. I suddenly felt guilty that he had become involved.

"I get it, Leonard," I cut in.

"I want to tell you something, Joplin," he pressed on, "about your book. I want to tell you that I think your father owed it to you. So hold on, okay? You'll get through this. So will Kessie."

It was heartfelt the way he said that. I blinked back an unexpected tear, and then another knuckle-rap on the door snapped me out of it.

"Someone's at the door, Leonard."

"Okay, Joplin. I'll be in touch as soon as I can. Bye."

I put my phone down and approached the door as warily as before, stole a look through the peephole and saw the property manager, her heavy arms crossed beneath a scowl that meant business. Did whoever-it-was forget to pay the rent? Couldn't be, it wasn't the first of the month until tomorrow.

I cracked the door and hesitantly peered out. The reporters hovered, ready to pounce. She flicked her eyes left and right at them, annoyed and ready to pounce herself.

"Mr. Dean," she huffed.

"Yes."

"Mr. Dean, you are causing an inconvenience for the other residents."

She spoke with a Spanish accent even though she didn't look Spanish. Her perfume was awful.

"*Me?*"

"Yes, Mr. Dean. These people are in everybody's way." She looked from left to right and deepened her scowl. "You need to tell them to leave."

"But...they won't do what I say."

"That is your problem, Mr. Dean."

"No it's not! *You* tell them to leave."

"That is not my job, Mr. Dean. If you do not make them leave then you will have to leave."

"But—"

"Immediately, Mr. Dean."

She had gotten red in the face, and when she turned and bumped into a reporter, I thought she was about to throw down on the spot. She muttered curses in Spanish and then bulled through the crowd.

*"Joplin?"*

*"Joplin?"*

*"Hey Joplin, are you being evicted?"*

*"Where will you go?"*

I slammed the door on that and swallowed bile. What was I supposed to do? I had been holed up in my apartment for days. I was out of food, low on coffee...I might as well have been stranded in the woods. Suddenly it was hard to breathe. My heart sped up until it ached, until I was sure I was having a heart attack, and that made it even worse. I needed to run, to get away. I had to get away or I was sure I was going to die.

I gulped breaths, pounded at the ache in my chest, went dizzily to my phone, my keys, my wallet. I bent over to be sick but came up with nothing but a straining contraction that left me drooling and about to pitch forward. I steadied myself, a hand on the wall, got my breathing going again and tried to shake the dizziness out of my head. I had to get away. I had to. I *had* to.

I must have looked like death as I shouldered through the throng to the Beemer. I could picture myself, ashen, disoriented, and yet not one of them asked me if I was okay.

*"Joplin?"*

*"Where are you going, Joplin?"*

*"Do you have any comment..."*

I threw myself into the Beemer, slammed the door and stabbed at the start button. They were pressed against the window glass, someone pounding on the roof, but sounds were dull, almost manageable. I felt a disassociated moment of security in the warm and familiar scent of the leather seats.

I started the engine with a roar, gunned it hoping to get them to back off. A few did, a few others pressed their luck, and a few more were running for their vans. I backed up sharply, ready to hit someone and not caring if I did, threw it into drive and peeled out of there.

Not that I had anywhere to go. I zigged and zagged my way onto West End Avenue, with at least one van keeping up and maybe a few behind him. I made it through a stoplight before it turned, cut sharply onto Bowling Avenue after I crossed 440, hurtled toward Woodmont Boulevard, and then turned right. At least one of them was keeping up with me somehow.

I hung a left on Estes Road and just about got T-boned. Horns blared, but I thought I was clear of the reporters, and then a van made the turn behind me like the A-Team.

Right on Hobbs, left on Linwood, leaving rubber stripes on the road and I still couldn't shake the guy. Right on Harding Place. Soon I was into Belle Meade's 30-mile zone, going about 60 past the golf course, flirting with getting pulled over by the Belle Meade police at any moment. The van didn't slow either, and neither of us got pulled over. Looking back, that's amazing.

It's possible that it was a subconscious thing that had steered the chase to that part of town, or maybe it was just a coincidence, but with the news van on my rear bumper, traffic backed up ahead, and the near certainty that I was cornered, Morgane's ugly office building came up on the right. I didn't think at all, there wasn't time. I whipped into the parking lot, slammed on the brakes, and more or less slid into a parking space. Behind me, the van pounded the curb to make the turn, rocking like it might tip as it scudded into the lot.

I got out and raced ahead of them along the sidewalk to the front door, burst through like a bandit, scared the hell out of the receptionist, dove into Morgane's office and slammed the door, gasping for breath.

Morgane was sitting at her desk, facing me with a look of absolute jaw-dropping astonishment. Her phone began to ring urgently and she picked it up.

"Yes?" She kept her eyes on me, now curiously. "No, not to worry. It is only Joplin here for some reason. No, it is no problem."

She hung up and now her expression shifted, mouth open skeptically, giving me an interesting new perspective on her crooked front tooth.

"Joplin, what are you doing?"

"They're chasing me," I said, still panting.

"Who is it chasing you?"

"*Reporters.*"

"Ah," she mouthed in awareness. "Yes, I see that you told them. I said you would do this."

Yes she had.

I dropped into a chair, wiped the sweat from my forehead. My hands were trembling. Morgane got up casually and brought me a bottle of water.

"Have this before you faint," she said.

"Thanks."

She stood close and watched as I sipped and tried not to choke. There was a commotion outside, the receptionist barking a demand, a muffled reply, a door slamming. Morgane seemed oblivious. I thought I'd had enough of the water, but as I lowered the bottle from my lips Morgane tipped it up with a slender finger and I choked down another swallow. I leaned forward after that, my face in my hands. Morgane smelled nice, that much made it through my frayed nerves.

"Why have you come here, Joplin?" she asked not gently.

"I didn't have anywhere else to go," I said into my hands.

There was a knock on her door. I looked up as Terri stuck her head in and gave me a quizzical look.

"Hey, Joplin."

"Hey."

She looked to Morgane and said, "I wanted to let you know that I'm staying at Brian's tonight." The salacious smile that followed was a clear confession that Brian was going to get lucky tonight.

"No problems," Morgane smiled in return. My jaw dropped.

Once Terri was out of the room I looked to Morgane, more confounded than a minister in a mosh pit.

"But...but..." I stuttered. "But I thought you were *gay*."

She rolled her eyes.

"Joplin, you are such a child."

"Huh?"

She rolled them again and sighed in exasperation.

"What is it that you need?" she asked stiffly.

It all welled up then, all of it, flooding into me and I couldn't stop it. I broke down like a kid with his thumb smashed in a car door.

*"I need somebody to tell me what to do."*

The trace of affection that softened her eyes held a calming quality like no other. She came to me and cradled my face in her hands, and if she'd asked me to jump out the window I would have done it.

"It will be okay, Joplin," she said softly. "I will take care of it."

///// 

I WAS AT THE MIAMI AIRPORT waiting for my next flight when Kessie called.

"Hey," she said.

"Hey."

An announcement over the loud speakers blared in my other ear.

"What is that?" she asked. "Where are you?"

"I'm at the Miami airport."

"Miami? What for?"

"Morgane set it up. I'm going to an island called Nevis."

"Where?"

"Nevis."

"Never heard of it."

"Me either."

"I heard about Knopf, though," she said.

"Yeah."

"I think it's wack."

"It's my fault."

"Maybe. Still, me and Marcia are going to talk to them about it."

"Thanks. And tell Marcia for me, too."

"I will." Her voice dropped a note. "Did you hear they pulled both our books from the National Book Award list?"

"They pulled yours too? Why?"

"They said the whole thing was too clouded now, like maybe you and I were in it together."

"But that's not fair!" I was tearing up.

"It's okay, Jop. I'm kind of glad in a way."

"*Glad?*"

"Yeah. I read Dad's manuscript. Oh my God, Jop, I didn't know you changed the names. *James Trevor Davidson?* And it was Clarissa all along? Who did he think that would fool?"

"I don't think he was trying to fool anyone, Kessie. I think he was just trying to see her the way other people would, and he couldn't do that if he was in it. And I think he wanted to see himself, too."

"But if he'd had a chance to publish it...I mean, everybody still would have figured it out."

"He wasn't going to publish it," I said, as sure of that as anything. "He wrote it for himself, so he could have her near."

"I don't know—" Her voice broke. She breathed heavily into the phone before going on. "I don't know if I feel sadder for him or for Clarissa."

"I feel sad for both of them."

"Yeah." She sniffed. "The parts you wrote...it was a lot, Jop."

"It wasn't that much."

"Yes it was. Evan and Hannah are so different from James and Clarissa."

"That's only because I didn't know what was up when I did it. I thought it was fiction. If you hadn't published Dad's stories I might not have changed anything."

"But you *did* change it. It's like you made up two completely new characters and put them in the same story, like a song and you change the words. It sounds the same but it's still a different song. Even makes those weird voices seem different."

I had never thought about it that way. It didn't excuse anything, but Kessie did have a point.

"Thanks, Andy," I said as sincerely as anything I had ever said to her. She sniffed again, and I got the sense that she was wiping her eyes.

"Sure, Jop. So call me when you get to wherever."

"I will."

*/////*

MORGANE HAD ARRANGED everything, from hiding me out at her place, to getting me the plane tickets and a place to stay on Nevis. Then there were water taxis and land taxis and an escort to the villa—by the time I got there it was night and I was alone in the dark with a bottle of coconut rum and mosquitoes buzzing in my ears as I gazed out from the veranda toward the inky sea.

A cluster of lights twinkled on the horizon, a cruise ship bright with everything familiar. There was no phone in the villa, and until someone came to turn on the internet, no blog, no social media, no email. There was only me, whatever that meant, some damp writing paper in a desk, plenty of pens, a spangled sky, and the hooting, scraping, chirping, clicking sounds of the jungle. The bed was funky from the humidity, the mosquito net smelled musty, and I have never slept as well as that first night.

///// 

THE DOUBLE DEUCE served Yorkshire pudding on Sundays, which was less of a meal than an event. You didn't want to miss it. I had made my reservation in plenty of time, and showed up just after noon so that I could get mine in the first round.

Shelisa was there. She smiled wide when she spotted me, passed behind the bar, and then came to my table with a cold Guinness and the set-up for my meal.

"How are you today, Joplin?" she asked me as she went about arranging everything.

"I'm doing great." I looked around. "Is Barber here today?"

"No." She didn't look up from her work until she was satisfied that the cream and sugar spoons were set just so. "He still be on Montserrat."

I laughed and so did she. I know she was thinking that he was having a dandy time with his dolly, while I was as certain as yesterday that he was right then on his scuffed knees chipping away with his archeological hammer at the lava layer that covered Plymouth, Montserrat's former capital.

"Too bad," I said.

"Not too bad for him," she smiled. "You have a big day today, ent it?"

"Yeah."

She looked around. The place hadn't begun to fill yet so she slid into the chair across from me and leaned forward on her elbows.

"So what are they going to do?" she asked.

"They're going to publish both of them."

"*Both of them?*"

"Yeah. Kessie made it happen, I don't know how. She probably threatened them with a Twitter war or something." I laughed.

"How will they do it?"

"They're using the same title for both, but calling them *Version One* and *Version Two*. Dad's version gets his name by itself, and mine gets Dad as a contributor."

Shelisa rubbed her chin and mused, "Two books, the same but different."

"Yeah. They're already bestsellers in pre-order, but what's really crazy is those first books they printed, the ones they pulled? Now they're collector's items."

"They be worth a lot of money?"

"Might be."

She hopped up. "I gawn to come back," she said, and then she hustled off.

I sipped my Guinness, which had become my favorite, and took in the sights around me, the international flags, the license plates and nautical stuff. I had come to love the place as if it were my own. As welcome as Shelisa and the others always made me feel, maybe it was in a way.

Shelisa returned shortly with a brown paper bag and a sly smile. She settled into her chair, put the bag in the middle of the table, and looked from it to me with a grin.

"What's that?" I asked.

She didn't answer, but made a show of it instead, reaching into the bag, making sure I couldn't see in, grasping something inside and then yanking the bag away as if she were opening a gift. Her bright smile was as wide as my gawking incredulity.

"How did you *get* that?" I asked in amazement.

"Barber sailed to Guadeloupe with his woman and found it." It was a first edition of *The Latter Half of Inglorious Years*, *my* first edition. "So you must autograph it for me."

I quailed a little at that. Signing books for strangers was one thing, but signing for someone you knew? If you didn't get it right they would be disappointed.

"Let me think about it for a few minutes, okay?"

That caused her brow to furrow, but her smile stayed in place. A large group came through the doors just then. The place would start filling up pretty fast now.

"I gawn do some work," she said. She stood, gave my place setting a side look, then reached across and adjusted my sugar spoon a little more to the right. "Leave it here when you finish," she added.

"Okay."

"And both of you will come to my house for Christmas, yeh?"

"Yeah," I laughed. "We'll both be there."

"Good," she nodded, and then she got to work.

It took a couple of Guinnesses to get me loose enough to come up with what I hoped was a good inscription. Meanwhile my Yorkshire pudding arrived from the kitchen. I ate and rehearsed, even practiced on a napkin. Once my table was cleared, I opened the book to the title page, lingered on my name, standing alone and no longer in shame. I wrote:

*For Shelisa*
*The soul of an island is seen in its stories; the soul of a friend is seen in mine*
　　*Joplin Timothy Dean*
　　*On Nevis*

Shelisa was bouncing from table to table, harried but never looking that way. I finished up, left her book on the table and headed for the door. We made eye contact as I went out. I gave her a short wave. Balancing trays of food, she dipped her chin in response, glanced at my table, saw the book and smiled. I smiled back and then stepped into the sun.

It was another glorious day, not as cool as recently but the humidity was manageable. I hopped on the scooter and made my way around to Oualie, steered through the alley between Oualie Resort and Winston's bicycle shop to the dock beyond. I sat on the scooter and waited, the sun feeling like an infusion of energy, the bay a glistening turquoise and with the tail of St. Kitts breaking the surface in rises and falls across the way.

I watched the water taxi ply through the strait, its wake fanning out in threads of foam. It slowed, coasted in, then bumped gently against the dock. Men jumped to work, tying the boat fast, pulling out luggage. Passengers began to step over the gunwale onto the wooden dock. They were hard to make out through the glare of the sun on the water, but then I saw her and waved. She waved in return, eagerly, excited, dressed perfectly for the weather and catching appreciative stares as a result.

I met her at the foot of the dock and we hugged as if it had been years, not bare months.

"Joplin," she said. "You look great."

"You too, Kessie."

I led her into the hotel restaurant, where we took a table overlooking the beach. The breeze was soft and salty. With a miraculous tan and her hair in rows, Kessie looked as if she belonged to the place.

"How was your trip?" I asked.

"It was fine. A lot of steps, though."

"Yeah, I think that's why I like it here so much. You can't just show up, you have to work at it."

"So is this where you're staying?"

"Oh, no," I laughed. "We'll be on the almost exact other side of the island."

"That sounds far."

I thought about that. Ten miles, maybe, but the distance of a lifetime.

"It's a good ride."

"Ride?"

"I brought the scooter."

"*Scooter?* But what about my stuff?"

"Don't worry, it'll get there."

"If you say so." She turned thoughtful, scratched at the table with a fingernail. "Do you really think we can do it, Jop?"

"I know we can."

She looked at me curiously and I grinned back at her.

"You're so different now," she said.

"I am?"

"Yeah, like maybe this all happened for a reason."

"Maybe," I shrugged. She mulled that.

"Are you sure you don't want to change the ending in Dad's version? There's still time."

"It wouldn't be honest, Kessie. They're his words."

"Yeah, I know," she sadly agreed.

"C'mon," I said, getting up. "Let's go for a ride and worry about this stuff later."

As we round the island, Kessie holding tight, I think about the shirtless man that day, hefting his bluefish by the gills, his story written into his body in welts and stripes. I'm thirty-seven years old and I've done more than I imagined. I have the scars, I can put them to words, and they can be as impressive as the story I tell.

Shelisa had sensed that story all along. It's not just my story though, Kessie is in it too, and my other sister, so we're going to write it together, all of us. I can see the paragraphs in my mind already, fully formed. Soon I'll join them to Kessie's and together we will create the story that Dad had struggled so hard to write.

We're going to call it *The Life of Clarissa*.

/////

*The sun rose to slant through his window, casting dark shadows on darker eyes. His worst demons gathered at sunrise. To live it again through his own brutal words was more than he could bear. No merciful errand of imagination would ever spare her, no amount of longing for a gentler end. There was no way to write past the truth, nowhere to send James now. She had given him the essence of herself, and to this he had added words—words of grace, words of passion, words of life. But his words could never describe what couldn't have been, only what would be, the dark shadows of sunrise and the latter half of his inglorious years.*

*The End*

/////

# Acknowledgements

From that first hazy idea a decade ago until the last nail-biting edit just recently, a lot of things had to serendipitously align in order for *The Latter Half of Inglorious Years* to take its present form, not the least of which was my sojourn on the island of Nevis. For that I have to thank my travel agent, Eloise Foley. She could as well have thrown a dart at a map for all I knew of Nevis beforehand, but she made the perfect call. Nevis is a remarkable place.

Shelisa Martin was an inspiration, and isn't her name lovely? She graciously consented to the character I named for her, although to be clear, my fictional Shelisa and the real Shelisa are as different as Clarissa and Hannah.

Other characters amble through in their fictional guises: Morgane, Kevin, Doreen, Julie, and the perspicuous Nelson; and others who didn't amble through but still left an impression: Suzanne, Winston, Star, and of course Bee Man.

Two editors steered me straight this time, Jill Thaxton and Monique Weston. The pair pared unapologetically, but the product was worth the pain. Many thanks to them both, and to Lou Ann, who was there at the inception although she probably doesn't remember.

Kirk Ward Robinson
*Smith County, Tennessee*
*March 2018*

## About the Author

KIRK WARD ROBINSON was born and raised in south Texas, and has since lived in every continental American time zone. He is an inveterate hiker and cyclist who prefers to travel and explore the world that way. His wide-ranging career has included roles as a chief operating officer, bookstore manager, stagehand, bicycle mechanic, and executive director of an educational non-profit organization in cooperation with the National Park Service. Robinson has been twice named to Kirkus Reviews' *Best Books*: in 2012 for *Life in Continuum*, and in 2015 for *The Appalachian*. These days he maintains a small ancestral farm in the hills of Tennessee.

www.kirkwardrobinson.com

www.ingramcontent.com/pod-product-compliance
Lightning Source LLC
Chambersburg PA
CBHW020959120726
47905CB00009B/2772